Nauti Boy

Lora Leigh

HEAT | NEW YORK

THE BERKLEY PUBLISHING GROUP
Published by the Penguin Group
Penguin Group (USA) Inc.
375 Hudson Street, New York, New York 10014, USA
Penguin Group (Canada), 90 Eglinton Avenue, Suite 700, Toronto, Ontario M4P 2Y3, Canada
(a division of Pearson Penguin Canada Inc.)
Penguin Books Ltd., 80 Strand, London WC2R 0RL, England
Penguin Group (Ireland), 25 St. Stephen's Green, Dublin 2, Ireland
(a division of Penguin Books Ltd.)
Penguin Group (Australia), 250 Camberwell Road, Camberwell, Victoria 3124, Australia
(a division of Pearson Australia Group Pty. Ltd.)
Penguin Books India Pvt. Ltd., 11 Community Centre, Panchsheel Park, New Delhi—110 017, India
Penguin Group (NZ), 67 Apollo Drive, Mairangi Bay, Auckland 1311, New Zealand
(a division of Pearson New Zealand Ltd.)
Penguin Books (South Africa) (Pty.) Ltd., 24 Sturdee Avenue, Rosebank, Johannesburg 2196,
South Africa

Penguin Books Ltd., Registered Offices: 80 Strand, London WC2R 0RL, England

This is an original publication of The Berkley Publishing Group.

This is a work of fiction. Names, characters, places, and incidents either are the product of the author's imagination or are used fictitiously, and any resemblance to actual persons, living or dead, business establishments, events, or locales is entirely coincidental. The publisher does not have any control over and does not assume any responsibility for author or third-party websites or their content.

First edition: March 2007

Library of Congress Cataloging-in-Publication Data

Leigh, Lora.
Nauti boy / Lora Leigh.—1st ed.
    p. cm.
ISBN-13: 978-0-425-21413-8
I. Title.
PS3612.E357N38 2007
813'.6—dc22   2006027717

PRINTED IN THE UNITED STATES OF AMERICA

10 9 8 7 6 5 4 3 2 1

Acknowledgments

For my CP, you know who you are. Special thanks to my advance readers, Melissa, Annmarie, Shelley, Janine, Susan, Chris, and Marty. Without you guys, I don't know what I would have done. You keep me on track, you keep me moving, and you have my eternal thanks.

PROLOGUE

How had he known she would be waiting on him, here of all places. Rowdy Mackay steered the Harley into its parking spot before lifting his glasses from his face and facing the demon sprite as she moved from the wood bench to stand on the sidewalk in front of him.

She was wearing one of those short, snug little T-shirts she liked so much. At least it wasn't one of his bigger shirts. He had lost two more on this trip home and he knew who to blame. She had been stealing his shirts since she was sixteen—when her mother married his father, bringing his favorite bit of trouble right into his home.

And he had been running from her ever since. Seven years of running.

He turned and tucked the sunglasses into the side of his Marine-issue duffel bag strapped on the back of the Harley before he bent his leg on the gas tank and watched her silently. Dawg and Natches were supposed to be here soon. Dawg was driving

Natches over so he could take the Harley back, but they weren't here yet. There was no one to distract him from the hunger driving him crazy.

She was twenty-three and her kisses were soft summer rain. They slid over a man's senses and drew him in, inviting him to get all wet and wild with her, inviting him to give her his worst. And in Rowdy's case, his worst might be a hell of a lot more than she could handle.

She stepped from the sidewalk. The low rise of her jeans didn't even come close to the tempting shadow of her navel. She made him sweat in the middle of damned winter. But it wasn't winter now, it was summer. A hot, Kentucky summer evening, and he was leaving again.

And this time, he knew beyond a shadow of a doubt that he wouldn't be able to walk away again. This was his last year away from home, he figured. Each year without even touching her, without taking her or tasting her kiss, she made him feel things he didn't expect.

His chest tightened at that knowledge. At the effort it was going to take to walk away from her again.

"You left without saying good-bye." She stopped beside the Harley, her dove gray eyes staring back at him with a shadow of hurt. "I didn't even get to see you this time."

No, she hadn't. He had stayed as far away from his dad's home as possible, spending the six weeks he was back on the boat he kept at the marina.

A playful breeze caught at the long curls of her golden brown hair and tugged at the lush waves of silk he dreamed of wrapping around his body. He had dreamed of her while he spent those lonely nights on the boat. Dreamed of touching her, kissing her, dragging her beneath his body, and taking her until neither of them could breathe for the exhaustion filling them.

Other women hadn't even figured into his lust. His stubborn body rejected them. He wanted Kelly.

His mouth was watering. He could feel the need to pull her to him, to wrap himself around her, nearly getting the best of him.

"Rowdy?" Her voice was filled with a young woman's hope, her dreams, and all the passion he knew burned inside her.

"You shouldn't have come here, Kelly." He sighed as he gave in to the impulse to reach out, to use the excuse of pushing her hair back to touch the soft warmth of it.

He really wanted to crush it in his hands, pull her head back, and devour her. Damn, he could do it too. She would let him. He could see it in her eyes.

"You didn't even say good-bye." It wasn't just hurt in her voice then, there was anger.

"If I had to say good-bye, I might not have left," he finally sighed. He was a man; he knew better than this. Kelly might be twenty-three, but she had no damned clue what she was getting into with him.

He'd kissed her three years before. Pinned her against the trunk of a tree and took her lips like the sweet drug they were. He had marked her because he couldn't help himself. He had made certain no one was dumb enough to think they could have Kelly. And his cousins would make sure it stuck while he was gone. While the Marines took their final year of this tour and he decided what the hell he was going to do about Kelly.

"You could have said good-bye," she whispered again.

"I could have been shot by my own father for the things I'd have done to you if I had just a measure of a chance." He tried to

3

smile, but he was too busy trying to keep his hands off the soft curves of her ass instead.

She was making him crazy. But hell, this was Kelly; she had been making him crazy for most of her life in one way or the other.

"I would have come to the boat—"

He laid his finger over her lips when he wanted to lay his own lips over them. Take them, lick at them, feel her open to him as she had that night at the lake.

"No." He shook his head. "You're here now." He had known she would be. Prayed for it.

He lifted his finger from her lips as he lowered his head. He didn't kiss her lips, he couldn't trust himself to rein in his hunger, his lust. It was impossible. He had a plane waiting on him, a job to finish, and he—

Sweet merciful God have pity on him. Her head turned, her lips touched his, and he was a goner. His hands slid over the ripe curves of her ass and he clenched, lifting her into the cradle of his thighs as his hunger overruled all common sense.

His head tilted, his lips slanting over hers, and he swore he saw stars as the sweet taste of her exploded against his senses. Blood began to pound in his veins as his thighs tightened, his dick thickened, and everything but the taste of Kelly receded beneath the force of his lust.

Pure, raw pleasure. That was what she was. She made him hard, made him primal, made him want to show her all the reasons why he should have never touched her the first time.

But she was his. His woman. His sweet, hot taste of paradise, and he could do nothing but beg for more. She was his drug, and God help them both, he was afraid the addiction might well kill one of them. He knew for a certainty it was going to drive him crazy.

Male catcalls and raucous voices had him finally dragging his lips from hers as he glanced up to see several servicemen watching him enviously. *Son of a bitch.* Here he was in the damned parking lot of the airport ready to tear her clothes from her body.

Glancing down, he watched her eyes drift open, saw the passion that clouded her gaze as she stared up at him.

"Don't forget me, Rowdy," she whispered as he set her back from him.

But he couldn't let go of her. His hands clasped her hips as his forehead settled against hers.

"Forget you?" he asked softly. "Baby, you're in every dream that drifts through my head. How the hell am I supposed to ever forget you?"

And that sucked. He couldn't forget her anymore than he could have her. Sweet, little, virgin baby, she had no idea what she was getting into.

ONE

One Year Later

So that was what had happened to that third shirt. Rowdy Mackay leaned against the kitchen doorway, tilted his head, and watched in amusement as Kelly shuffled over to the refrigerator and opened the door to peer into the interior.

The long, gray Marines T-shirt swallowed her slender frame and hung well past her thighs. A pair of his matching gray socks covered her small feet, and gray sweatpants hung from her hips. Not his, he thought in amusement—obviously hers but loose enough to make a man wonder why the hell she was suddenly hiding that curvy little body he knew she possessed. Especially when she had never bothered to do so in the past.

This outfit was a far cry from the snug shorts and T-shirts she used to don for summer sleepwear. Long, honey brown curls fell from the crown of her head to the middle of her back, the loose ringlets tousled and still a bit tangled from sleep, and damn if she didn't look like she had just dragged herself from a lover's bed.

He knew better, of course. His father's rules were strict. Rowdy might live under his roof during the brief times he was home, but he didn't bring his women here for the night, and he knew damned good and well Kelly wouldn't bring a man here.

The treasured princess of the house might be spoiled beyond bearing, but she respected her mother and stepfather. So dragging herself out of a lover's arms before making her way to the kitchen for a snack wasn't a scenario that was likely to happen here.

It was one of the reasons he had stayed away as much as possible since she had come of age. One of the reasons he had taken that last tour with the Marines. Some things a man just knew he was too weak to resist, and he had accepted long ago that he was too weak to resist Kelly.

That realization had come along about the time she grew breasts and he began noticing those breasts. Somewhere around the time that she started teasing him with innocent smiles and brushing against him, and he began enjoying it.

It was then he joined the service just to get the hell out of the house, to get away from her. College wasn't providing him the escape he needed. She was still there, and so was he, too often. And he was weak. Weak men were dangerous creatures. A twenty-two-year-old man had no damned business touching a sixteen-year-old, and he had known it. The only other option had been leaving. So Rowdy had left.

His time in the Marines had taught him self-control, finished his education, and brought him into manhood. But his greatest weakness was still his greatest weakness. *Kelly.*

"I don't wanna cook."

His lips quirked at the early morning grumpiness in her voice. She was talking to herself. Some things never changed. The sun would rise in the east and set in the west, and Kelly would always mutter to herself when she was irritated.

And the sound of her sweet, husky voice would always make his dick threaten to burst the zipper in his jeans.

"There's cereal in the cabinet." Rowdy expected her to turn with a smile bright enough to rival the sun. His arms were ready to open for the handful of woman barreling toward him. He wasn't expecting what he got, though.

Kelly screamed. The refrigerator door slammed closed hard enough to rattle the contents as she turned to dart through the opposite doorway.

Her face had gone paste white; her wide gray eyes were filled with fear.

Who had she been expecting?

She was poised to run but fighting to stand still. Conflicting emotions ran across her expressive face as her eyes met his, and the room filled with a tension that had never been there before.

Fear filled her eyes.

Rowdy narrowed his eyes on her, his body stiffening. No, it wasn't fear. For a moment, there had been pure, shocking terror. A woman aware that she was alone with a man, that she was weak, that her security wasn't assured. He'd seen it overseas in the eyes of a thousand women, and he saw it now.

"Rowdy?" Her voice was high, thin, her hands bunching in the front of her shirt, fisting the material as she shuddered. "What are you doing here?"

The husky, fear-laden voice twisted at his guts and had pure, unbridled fury simmering in his mind. What had happened to Kelly?

"It's home, isn't it?"

He had been ready to catch her as she ran at him. She always ran to him, throwing her arms around his neck, pressing her tight little breasts against his chest, and slapping a kiss to his cheek. For eight years, he could count on Kelly's greeting. Until today. He wondered in which direction the sun would rise now. Some things should just never change.

"Oh. Yeah." She nodded, her eyes darting around the room before a nervous smile tilted her soft pink lips, trembled there for a moment, then disappeared. "We weren't expecting you. Did you tell Mom and Ray you were coming?"

"No. I never do." His battle instincts were humming now. This wasn't normal. It was so far from normal that he knew with a clench of his gut that he wasn't going to like whatever the hell had been going on here.

Suddenly, nearly a year of his father's discomfort when they talked on the phone rose within his mind. Every time he had asked about Kelly, Ray Mackay's voice had tightened. When Rowdy asked to talk to her, he was given excuses.

The letters he had received from Kelly had changed, too. She no longer sent pictures, no longer filled the exchanges with innuendo or teasing comments. She had still written, but it was different, a difference he couldn't put his finger on, couldn't explain. He had felt it, though.

"No, you're always sneaking up on us." There was that nervous smile again, the way her eyes darted around the room.

Rowdy held himself where he was, leaning against the doorway, arms crossed over his chest. He could be a patient man when he had to be. But he had also learned that sometimes, there was no choice but to forge ahead and confront whatever enemy waited in the dark. He'd learned to forge ahead just as well as he had learned to wait.

"What's going on, Kelly?" He straightened from the doorway,

dropped his arms, and tucked his thumbs in the waistband of his low-slung jeans.

His chest was bare, the cooling breeze from the air conditioner drying the sweat that had dampened his flesh. He'd been cleaning the Harley, polishing his baby and getting her ready for her first ride in over a year. He'd dumped his duffel bag in his room and headed straight for the garage, knowing his father and stepmother would be at the marina, and figuring Kelly would be there as well.

The fact that she wasn't was interesting. Her reaction to him even more so.

"Nothing's going on." That damned quick, nervous little smile was starting to get on his nerves.

She was scared of him, and it was eating a hole in his soul. Kelly had never been scared of him, not once, he had always made certain of it. Now she was watching him as though she were terrified he was going to jump her any second.

"You're a lousy liar, baby," he grunted, heading for the fridge and watching as she edged out of his way.

She kept her eyes on him, watching him suspiciously as he opened the door and grabbed a bottle of water. Uncapping it, his gaze locked with hers, he brought it slowly to his lips.

Now there was a glimmer of the girl he had left eight years ago. Shyly watching as he drank from the bottle, her little tongue flicking out to swipe over her own lips, as though she were thirsty. A hungry little gleam filled the soft depths of her eyes, darkening them, making them appear stormy, cloudy as it mixed with the fear.

"When did you get back?" She crossed her arms over her breasts, tearing her gaze from his. "Do Mom and Ray know you're home?"

"Not yet." He recapped the bottle and set it on the kitchen isle as he continued to watch her. "I had Dawg pick me up from the airport this morning. We pulled in here about seven."

She nodded, a jerky little movement that had his fingers tightening as he watched her. The suspicion growing in his mind sent black anger swirling through him. Something had changed her, something dark and ugly, and he could see it in her eyes, in the regret and the anger and the fear that filled her expression.

The girl he had loved nearly all her life was terrified of him. She wasn't wary, or nervous, she was flat out scared. This was the same girl he had held as a child when her father died. He'd been a scrawny teenager, she had been too young to understand the sudden death that had rocked her world, and had sought out the boy who ruffled her hair, teased her about her skinned knees, and protected her from the bullies.

This was the same girl he'd taken to her senior prom when her date had stood her up. The one he had danced with on the dance floor and had to hide his erection from because he knew he couldn't touch her, couldn't have her. The girl he had kissed one night when he'd had too much to drink, the one he had touched too intimately before he headed back to base four years before. She was his girl, and suddenly, she was terrified of him.

"So where's my hug?" He leaned against the middle counter, watching her closely.

What little color had returned to her face, drained. Her eyes jerked to his, then away, her throat working as she swallowed tightly.

"I have to get dressed. I have to get to work." She turned on her heel, moving for the doorway.

"Kelly." Knowing he was making a mistake, feeling that knowledge to the soles of his booted feet, Rowdy reached out to catch her wrist.

His fingers touched her, curled around the bare skin when she shrieked, turning on him with a flash of fear as she jerked away from him, her body tightening defensively.

"What?" She gave it a good fight. She tried to cover her reaction, but the way she suddenly backed away from him and the fear on her face gave her away. There was no hiding the fact that his touch had terrified her. "Kelly, where's Dad?" He kept his voice cool. But fury was racing through him. Only one thing could cause a reaction like this, only one thing would have changed the teasing, tempting little minx he had known into a terrified, scurrying little rabbit.

"The marina." She licked her lips again, her gaze jumping away from him, her expression warring between fear and frustration. "I have to get dressed. I'll . . . I'll be down later."

She ran from him. As quick as that she turned tail in those sloppy, ill-fitting clothes she was wearing and moved from the kitchen to the staircase in the entryway and rushed upstairs.

She left him alone in the sunlit kitchen, his fists clenched, anger surging in his gut, and his suspicions all but confirmed.

He turned abruptly and stalked to the phone, ripping it from its base, and punched in the marina's number.

He waited through four rings impatiently, one hand propped on his hip, the other clenched around the phone with a force that should have shattered it.

"Mackay Marina." His father's booming voice suddenly came over the receiver.

"Hey, Dad, how's it going?" Rowdy kept his voice calm, controlled.

"Hey, Rowdy, not too bad." Ray Mackay chuckled. "How did you get to call so early? That CO of yours sleeping on the job?"

"Hell if I know," he drawled. "I didn't sign up for another tour, Dad." He had planned to, had every intention of doing so until his last birthday passed and he realized that running from some things wasn't working. "I'm home. Showed up about seven this morning." Tension suddenly sizzled across the line.

"You're home?" His dad's voice was deliberately bland, the tone mild. But Rowdy knew his dad, sometimes too well.

"Yep. Saw Kelly too."

He wasn't a fool, but even if he had been the muttered curse that came across the line would have warned him.

"We're on our way home." Ray confirmed his worst fears. "We need to talk."

Rowdy hung up the phone, stared around the kitchen, then breathed out heavily.

Damn. He came home to court his favorite girl, to settle down, to stop fighting what he knew was a losing battle. Had he come home too late?

Kelly let the hot water from the shower flow over her, wash away her tears, though it couldn't wash away the feeling of hands holding her down, of fetid breath on her face and hard, wet lips covering hers.

It couldn't drown out the rage and anger, or the fear. The water turned her skin pink from the heat and stung her tender flesh, but it couldn't ease the need that lay just below the memories of a night she feared had changed her life forever.

Rowdy was home. All six feet, four inches of hard, muscled flesh and teasing sea green eyes. He was home after more than a year away, a man full-grown, mature, and sexy as hell.

She wiped at her tears again, her breath hitching in her throat as she remembered one of the few nights she had followed him to the lake. The houseboat was Rowdy's pride and joy, and it was his escape. And she knew where he would head, to the Point, a serene cove where he and his buddies gathered on the weekends to drink, fish, let off steam, and party out the excessive energy they always seemed to have.

"Dad'll kill me." He had been just a little drunk, and way too sexy. His sea green eyes had darkened, his expression growing heavy with desire as he pressed her against a tree.

They had been hidden in the shadows from the rest of the group, sheltered. The heat of summer and lust had wrapped around them. He had been a man, and she had been too innocent, too uncertain in how to contain the need that pulsed in every cell of her body.

"I won't tell him," she had whispered, her palms smoothing up his chest, feeling the prickle of the light growth of body hair that spread over his torso as his hands gripped her hips, pulling her against his thighs.

"He'll know I touched you." His lips had quirked into a smile. "You're like pure, raw liquor, Kelly. And you go to my head faster."

She had fought to breathe, to contain the explosion of satisfaction and joy that rushed through her bloodstream.

"I'm leaving again tomorrow, baby." At first the words hadn't made sense. "I took another tour. Damned good thing, because sure as hell I'd end up doing this, and fuck us both up for good."

Agony had washed over her body even as pleasure had exploded into fragmented, flickering rays of sensation. His lips had covered hers, his tongue teasing her as he sampled her kiss then tasted the tears that fell from her eyes.

"One kiss, baby. Just this. Damn, you're going to break my heart."

He had kissed her as though he were starved for her. One hand had curled in her long hair, the other had cupped her breast, his thumb rasping over her engorged nipple, their moans blending together as the summer night enfolded them.

The hard length of his cock had pressed between her thighs. Even through the heavy material of his jeans she had felt the throb of his erection, the length of it, the promise of passion and satisfaction.

"Don't leave," she had whispered as he drew back from her. "Don't go, Rowdy."

"If I don't, I'll ruin us both forever . . ." He had set her from him, staring down at her, his eyes raging with lust. "Don't forget me, darlin', because sure as hell, I don't think I'll ever forget you."

He had never touched her again. He had taken her back to the shore and walked her the short distance to the small parking area above the Point. He had put her in her car and sent her home. And the next morning, he was gone. And he had not touched her since. She had lived on fantasy and dreams, because Rowdy made certain there was no chance of a repeat performance. And she had plotted and planned for his return. She had moved out of her mother's home into a small apartment in town. She had begun monthly visits to the local spa where she was plucked, waxed, toned, and lotioned on a regular basis. For too short a time.

Within three months of moving out all her dreams had turned to ashes and fear had taken their place. Her own foolishness had led to her downfall, and pulling herself from the shadows of the terror she had experienced was taking all her strength. She didn't know if she could survive dealing with Rowdy and her need for him, on top of it.

She leaned her head against the shower wall, her breath hitching as she fought back tears. He knew something was wrong. There was no way to hide it. She looked at him now and she didn't just see the man she had been in love with since she was a kid. She saw someone she couldn't fight, couldn't struggle from if she needed to. She saw a threat.

Her fists clenched as she pressed them against the tile, anger building in her chest until she wondered if she would be able to hold back the screams that pressed at the back of her throat.

She loved him. She had loved him forever. Dreamed of him, ached for him, waited for him. And now she was too damned scared to even welcome him home.

Are you my good girl, Kelly?

She flinched at the memory of the scratchy voice at her ear as a hard male body held her down, as the slickened fingers of the other hand probed between her buttocks, ignoring her struggles, her muted screams through the gag over her mouth.

She had been bleeding from the numerous cuts he had made on her body after he tied her spread-eagle on her bed. The wounds had burned like fire as they bled, the adrenaline pumping through her making the blood race and pour from the cuts. It had made her weak, made it hard to think, to work the hastily tied gag loose enough for one piercing scream as she felt him attempt to penetrate her rear.

God, she hated the memory of it. Hated the feeling of helplessness that followed her, even now. She had been unable to fight; unable to protest anything he did to her. And the nightmares that alone brought left her shaking in the darkest hours of the night.

She had been terrified of Rowdy knowing. Fearing he would blame her.

But even more, she had feared *for* Rowdy. He would have never stayed on duty if he knew what was going on at home. He would have left, with or without permission, and returned for vengeance. Rowdy protected those he cared about, and Kelly knew, beyond a shadow of a doubt, that he would have come racing home, even if it meant going AWOL.

But now Rowdy was home. And Kelly knew, once he learned the truth, he would never let it rest. He would find the stalker tormenting her, or he would die in the effort. And the fear of his death overshadowed even the fear of the threat she faced herself. Because life without the promise of seeing Rowdy, of hearing his laughter and the dark promise of passion in his voice, was a life Kelly didn't want to contemplate. A life she knew she didn't want to face.

TWO

At fifty-seven, Ray Mackay was still a powerful man, with hazel eyes and hair that still retained much of its raven black color. His weathered face was starting to crease with deep laugh lines at the sides of his eyes. Eyes that were usually cheerful, always warm and friendly, were now somber.

Rowdy was waiting on the front porch of the two-story white and red farmhouse when his dad pulled into the driveway, the dark green Jeep Laredo parking beside Rowdy's Harley.

Maria Mackay was out of the jeep before Ray turned the engine off, rushing up the cement walkway, her gray blue eyes concerned as she met his gaze.

"Is Kelly okay?" Maria Salyers Mackay was still slender for her forty-seven years of age. The summer shorts and crisp, white cotton shirt showed off her tanned legs and arms attractively.

"Why wouldn't she be?" He leaned against the railing, watching her with narrowed eyes. "And why do I have a feeling that if I had warned ya'll I was coming home, that I might have found my way barred?"

He could see it in her face, in his father's heavyset expression. They hadn't expected him, and they weren't comfortable with him being there alone with Kelly. And that just pissed him off. Whatever the hell was going on, one thing should have been set in cement in their heads, and that was the fact that he would die before he hurt Kelly.

"I'd never bar you from your own home, Douglas."

He winced. Maria was the only person who called him Douglas, and the snap in her voice when she said it now was as sharp as a knife. No one called him Douglas, ever. But hell, she had taught him in school and breaking her of the habit wasn't easy.

He crossed his arms over his chest, staring down at her intently as she stepped onto the porch.

"I'm going to check on Kelly." She moved for the door.

"Not yet." He didn't move; he didn't intend for his voice to lower warningly, or his body to tense as he watched a main source of information attempt to escape. But he wanted answers, and she wasn't running off until he had them.

"Go on, Maria." Ray stepped up behind her, his large hands settling on her shoulders as he gave them a comforting squeeze. "I'll talk to Rowdy. We'll be in soon."

She glanced up at Rowdy, worry and regret shimmering in her eyes before she turned to her husband, kissing his cheek gently before moving into the house.

Rowdy's attention fixed on his father, watching as he swiped his fingers through his hair before burying his hands in his jeans pockets.

"Was she raped?" Rowdy lifted the bottle of water to his lips, taking a long sip as he watched Ray's eyes darken with pain.

Ray breathed out roughly, his shoulders shifting as he lowered his head.

"Attacked," he finally muttered. "She wasn't raped. But she was cut up pretty bad, traumatized." He lifted his head and Rowdy wondered if his father could see the pure murder burning inside him now.

"Who did it?" He kept his voice even, cool nonetheless.

Ray shook his head slowly, his expression heavy.

"She didn't see his face; there were no leads on who he was or why he attacked her."

The water bottle crumpled in Rowdy's hand, water sloshing over his fingers before he realized what he had done. Forcing himself to release the plastic, he set it on the railing and focused on his father.

"Where did it happen?"

"She moved out right after your last visit," Ray sighed roughly. "Nice little apartment in town, next to one of her friends. Few weeks later she started getting crank calls. Caller ID couldn't trace them. We put new locks on her doors and windows, but you know how she was." Ray shook his head wearily. "Liked sleeping with her window cracked. She thought she was safe. Thought she would hear it if someone snagged the fire escape ladder. But she didn't. Her neighbor's boyfriend heard her screams and knocked the door down, but he'd already hurt her. The attacker got out the window before the boy could catch him."

Short and to the point. And he was hiding something, Rowdy could feel it. He stared back at his father, silent, probing, knowing he would tell him eventually. Rowdy wouldn't give him a choice.

Ray glanced back at him, then away. His teeth clenched, rage glittered in his eyes.

21

"It wasn't a normal attack," he finally muttered.

Rowdy felt a chill race up his spine.

"What do you mean by that?" He had to force the words past his throat.

Ray coughed nervously. "He meant to rape her anally. He almost managed it."

"Motherfucker! God. Damn!" Rowdy flung himself across the porch, his hands running over his head before he gripped the back of his neck in fury. "Son of a bitch!" His abdomen tightened as he fought to hold back a howl of pure rage before jerking back to stare at his father. "Why the fuck didn't you tell me?"

"Hell Rowdy, what could you do?" Ray snapped, anger suffusing his face. "She begged us not to tell you. You were clear across the world with no hope of coming home anytime soon. There was nothing you could have done."

"Like hell," he snarled. "They would have let me come home or dealt with the consequences. That's no excuse."

"Exactly." His father's face flushed with anger. "You would have gone AWOL to come home, and caused even more of a mess for that kid. Do you think we didn't know what the hell was going on before you left the first time? You couldn't keep your eyes off her and she was just a fucking kid. Four years later you were back for three months and it was worse. She didn't need that. The attack was too brutal and she was too damned vulnerable. I opted to wait till you returned, and I stand by that decision."

"Damn." Rowdy pushed his fingers through his hair before rubbing at the back of his neck with an edge of violence. "Son of a bitch, Dad. Who would do that to her?"

Ray shook his head. "There was a rash of rapes last summer. Several girls in surrounding counties were attacked, all anally. No one caught the bastard and the sheriff has no leads. She's finally coming out of it, Rowdy, getting a grip on herself. But it was bad for a while. Bad enough that we wondered if she would ever leave this damned house again."

And no one had told him.

"Look, Son," Ray finally breathed heavily. "I know how it was with you the last time you were home. With her." He shifted uncomfortably. "I know about the games you, Dawg, and Natches get up to. And so does Kelly. Don't expect anything from her. You hear me?"

Rowdy stared back at his father in surprise. Damn, this was just what he needed right now.

"What do you want me to say?" he asked his father softly.

Ray shook his head. "I don't want you to say anything, Son. I want you to let Kelly come to you. She's been scared to death of your return, and I don't know why myself. I know you wouldn't hurt her, but I know for a fact she knows about some of those little affairs you and your cousins have participated in."

And his father suspected she was scared of him now. Rowdy could see it in Ray's eyes, feel it in the air around them.

And he was probably right. God help the bastard that touched her, because if Rowdy ever found him, he would turn him into dog meat.

"I'll head to the boat." Rowdy breathed in roughly. He needed time to think, time to figure this one out.

Ray blinked several times, his expression twisting in emotion as he turned quickly away from Rowdy and headed to the house. Pausing at the door, he turned back to his son and said, "Did I ever mention how proud of you I am, Boy?"

Rowdy snorted. "Stop calling me a boy, Pop. You're going to kill my rep, you know."

His throat tightened with emotion as well. He knew what his father was saying.

"I'm proud, Boy," he muttered. "Damned proud."

And Rowdy felt like a failure. He had failed to protect the only woman who had ever held his heart because he was too damned busy running from her. He should have been home, he should have been holding her in his bed, loving the hell out of her. If he had staked his claim, she wouldn't have been in that damned apartment.

He breathed in roughly before turning to the door himself. His duffel bag was in his old room. Not that he stayed at the house much when he was home in the summers. He had thrown the bag in there for convenience; now he was going to have to collect it.

Rowdy jerked the door open, stalking into the house before coming to an abrupt stop. Kelly stood at the top of the landing, her face paper white, her long, damp hair hanging over that fucking shapeless T-shirt, her hands clenched in front of her.

Her lips were trembling, her eyes big and dark and filled with tears.

Rowdy glanced away, fighting for control before he turned back to her and began to walk steadily up the steps. The tears gathered in her eyes, until one dropped as she stepped back, allowing him to stand beside her.

God, he wanted to wipe that tear away, wanted to erase the shattered pain he saw in her eyes.

"I'm sorry," she whispered, her voice ragged. "I'm so sorry, Rowdy."

"Why?" He asked the question softly, aware of her mother standing farther up the hall, his father in the entryway.

"I wasn't careful—"

"No." She flinched as he snapped the word out. "Don't be sorry for that, baby. That wasn't your fault." His arms hung limply at his side, his own world lying broken at his feet, and he couldn't even hold her. Couldn't comfort her. It was ripping his guts to pieces. "I'll be at the boat if you need me. I'll always be here if you need me."

And for now, that was all he could give her. Right now, it was all he had. He moved away from her, turning and stalking to his bedroom, ignoring Maria's whispered "Douglas?" as he pushed the door open.

His duffel bag was still on his bed, unpacked.

"I'll get the rest of my stuff later." He picked up the Marine-issue bag and turned to face his father as the other man followed him into his room.

"Make sure you're home for dinner," Ray growled, his voice rough. "Don't forget you have family here at the house too."

Rowdy forced a smile to his lips as he jerked the duffel bag from the bed and headed to the door.

"Dinner for sure. Tomorrow." He nodded. "I have things to do tonight."

He paused outside the door, staring at Kelly where she stood on the landing, her eyes wide with pain.

"Come down to the boat whenever you need to," he told her softly. "Anytime baby."

He came back for her. He wasn't hiding that, not from his father and not from her.

A glimmer of surprise filled her eyes as a little flush moved beneath her pale skin. At least she didn't look terrorized anymore. It didn't mean he had recovered though. Rage was eating a hole into his gut and pounding through his bloodstream with enough force to make him wonder exactly how good his control was now.

He wanted to kill the bastard who had hurt her. He wanted to wipe away the memory of her pain and fill it with pleasure. And until he got a handle on himself, he didn't have a hope of doing either.

THREE

An hour later, Kelly pulled her car into the parking lot of the marina and stared out at the boats lined at the end of the docks. The Nauti Boys were all there. The *Nauti Buoy*, *Nauti Dawg*, and *Nauti Dreams*. She could see Rowdy on the upper deck, dressed in cutoffs, bare chested and looking like a sun god as he straightened and stared out at the parking lot.

She had to talk to him.

She laid her head on the steering wheel and closed her eyes as she felt her heart thumping erratically in her chest. Fear or excitement? *Both*, she admitted to herself.

The knowledge that he was back sent heat rushing through her even as fear shadowed the arousal. She was a virgin, but she wasn't ignorant. She knew what the tension between her thighs was, and it was stronger than it had ever been. She grabbed her purse before opening the door and stepping out onto the parking lot. She looked around, feeling the snaking fear that always followed her when she left the house. Squaring her shoulders, Kelly turned and headed toward the docks. Her head lifted as her gaze locked on Rowdy. He was watching her, standing beneath the rays of a sun that lovingly painted his hard, muscular body. He made her breathing hard, made her mouth water and her hands shake with nerves.

Pulling her gaze away, she moved onto the floating walkway, heading for the back edge of the docks. There were half a dozen rows of docking slots on this quarter of the marina. They were the least expensive slots, and the farthest away from the marina's office.

Rowdy's, Dawg's, and Natches's boats were in the last three slots, and incidentally where the majority of the ducks tended to congregate. Dawg was notorious for feeding them throughout the day.

As she neared the *Nauti Buoy*, the sliding deck door opened and Rowdy stepped out. Dark gold flesh gleamed with sweat as he leaned against the doorway, his thumbs tucked into the pockets of his ragged cutoffs as he watched her.

"Permission to come aboard?" A nervous smile trembled on her lips.

"Always." His deep voice raced across her nerve endings, sending frissons of heat to lick at her flesh.

He moved back into the interior of the houseboat, his lashes lowering over his brilliant eyes as he watched her.

Kelly stepped onto the small deck, trying to ignore the shaking in her knees as she crossed it and entered the main section of the craft.

She had known for four years that when he came home for good, he would claim her once and for all. She had waited for him like an immature child, weaving dreams and fantasies of what would happen when he came home at last. Somehow she had known that would be his last tour, despite his threats to reenlist. A year ago, she had felt it. Something had changed in him, the way he watched her, the tension that emanated from him whenever they were together.

As it was now. She could feel it tightening in and around her body, reminding her of all the desires and explicit fantasies that had tormented her through the years.

"Thirsty?" He moved to the low fridge, opening it to pull out a beer and lift it to her in invitation.

"No." She shook her head as she pushed her hair from her shoulder and faced him awkwardly.

God, she had no idea what to say to him.

He continued to stare back at her intently.

"I'm sorry," she sighed; she didn't know what else to say. "It was my fault Ray didn't tell you what happened."

His lips quirked as he lowered his head, hiding the hurt she knew he must have been feeling.

He finally shrugged as he lifted his gaze. "Why didn't you let him?"

She blinked furiously at the tears that threatened to fill her eyes.

"You couldn't do anything." She shrugged heavily. "You were a world away, Rowdy. You weren't free. I didn't want you to worry."

He snorted at that. "I would have come home, Kelly. I could have come home without repercussion."

And that was what had scared here.

She breathed in roughly. "I'm doing okay. I've been seeing a therapist and she's really helped. It's just, sometimes, I still get scared." She shrugged helplessly. "I feel like such a wimp."

And she felt watched. Stalked. Not that she had told Ray or her mother how she felt. Her therapist assured her it was normal, under the circumstances. But it eroded her confidence, kept her awake long into the night. His eyes darkened as he moved slowly toward her.

She stepped back instinctively.

"You're scared to death of me," he said softly.

She could hear the dark torment in his voice, see it in his eyes.

"I'm not scared of you." She fought the trembling of her lips as she stared up at him, fought to stand in place rather than running as she wanted to.

"Then what are you scared of?" He reached out, his fingers running down a long curl that fell over her shoulder. "Why are you trembling, Kelly?"

"You've always made me tremble." She bit her lip at the admission. "Now . . ." She stared back at him miserably. "I'm not scared of you, Rowdy, but forgetting . . . sometimes, I can't forget."

His thumb smoothed down her cheek, nearly taking her breath with the latent sensuality of his touch.

"Are you going to keep running, Kelly?" he asked then. "You knew if you told me what happened I'd come home. You knew I would have never stayed away. What couldn't you handle about that?"

"You couldn't come home—"

"Bullshit," he growled. "I would have found a way back to you, you knew it. But you swore my dad to secrecy and, it seems, my cousins as well. You were scared of me."

"No . . ." She shook her head again, desperate to make him believe her now.

"You knew what I wanted from you, Kelly." He turned away, stalking across the room before turning back to her. "You knew I wanted you in my bed. You knew what was going to happen when I came home. Didn't you?"

"I knew." She couldn't deny it.

"Did you think I'd try to take you while you were raw from an attempted rape?" Disgust filled his voice.

"That's not true." She couldn't let him believe that.

Moving across the room, she gripped his arm, holding him in place when he would have moved from her.

"I knew you wouldn't, Rowdy," she cried fiercely. "I know you would never, ever hurt me. I can't help it. You don't know how long I waited for you to come home, how much I needed you to touch me, and now I don't know what to do. I don't know how to make sense of any of it."

She stared back at him, desperate for him to understand, on the edge of crying and knowing the tears would do her no good.

"What you made me feel has always scared me," she finally admitted, her voice trembling. "How much I needed your touch always terrified me. And now, it's like all the fears are swirling together until I can't make any sense of any of it."

His expression twisted into a grimace of raw pain as his arms came around her. Slowly. Powerful, naked, sun-heated, he pulled her against him as her hands clutched at his waist as the scent of him infused her senses.

"Kelly. God, baby, do you have any idea of what it did to me to realize I wasn't here to protect you?" he whispered against her hair, one big hand holding her head against his chest as the opposite arm wrapped around her back. "If I had been here, I would have been in your bed that night. No one would have touched you."

"This isn't your fault," she snapped, her head lifting, a frown tightening her brow as she glared back at him. "I knew you were going to think that."

"I don't think it, I know it," he growled, holding her tighter, pressing his hips against her lower belly as she felt the breath slam out of her chest.

His erection, impossibly large, hot even through the denim, pressed against her as he stared down at her with heavy-lidded arousal.

"I know, Kelly." His hands moved to her hips as she felt the familiar weakness sweeping through her body. "There's not a damned thing that could have kept me away from you. Why the hell do you think I spent so much time in the Marines? I stayed away because I couldn't keep my hands off you."

His hands were on her now, clasped at her hips as hers flattened against his bare chest and she stared back at him in shock.

"I want you until I can't breathe for it," he whispered then. "But I would never hurt you. And I would never take what you can't give me, Kelly. Ever."

"I know that, Rowdy," she cried, the aching need and shadowed fears that rose inside her clenching in her chest. "I never thought you would."

"I wanted to hold you this morning." His hands smoothed over her back, her hips. "I wanted to pull you in my arms and put myself between you and the world to keep anything, everything, from threatening you ever again."

She shook her head. God, what was she going to do? He wasn't even concerned with what his father had said, the fact that he had been thrown out of his home. He wasn't angry with her or with Ray. He was angry with himself for not being there.

Kelly stared back at him, dazed, uncertain. Rowdy's expression was fierce, arrogant, equal parts frustration and determination mixed with pure, hot lust.

"Rowdy—"

"I want to take all the fear out of your eyes, Kelly," he whispered, his head lowering, his eyes holding hers. "I want it gone. I want to see all that fire and arousal and need that's always been there. That I see now."

She breathed in roughly, fighting to find reality, to make sense of the influx of sensations racing through her body.

"I want to kiss you, Kelly." Her lips parted.

Beneath her hands, his heart raced, just like hers. A hard, rushing throb that transferred to her veins, her nerve endings, and washed through every cell of her body.

"Did you miss me, Kelly?" he whispered.

"Yes." Her vision was filled with his lips. Sensually full, a treat she had dreamed of for too many years, had ached for with everything in her woman's body.

"No. Keep your eyes open." He stopped as her lashes drifted closed. "Watch me, baby. See me. It's just Rowdy. Just my kiss, remember how much you liked my kiss?"

She loved his kiss. Her lips parted in anticipation, but perhaps she hadn't fully remembered what being kissed by Rowdy meant. Somehow, she must not have remembered just right, exactly how it felt that night on the lake.

Because this was nothing like that brief, hungry kiss four years before. This was seduction. It was coercion on its most basic level. The whisper of his lips against hers as his heavy-lidded eyes stared back into hers, darkening, flaming with need as his mouth possessed hers with devastating sensuality. Rough silk caressed her lips, stroking over them as he denied her the deeper, darker possession she was craving. This wasn't a hungry consummation, it was a dream washing over her, easing her from the shadows haunting her and pulling her inexorably into a steadily building whirlwind of sensation.

"So beautiful," he whispered against her lips, sipping at them, making her ache for more. "There you go, just watch me, Kelly. Watch me and feel."

A whimpering moan tore from her throat as she felt his hands lift the hem of her shirt, felt his hands, calloused and hot against the bare flesh of her back. Curling her fingers against his chest she allowed herself to settle into his body, her head falling back as one hand cupped the nape of her neck and his kiss became deeper.

"Keep your eyes open."

Her eyes flew open as he pulled back, her breathing becoming jerky at the hunger in his face.

"Watch me, Kelly."

"I can't," she gasped. "It's too good."

His eyes dilated at the admission.

"Watch me, or it stops," he growled firmly. "See who's touching you, baby. It's me. You've been mine forever, Kelly. We're just going to ease into it now. Let me show you what I've dreamed about for the last eight years."

She was shaking in his grip, but not from fear. Hunger was consuming her as his lips covered hers again, and she struggled to keep her eyes open, to keep her senses from drowning beneath the full-lipped kiss that threatened to dissolve the strength in her knees.

Twining her arms around his neck, she arched against him, barely retaining enough thought to keep her eyes open. If she closed them, then the incredible pleasure tearing through her would be gone. His lips on hers, his tongue stroking along her lips as hers licked back, desperate for more.

Her hips tilted to him, arching as his knees bent enough to tuck his erection at the notch of her thighs.

Oh, that was good. She whimpered as she twisted against him, feeling the heavy rasp against her clit as he lifted her to him, turning her and bearing her to the counter behind them.

"There. No need to worry." He stepped between her spread thighs, pressing firmly against her as her back arched and her hands clenched at his shoulders.

"See how good it feels." His hips moved, dragging a ragged cry from her throat as his lips covered hers again.

Oh yes, it felt good. It felt as though tiny electrical charges were exploding across her flesh, sensitizing her.

His hard, bare chest pressed against her breasts, the lacy material of her bra scraping over her hard nipples, making them ache for a harder, firmer touch. This part of her hunger for Rowdy had always frightened her. The part that refused to accept a gentle touch, that ached, screamed out for more.

Powerful, possessive, Rowdy's kiss consumed her, but his hands didn't touch her. They were flat on the counter beside her, despite her need for them on her body.

"Rowdy," she gasped as his head lifted.

"See how sweet it can be, baby?" he crooned. "So sweet and easy."

"No." She shook her head fiercely. "Touch me. I need you to touch me."

There were no shadows of fear now. The overriding hunger Rowdy filled her with left no room for fear, no room for shadows. There was nothing but the demand for his touch, and that demand was rising by the moment.

"Where?" he whispered the question against her lips. "Where do you want me to touch you, Kelly? Show me, baby."

His powerful biceps flexed at her side as he held back. She shuddered, realizing the demand in his voice and the fact that whatever she wanted, she was going to have to initiate.

Her lips curled at the corners in amusement.

"You think I won't do it?" Her body was humming with need now.

"I think you could make me lose my mind if you wanted to try." Heavy-lidded eyes, his lips full and sexy, he stared back at her with wicked intent. "But will you?"

The muscles of his chest twitched; the blood pulsed in his neck. A small rivulet of moisture rolled from his neck, drawing her gaze and her hunger. Leaning forward, she moved her tongue against his skin, licking at his flesh and drawing in the salty male taste.

The groan that rumbled from him had a shiver racing up her spine.

"Touch me," she whispered against his neck, her teeth raking over the hard column.

"Show me where." His voice was tight, dark with lust. "It's up to you, baby."

Up to her. She breathed in deeply.

"I want your lips on my nipples." Her breathing grew harder as she let him hear the words, words she had only whispered in her dreams. "Then your teeth—"

"Sweet mercy." The heavy groan tore from his lips. "Oh, baby, the things I'm going to do to those tight, hard little nipples. Lift that shirt for me, baby. Give me those pretty breasts."

Her hands fell to the hem of her shirt, lifting it as she leaned back to stare into his eyes, wanting to see the lust and need flaming in the green depths.

As the shirt cleared her belly and began edging over her bra, a shockingly familiar voice drawled from the doorway. "The door's open; does that mean I can join you?"

Laced with amusement, heavy with interest, Natches's voice had Kelly jerking the shirt down and staring back in shock at the deepened lust in Rowdy's eyes.

There was no anger that Natches had invaded the moment, there was added arousal, a deepening flush of lust on his hard face.

"Ever been watched?" he whispered, his expression heavy with dark desire.

Breathing heavily, Kelly stared back at him. She wasn't shocked, she realized. She had heard too much about the Nauti Boys. Too many tales of their sexual excesses, their uninhibited immersion into their sensual games.

She swallowed tightly, staring back at him as the flames between her thighs began to burn with insistent demand.

"Rowdy . . ." She shook with indecision. She had guessed over the years that the day would come when she would face this choice. That she would run headlong into the hungers the three men shared; she just hadn't expected it nearly this soon.

"As much as I would love this," Natches sighed, "and I surely would love it, I just came to let you know Uncle Ray is headed this way. And he has that bulldog look on his face for sure."

Was it relief or regret that raced through her mind? Whichever it was, there was no doubt her body was howling in protest.

"Well hell." Rowdy dropped a quick, hard kiss to her lips as he stepped back, his hands gripping her waist as he sat her gently on the floor. "Guess the cavalry is going to rescue you, baby."

She didn't need rescuing.

"I'll talk to him," she whispered.

"No talking needed, baby." He shook his head as he sighed wearily and tucked her hair behind her ear, then ran his fingers gently down her cheek. "Go on to the marina. I'll check in later. Okay?"

"He doesn't understand."

"Go, baby." He shook his head. "Me and Dad don't have a problem here. He's just being who he is, that's all. And who he is means he's going to worry about the little lamb staying too long with the big bad wolf." And that was her fault. She had been so hysterical over Rowdy knowing about the attack that she knew Ray was now worrying about her being alone with Rowdy at all.

She had sworn his cousins to secrecy, begging them to hold their silence on the attack, pleading with them not to tell him.

Reluctantly, they had agreed. And now Kelly knew why the reluctance had been so thick. They knew Rowdy, and they knew he'd be angry with all of them. And he was. He was hiding it well, but she saw the flash of it in his eyes, mixed with the hurt. Being kept in the dark never had sat well with him. He was the type of man who faced the monsters and fought them back however much it took. He wasn't a man that appreciated being protected or deliberately left out.

"I better go," she sighed, glancing at the door. "Will you be at the house tonight for dinner?"

"Tomorrow," he promised easily, reaching up to tuck her hair behind her ear. "Wear something pretty for me."

Something pretty. She hadn't done that for a year.

"I can do that." She moved away from him slowly. "I'll see you tomorrow."

"Count on it, baby." He leaned against the counter, his gaze heavy lidded, his body hard, aroused as she slid past the doorway.

Her heart was racing in excitement, drumming with latent fear, but for the first time in a year, she felt alive again. Rowdy was home now. A smile edged at her lips. He was home, everything would be fine now.

FOUR

The Nauti Boys were together again. Rowdy finished off his beer as he stared at the other two men who had followed him topside later that evening.

Natches, the youngest of them at twenty-nine, tossed the pizza box on the table and moved into one of the chairs that set beneath the awning. Dawg, the oldest at thirty-one, flipped on the CD player he had carried up and set it on the spare chair. The better to drown conversation. They had learned young to watch their discussions here at the marina and on the lake. Sound carried on the water, and they had learned more than one secret eavesdropping themselves.

"You're pissed." Dawg sprawled back in his chair as he stared at Rowdy through narrowed, green eyes.

Rowdy took his own chair and stared back at the two men. They had run wild through town and the Marines together, though Dawg and Natches had gone reserves after their first tour rather than staying in longer. Dawg managed the lumberyard his father left him, while Natches had opted to permanently distance himself from his parents' thriving restaurants and owned a garage of all things. His dad stayed elbows deep in flour and Natches was a grease monkey. The family fights over that one had been interesting.

"I'm pissed." Rowdy shrugged, knowing there wasn't a damned thing he could do about it.

Uncapping another beer from the cooler beside him, he stared at his cousins soberly, wondering if he would have made the same choices.

They were the bad boys of the county. The three of them had been the terror of Somerset, Kentucky, when they were young. Fathers locked their daughters up at night in fear of the three of them. They hadn't exactly gained a good reputation where women were concerned.

"Damn, Rowdy, I'm glad you're back." Dawg shook his shaggy head, his raven black hair reflecting the lights of the marina. "Even pissed, it's a hell of a sight better than dealing with this without you."

Natches sipped at his beer, his own black hair not nearly as shaggy as Dawg's but longer. It was pulled back in a ponytail at his nape, giving his features a harder, more savage appearance.

They knew why they were there.

Rowdy turned back to Dawg.

"You could have told me when you picked me up," he informed his cousin, his lips flat, anger tightening his skull.

Dawg shook his head, lowering it briefly before sighing.

"Some things you just don't know how to tell a man." Dawg grimaced. "I figured you'd get a hint soon enough. It's not like she's the same girl she was last year."

Rowdy bit back the angry response burning on his lips, but hell, this was Dawg. When Rowdy hadn't been around to watch out for

Kelly's skinned knees and the bullies who liked to pick on her, then Dawg had been there.

"We've pulled all the info on this that we can find, Rowdy." Natches straightened in his chair and reach for the pizza. "We've been working on it since it happened, trying to figure out who the bastard was."

"And?" If anyone could figure it out, it was Dawg and Natches.

"Not much," Natches admitted. "We've had four other rapes in surrounding counties over the last two years. All anal rapes, beatings, cuts, much more severe than Kelly's. She got lucky. Her neighbor's boyfriend heard the single scream she was able to get out. The boyfriend was a tough guy, broke in and tried to apprehend the bastard, but once he caught sight of Kell he let the guy go to help her."

"All this shit going on at home and neither one of you were good enough to tell me what the fuck was happening?" Rowdy snapped.

He had talked to both of them over the past year and never realized that the distance he had felt had been something they were hiding rather than his own impatience to finish his tour.

"What could you have done, man?" Dawg tilted his head to the side and stared back at him questioningly. "We didn't want the trouble of hiding an AWOL Marine the rest of our natural lives and didn't figure Kelly needed that on top of everything else. We took care of her until you could get home."

"Were there any rapes after Kelly?" He asked.

"Nothing with the same M.O." Dawg shook his head. "It's like the son of a bitch just disappeared. I'm hoping he did."

"Ray keeps us up-to-date on Kelly though," Natches sighed. "And we take turns being here at the marina when she's working. She's retreated so far into herself that sometimes I've wondered if we could find the girl she used to be. The closest I've seen was when you had her backed into the counter this afternoon." Natches's lips twitched at the memory. "She looked real comfortable there, Rowdy."

"Asshole," Rowdy grunted.

Rowdy stared at the other two men as he wiped his hand over his face and considered the situation for long moments.

"He's not gone," he finally sighed. "I want to believe he is, I really do. But I can feel it. He's waiting."

"Are you two free?" He looked at them and knew they would be, whatever it took. "We're free. We made sure of it." Natches nodded firmly. "How do you want to play it?"

"I need one of you watching our back whenever we're away from the house. I can feel that bastard watching her. I felt it today when she was on the boat, like a damned itch just under my skin."

Dawg frowned at that. "There's been no sign of him, Rowdy. We've been watching her every second that we've been able to. No phone calls, no strange accidents. Nothing."

Rowdy clenched his jaw at Dawg's argument.

"Rowdy's right," Natches muttered over the music. "I've felt it all evening, especially since we came up here. That's a feeling you never forget, Dawg. I've had a bead on me in the service enough times to know the feeling."

"Hell, and here I was hoping it was just my overactive imagination," Dawg grunted. "But if he's watching, it's the first time he's watched close. I've only had the willies once or twice since all this hit the fan."

The willies. It was the perfect description for that odd, warning tingle at the back of the neck, the knowledge that something, or someone, intended to take your head off if they had the right chance.

"Dawg and I made sure we were both fairly free this summer,"

Natches stated. "We're staying on the boats. We'll watch for unusual movement or watchers. We haven't seen anything so far, but with crazies like this, who the hell knows what set them off."

They knew each other too well sometimes, Rowdy thought. His cousins had already anticipated what he would need.

"I've been thinking," Dawg said, his voice graveled, suspicious, "whoever he is, he has to know her. Kelly's not a creature of habit. She's impulsive, unpredictable, and never where you expect her to be. He knew she would be home. He knew she liked to crack her window at night. You can't tell it's cracked from the street. He had to have known."

"He studies his women," Natches said. "Gets to know them somehow. We've been talking about this." He nodded to the others. "Playing it out. I think he's local."

"Why?"

"The rapes are in a four-county radius around Somerset. Until Kelly, Somerset hadn't been hit. She fits the profile of the other girls, though. The others he'll call every now and then from what the detectives on the case told me, and ask if they're being 'good girls,' but he hasn't called Kelly. The only reason he wouldn't call her, is because he's close enough to watch her," Natches pointed out.

"The guy lost it when he was interrupted. The others"—Dawg cleared his throat, fury flashing in his eyes—"he made them beg. First to live, and then for him. Kelly wouldn't beg—"

"And he was interrupted—Shit!" Rowdy ran his hands over his head.

"But she's still a 'good girl,'" Natches pointed out. "When she stops being a good girl, what will he do?"

Rowdy felt his stomach pitch at the thought of that. This was why Ray was so pissed at his son's return. Because he knew Rowdy had returned to claim Kelly, which was most likely the one thing guaranteed to push her stalker over the edge.

"The redneck code, cowboys," Natches drawled. "You don't fuck the good girls unless you mean it. He doesn't rape them normally, he takes them anally. He's not serious 'bout them. And he's not going to 'dirty' a 'good girl.'"

It was sickening, and the truly horrifying part was it all made sense. There were unwritten rules sometimes, a code, a way of dealing with women. Good girls versus "bad" girls and the rules of engagement. This rapist was twisting those rules. Perverting them in ways guaranteed to give a sane man nightmares. He was targeting good girls, or his perception of a good girl.

And Kelly gave the impression of the perfect good girl. But she was *his* naughty girl. He had seen it in her eyes eight years ago; he saw it there now. She wasn't a fool, and she might very well be a virgin, but Rowdy knew that his naughty girl was in there, waiting for *him*. And he was going to claim her, love her, protect her.

No matter what it took.

"Rowdy, you start fooling with her and the bastard is going to come after her stronger," Natches pointed out. "We can control it if we use it, control him and take him."

"But only if he thinks Kelly isn't a 'good girl,'" Dawg injected. "Good girls can tame the bad boys. Unless he thinks Rowdy is up to his past games with Kelly, it might not push him over the edge in time."

Rowdy stared back at his friends. He heard the question in Dawg's voice, the suspicion. He leaned forward, bracing his arms on the gas tank as he watched them. He ignored the tightening, low in his stomach, the vague disquiet he felt at the thought of sharing Kelly. Of allowing his cousins to touch her, to hold her. He had waited for six years, ever since she turned eighteen, for the chance to show her just how much pleasure he could give her when he took her to his bed. He refused to remember the arousal she inspired two years before that. You didn't lust after babies, and sixteen-year-old, wide-eyed virgins were just that. Babies. But the minute she turned eighteen, he had known his days of freedom were numbered.

"I haven't changed." He stared back at them with an edge of humor, of determination, as he ignored the odd, unfamiliar tightening in his chest. "Have you?"

Snorts of wry amusement met his question.

"Yeah right, and pigs started flying over the lake when it happened." Natches laughed. "We've been waiting on you, Rowdy, you know that. You think that little girl would have stayed unclaimed if any of us had changed over the years?"

They were unique, maybe. Sexual fulfillment and pleasure wasn't a game. It was something they took seriously, something they worked at. They all cared for Kelly, in different degrees. She was Rowdy's life. But the others, hell, they loved her too, and they always would.

Loving Kelly himself didn't change that. He'd kill any other man who dared touch her, but he hoped, prayed, he wasn't wrong about Kelly and the fact that her needs would mirror his own.

The need was an enigma, even to the three men. Maybe they were too close, left on their own too much as teenagers—who the hell knew. They didn't question it, they didn't fight it. If Kelly didn't want it, then it was a no-go, but he had a feeling about Kelly. She was a little sex kitten waiting to purr, and they were ready to stroke her.

So why was he suddenly tensing at the thought of Dawg and Natches inspiring that pleasure, that need within her?

He nodded slowly. She was his; there was no contest there. He would fight any man for her, even a friend. But here, there was no need to fight. Dawg and Natches didn't own her heart, Rowdy did. And the pleasure he knew the three of them could bring her outweighed the subtle warning shifting through his chest.

"Will she agree?" Dawg asked the hardest question to answer.

"Before the attack, I would have said yes." Rowdy sighed roughly. "Now, who knows?" He shook his head before wiping his hand over his face in a gesture of frustration. "We'll see. It will have to be her decision."

They nodded in reply.

"We get her over the attack first, take care of the attacker, then see where we go from there," Rowdy said. "She's not ignorant of the rumors, she suspects what's coming. But"—he swallowed tightly—"she's going to be scared now. And for that alone, I'll kill the bastard."

FIVE

Ray stepped into the bar the next evening, several hours after Rowdy called to say he wouldn't be home for dinner after all, with the excuse that he had to take care of business. Ray feared that somehow Rowdy felt he couldn't come home. And he wasn't having that. That was Rowdy's home, no matter what was going on, and he needed the boy to know that.

Ray hadn't been in a bar in over ten years. Not since he started dating Maria. He had known her forever. She and her husband had been regulars at the marina, their boat docked close to the office. Hell, during their younger days, when pleasure had been all that mattered, he and James, Maria's husband, had shared Maria at one time. Once, long ago, Maria should have belonged to him, but his own ignorance had been Ray's downfall.

That was how Ray knew his son had come by his darker passions naturally, how he knew what awaited Kelly if she became his son's lover. And yeah, he knew Rowdy would never hurt her, but he also had seen the horror the girl had been through. Kelly was a warm, vibrant girl, just as her mother was, with a capacity to love that would humble any man. The thought of Rowdy tarnishing that love with his games, as Ray had once tarnished Maria's love for him, scared the hell out of him.

Ray's first wife, Layne, had been an aloof woman. He'd cared for her though, loved her in a lot of ways, and the child they had together was a fine man. Ray knew that. But he was a man, in every sense of the word.

Ray stared around the smoky establishment, looking for the boy. Rowdy was sitting alone at a far corner, a beer bottle between his hands, his head lowered. The weight of the world was settled on his son's shoulders, and Ray understood why. Rowdy came home expecting open arms and found a mess instead.

Ray stopped by the bar and purchased a bottle of Jack Daniels, snagged two glasses, and made his way across the room. It was time to talk man-to-man, with no shame. That called for an iron backbone. Or plenty of whisky.

He slammed the bottle on the table as Rowdy lifted his gaze. Deep green eyes spat with fury, blazing from a sun-darkened, roughly hewn face. Yep, the boy was pissed off, clear down to his bones, and Ray didn't blame him.

He pulled out a chair and sat down.

"Some things just call for a good drunk," he said heavily, uncapping the whisky and pouring two small glasses full. "Childbirth. Your son's first date. Your daughter's near rape." His throat tightened with the pain as he tossed back the dark liquid and poured another shot of courage. "And when a man screws up because he feels helpless, and hurts the people he loves the most."

He stared straight into Rowdy's dark eyes, feeling his son's pain as though it were his own.

Ray sighed. "I swore to her I wouldn't tell you. And it's weighed bad on me ever since. While she was all doped up on the pain medication, and hysterical, she told her mom about what happened at the airport with you before you left that last year. She loves you. Always has. We've known that." He swallowed tightly. "And I knew how bad you wanted her." He paused, glancing away for a long second before pulling his gaze back to his son's. "I never told you how much pride I had in you when you walked away, did I?"

He saw his son's surprise.

"I didn't figure you knew why I'd left." Rowdy leaned back in his chair before picking up the whisky and throwing it back. He grimaced but held the burn of it.

"I knew." Ray sighed heavily. "I knew when you were twenty-two and as though overnight, she turned from a clumsy little urchin into a woman-child. I saw your face the day you realized it."

He watched the flush that rose over Rowdy's face, the discomfort.

"She was a kid." He cleared his throat uncomfortably. "She's not a kid anymore, Dad. She's twenty-four, and a grown woman."

"And you were and still are a man." Ray shook his head wearily before sipping at the whisky. "A good man. One any father could be proud of. You didn't touch her, you did what you had to do and didn't make any excuses or cast any blame. Though you could have. You left your home because of the girl—many men would have resented her. You would have been well within your rights to have protested how much Maria and I spoiled her."

"You should have told me that then," Rowdy grunted. "She

kept stealing my damned shirts. She still does it. I should have made you throw both Kelly and Maria out."

A grin tugged at his son's lips. Ray shook his head. Rowdy was willing to forgive, no questions asked. And Ray didn't know if he could have been as gracious if someone had hid something so important from him.

Ray cleared his throat again.

"I should have told you." He rolled the glass between his fingers, staring at it rather than his son. "But I knew you'd get home one way or the other and I wasn't sure Kelly could face that. She needed time to put the attack into perspective before she faced what was between the two of you." Damn, he needed another drink.

He poured another, aware of the way his son watched him, his eyes narrowed, his expression thoughtful.

"Hunger like that goes beyond lust, Dad," Rowdy finally sighed. "I've fought it for too long. I don't know what it is yet. I don't know how deep it goes. I know I came back for her." He shook his head when Ray started to speak. "Hear me out. I had no intentions of living in that house, of breaking so much as one of your rules, but that bastard's still out there." Ray's gut clenched. "I'll camp outside her bedroom window if I have to, but you won't keep me away from her."

Rowdy leaned forward, his arms braced on the table, his fists clenched. Ray looked away from his son for long moments, wondering what he was supposed to say. Hell, he felt tired and helpless and not sure how to defend those he loved.

"You've been checking into it?" Ray knew he had. Rowdy had spent the afternoon at the police department before he met up with his cousins.

"I've been checking into it." Rowdy poured himself another shot. "I talked Betty Cline into letting me see the hospital records, and the sheriff gave me everything they had on the other girls. He's calling them. He doesn't call Kelly. He's local, Dad."

For a second, fear sliced through Ray. If the bastard was local, then he wouldn't have to call Kelly. He could watch her. Anytime, anywhere.

Then pride suffused Ray. Hell, that was his boy. Hard-eyed, determined, and ready to fight. He was more man than Ray had ever imagined. Rowdy wasn't drinking himself silly because Kelly had been attacked, but instead, he was plotting and planning justice. It was enough to make a father proud.

Ray breathed in hard. He had discussed this with Maria earlier, knew what he was about to do was hard on her; it would be harder on Kelly.

"Come back home, boy," he muttered. "I'm a damned fool when I get riled and we both know it. That's your home. As much as it is mine. And you're my kid. I want you there."

Rowdy's lips quirked. "The duffel bag is still on the bike. I was coming back tonight anyway."

Ray cleared his throat again. "I trust you, Son."

Rowdy's face changed then. If Ray thought it was hard before, it was more so now. Rowdy leaned forward, his eyes meeting Ray's straight on.

"She's mine, Dad." He kept his voice low, fierce. "Any other time I would have never disrespected your rules or your home. But I won't pull back now. I won't lose her because some bastard tried to destroy her. And I won't play footsie under the table because of your sensibilities. Do you understand that?"

Anger flared in Ray. He rubbed his hand over his lower face before breathing out roughly. "Hell. Fine. Whatever. But"—he glared back at the boy—"you don't play with that girl, Rowdy. You better be damned serious before you end up having sex with her.

Son or no son, I taught you respect. She's not one of those little tramps you, Natches, and Dawg screwed with when you were younger."

It was a warning he'd made when he first realized how sexual his son was. Good girls were solid gold. A good girl understood responsibility, values, and herself. A woman like that wasn't a toy, she was a partner.

"I know how to treat a woman, Dad," Rowdy grunted. "All women. Not just Kelly."

Unlike Ray's generation, Rowdy didn't differ how he treated women in regards to their sexuality. One didn't deserve less respect, or more, for the amount of experience they had in bed. Rowdy had argued that with his father many times. But love . . . that made a difference, and Ray knew it. And he knew his son was learning it.

"So you'll come home?" Ray's throat was tight with emotion. Damn, he hated that. Hated knowing there was more he should say and not knowing how to say it.

Rowdy looked over at him, his expression somber, his eyes, that deep sea green, serious and thoughtful. "I missed you too, Dad," he murmured.

If that knot in his throat could have gotten tighter, it would have. Ray swallowed, then tried again. "I love you, boy." His voice was so rasping he was ashamed of it. "And I'm damned proud of you. Damned proud."

"I love you too, Dad." That was his boy. Equal parts hellion and warrior but never afraid to say the words. "And I'm proud of you, too."

He poured the glasses full again; they toasted each other and settled down for a serious drunk. Hell, Ray had been waiting on this day for nearly thirty years. There just wasn't anything like having that first good drunk with your son, and knowing it meant something. Meant something damned fine.

Kelly heard the Harley coming up the drive with her stepfather's truck as the clock flipped over to two in the morning. Her mother had been pacing the house, muttering to herself, worry creasing her brow.

Maria turned to Kelly, her eyes dark as she watched her.

"Are you sure?" Maria asked, her voice soft, uncertain.

"For God's sake." Kelly felt like snarling the words. "Mom, have you and Ray lost your minds?" Sometimes Kelly thought the attack had been more traumatic on them in a lot of ways. Kelly was never really certain how she felt about it. Frightened, yes. Terrified sometimes. Knowing her attacker was still out there kept her nerves on edge.

"He's always wanted you." Maria had never been comfortable with that. Kelly had known it, though they never talked about it. Just as her mother knew Kelly had always wanted Rowdy. It was like some odd fact of life.

"I'm not a little girl anymore," she sighed, curling up on the sofa, watching her mother pace the living room as the vehicles shut off. "You know they're both drunk, don't you?"

One of Rowdy's friends had called from the bar. He hadn't been too sober himself, warning them that the two men were heading home, thankfully being driven by friends rather than driving themselves.

"Ray hasn't been drunk since before we got married." A smile curved her mother's lips, and Kelly swore she looked a little too sensual to suit her. *A daughter shouldn't see things like that*, she thought with a burst of humor.

"Well, he's drunk now." She winced as it sounded like a load of bricks fell on the porch.

"Hell boy, I thought you were holding me up." Ray's voice drifted into the house.

"Thought you were holding me up." Rowdy's laughter was muffled.

Maria moved for the doorway and pulled it open with a quick jerk as Kelly rose from the couch to stand just inside the living room.

The two men were attempting to hold each other up as they paused in the doorway to get their bearings. Rowdy's expression was relaxed, his gaze a little heavy lidded and so darned sexy he took her breath.

As her eyes met his, a slow, sexy smile curved his lips and made her knees weak. He gripped his dad's arm tighter and led him inside the house. Neither of them were too steady on their feet.

"Maria, he's a lousy drunk," Rowdy grunted as his father threw his arm over Maria's shoulder and planted a loud, smacking kiss on her cheek. "He didn't even make it through the first bottle."

Kelly wrapped her arms across her chest, a smile tugging at her lips as Rowdy winked at her.

"He never did, Douglas, you just keep forgetting," her mother chastised him firmly.

Rowdy winced. "That's not my name."

"That's what your birth record has. I didn't see a *Rowdy* there anywhere, Douglas."

Rowdy gave her a mock glare. "You're not being nice to me, Maria."

"That's not my job," she pointed out calmly. "Now move your big feet out of the way so I can get him upstairs. You two should be ashamed of yourselves."

"I can be ashamed later," Ray piped in as she led him to the stairs. "Hell. We had fun, sweetheart."

"I can tell." Maria laughed softly.

Their voices lowered as they moved away, and finally disappeared. A few minutes later the door at the back of the hallway closed and everything was silent.

Kelly watched Rowdy. His hair was still too short. The spiked military cut suited him, but she had loved his long hair when he was younger. The way it framed his face, emphasized his green eyes. He looked like a fallen angel come to tempt mortal women when his hair was long. Short, he looked like the warrior she knew he had to be. A fighter, a Marine. Tall and tough and hard.

He turned to her, placing his hand over his chest, the dark blue material of his cotton shirt stretching across his shoulders.

"Kelly, darlin', you look like an angel standing there." His smile was a tad goofy and too damned sexy.

Unfortunately, she knew better. She was wearing another of his shirts, one she had stolen the last time he was home. A pair of loose sweatpants and socks that bunched at her ankles. She looked messy and frightened, and she knew it.

She licked her lips nervously. Facing him after what had happened at the boat earlier wasn't easy. She wasn't ashamed, but neither was she comfortable with some of the feelings Rowdy caused to burn inside her. "I missed you, Rowdy," she whispered, trying to still the trembling of her lips. "I'm glad you're home."

His expression sobered as he moved toward her slowly. She forced herself to stay still, not to retreat. But he was so big, and powerful. Strong. The memory of hard hands holding her down, a rough voice muttering in her ear as her face was pressed into the pillow, haunted her.

"So where's my hug?" He stood in front of her, his arms at his sides, his eyes dark and glittering with hunger.

He still wanted her. She could see the memories of the heated exchange they'd had earlier in his eyes.

"I . . ." She swallowed tightly, glancing away as her hands tightened on her arms. God, what was wrong with her. She had nearly bared her breasts for him, but now she felt as uncertain, as frightened as she had the moment she stepped into the houseboat.

"Just a hug, Kelly-baby?" He whispered the words, his lips quirking gently. "I dream of your hugs, darlin', just as much as I dream of your kiss."

She stared back at him in surprise.

"You don't believe me?" He reached out, his arm lifting slowly, his fingers reaching out to lift a strand of curls from her shoulder.

She glanced quickly at where he held her hair, biting at her lower lip as she tried to still the pounding of her heart. She had dreamed of his touch for so long, waited for him, longed for him. *Oh God, this isn't fair*, she wailed silently. She had waited for this for so long, now her own insecurities were eating her alive. It didn't matter that her therapist had warned her to expect this. She felt as frightened, as off balance as she had the first months after the attack.

"Rowdy . . ." Her throat tightened as she fought herself, the fear and need warring inside her.

"It's real easy, baby," he crooned, his dark velvet voice washing over her. "You just lift your arms and put them around my neck." He let go of her hair, fingers curling around her wrists as he lifted her arms, urging them up until they curled around his neck. "Then you come up real close to me, so I can hug you back." His arms went around her, slowly, so slowly, pulling her against him until her head rested on his chest.

"There we go."

She was shaking, but was it fear or something more? She didn't know what she was feeling, didn't know how to assimilate the sensations and emotions washing through her.

"I came home for you, Kelly," he reminded her, his breath caressing her ear as she jerked against him. "I came home to touch you, to taste you, to claim you. Do you know what I would have done if I had known you were home when I pulled in yesterday morning?"

She shook her head, a jerky movement as a small whimper left her lips. He felt so good. A man shouldn't feel this good, powerful yet protective, hot and so blessed sexy.

"I would have come to your room and kissed you awake. I would have seen your pretty eyes opening, knowing it's me beside you, my lips touching yours. I want that real bad, Kelly. Even though I know if Dad caught me he'd skin me alive." He breathed in roughly; the feel of his chest rasping against her breasts sent a shudder racing through her. "Now," he whispered, "I really don't care if he does skin me."

She stiffened against him, needing to draw away, needing to get closer to him. God, she hated this. Hated the fear holding her back, hated not knowing, not understanding the emotions raging through her mind and body.

"Rowdy—"

"Shh." He stilled her protest as he rubbed his head against hers. "Just settle here against me, baby. Let me hold you for a minute; let me know you're okay. Just that."

"But I'm not okay." Her hands clenched in the fabric of his shirt as she finally admitted it to herself. "I'm scared, Rowdy. I'm so scared." She pressed her head against his chest, the words slipping free after nearly a year of burying them. She was terrified.

"I know, baby." He kissed her head, his hands running over her back. "But I won't let you be scared of me."

She heard the pain in his voice, felt it tighten her chest. No, Rowdy would never hurt her, but fear was an insidious disease, and fighting it took more courage than she thought she had.

"We're going to take this nice and easy," he crooned. "We're going to go upstairs and you're going to sleep, baby. I'm going to lie right beside you so you know no one can get to you, no one can hurt you as long as I'm there. Okay?"

"In my bed?" She jerked back, staring up at him. "Ray will skin us *both* alive."

"Dad will deal with it." His expression hardened, determination glittering in his eyes. "He already is. You're not sleeping; you're not eating. We're going to change that, starting tonight."

"Oh, are we now?" The high-handedness in his voice pricked at her.

"Kelly." He tilted his head, staring down at her, a smile quirking at his lips. "Are you going to fight me, baby? Really? Remember the last fight we got into?"

"You put another snake in my drawer, and I'll start calling you Douglas," she sniped. "I can't believe you'd threaten me like that."

He smirked, his gaze drowsy, his expression so sensual it was enough to make her panties damp. And they were damp. Yeah, she was scared spitless at times at the thought of touching him, having him touch her, but he could make her so wet, so fast, that it wasn't even surprising anymore.

"I'm just going to lie beside you, that's all," he whispered. "If you can't sleep, then I'll lie on the floor. But I'll be there, Kelly. Will you trust me enough to let me be there? Remember yesterday morning, baby? You trusted me enough to almost bare those pretty little nipples for me. Keep trusting me, Kelly."

She was breathing roughly; the realization of it forced her to try to regulate it. She hated this weakness, this fear. Even the sessions with the psychologist hadn't been able to erase it.

"I would trust you with my life, Rowdy," she whispered, knowing she did.

"Come on then." His arms wrapped around her as he led her to the stairs. "Let's go on up and see if we can get some sleep. I don't know about you, Kelly, but I'm dead tired."

She hadn't had nightmares in months, she thought as he turned out the lights and led her upstairs. She wasn't sleeping well, but when she did sleep, she wasn't waking screaming as she did in those first months. It should be safe. She could have something she had always dreamed of. Rowdy in her bed, sharing his warmth with her. Maybe even holding her. Surely she could handle that?

SIX

Kelly wasn't really surprised when Rowdy stopped at his bedroom to get a pair of soft, gray cotton sweats similar to her own. He slept in the nude, so the concession he was making wasn't lost on her.

"Okay?" He led her to her bedroom door, opening it carefully before stepping in ahead of her.

Kelly drew in a deep, sustaining breath, battling the confusing emotions racing through her. She had waited for Rowdy for so long that she wasn't certain how to adapt to this abrupt shift between his careful distance and his sudden closeness.

"I'm fine," she answered as she stepped in behind him, noticing the tension in his body.

"I'll change in the bathroom." He closed the door behind her.

Kelly fisted her hands in her T-shirt as she bit her lip, fighting to hold back her nerves as Rowdy disappeared into the other room. She gazed around her bedroom, taking in the frilly curtains over the dark shades, the white lace of her comforter. It wasn't exactly a man's room.

Yet, Rowdy hadn't flinched at it. He had filled it, overpowered it, and pulled all focus toward him. Not that she had expected anything less.

She was still standing in the middle of the room when he came from the bathroom long minutes later. She couldn't stop her gasp, couldn't help the leap of her pulse at the sight of him.

He was obviously aroused. In those pants, there was no way to hide just how well-endowed he was either. She swallowed nervously as her gaze moved over hard, flexing abs, sun darkened and powerful, to a wide chest and an expression blazing with hunger.

She took a step back, watching as his eyes narrowed on her.

"Come on, baby. We passed this point." His voice was rough, deep, a rasp of black velvet across her raw senses.

"I'm fine." Her hands knotted in the material of the shirt as she felt the flesh between her thighs heating further, dampening.

And her breasts. They felt heavy, swollen, her nipples almost painful with their sensitivity.

"I don't think I can sleep with you, Rowdy." She fought to keep her breathing under control. "I don't know if I can stand it."

He didn't argue with her. He stepped over to the bed and pulled back the blankets before staring back at her.

"I'd never hurt you," he whispered. "Come on, get into bed. Surely you're not going to let something like a hard-on scare you off, Kelly."

That wasn't just a hard-on. It was Rowdy's hard-on, and she was dying for it with the same intensity that she was terrified of it. Not because she was afraid he would hurt her, but because she was afraid of her own emotions, her own desires.

But when he extended his hand to her, she was helpless. Flushed, uncertain, she moved to the bed, crawling into it stiffly and lying down as he moved in beside her and reached over to turn out the small bed lamp.

And there he was, lying on his side beside her as she stared up at the ceiling, fighting to keep from touching him, from begging him to touch her.

"I told Dad I came back for you, Kelly."

Her gaze flew to his eyes, barely making out the glittering depths in the darkness of the room as she felt his hand move, felt it as it moved gently to her stomach.

"Rowdy . . ." She couldn't breathe. His hands was like a flame through the material of the shirt she wore, pressing against her stomach as she felt her womb spasm with need.

"It's nice and dark," he whispered then. "Like a sweet, warm dream. Your dream, Kelly. What would you do in your dreams? What would I do to you?"

She couldn't help the tiny moan that fell from her lips. She had many, many dreams of what she wanted Rowdy to do to her, with her. The things she would do to him, if she only knew how.

"This is dangerous." Her voice sounded strangled in the darkness around them as her hand gripped his wrist.

"Do you trust me?" The question had her breath catching on a sob.

"With my life," she answered readily. And she did.

"Trust me to touch you. To bring you pleasure, Kelly. Let me touch you."

His hand moved, his fingers bunching in the shirt to drag it over her stomach.

"They'll hear me." Her hands clenched harder around his wrist. "You don't know what you do to me, Rowdy. You can't understand—"

"Do you know what I want to do to those pretty breasts?" He shocked her to silence again. "I want to take this shirt off you, Kelly. I want to bare them and touch your hard little nipples with my fingers, then with my mouth. I want to show you how good just a touch can be."

The material of her shirt began to rise as she tried to draw enough oxygen into her lungs to protect the incredible sensuality of his statement.

"But you might get loud," he whispered with a thread of amusement. "And I think I'd like you loud, Kelly. I want to hear you screaming in pleasure, begging me for more and more until you know you can't take more, but you want it anyway. And that's when you need a harder touch, more sensation. That's when pleasure becomes almost painful and when the pain becomes ecstasy."

She shuddered as his hand moved against bare flesh and the shirt rasped over her hard nipples as he drew it slowly from her.

"Excellent," he crooned. "I'm going to get you naked before the night's out, baby. I'm going to hold you against me and feel the sweet, sleek warmth of your body. Would you like that?"

His hand cupped the hard swell of her breast as her breath rocked from her body and she arched, jerking against the touch as a million sensations began to riot through her.

She had to bite her lip to keep from crying out.

"How pretty," he sighed, looming over her, his gaze on her face despite the warmth of his fingers caressing the globe of her breast. "What will you do when I get my fingers on those tight little nipples? Or my mouth between your soft thighs?"

"Rowdy, please"—her voice was a breath of sound as she shuddered beneath him—"I don't know . . ."

"Shhh. Just lie here with me," he whispered. "Let me feel you come for me. Just here in a bit, baby. Let me touch your sweet body and show you how good it can feel. Then you can sleep, right here against me."

Let her come for him? He was going to make her come? Here? In her bed?

Then she almost did come. His finger began to circle her nipple, drawing an incredible circle of fire around it as his head lowered, his lips barely touching hers.

"Get ready," he whispered. "Let's see how much you like this."

His thumb and forefinger gripped the violently sensitive peak and exerted just enough pressure to throw her into a maelstrom of sensations. Fire tore from her nipple to her clit, surging to her womb as she felt it flex in hunger.

Her lips parted on a fractured cry that he took into his own mouth. His lips covered hers easily, gently, absorbing her cry as they moved against her with restrained hunger.

His fingers were tugging at her nipples, both of them now, shifting against her until he rose half over her, surrounding her with his heat.

"God, I would have loved to have heard that cry," he groaned against her lips.

Kelly could feel the tremors racing through her body, feel the soft wetness gathering between her thighs. Her hands lifted to his shoulders, her fingers pressing into the hard muscle as his lips smoothed over hers again.

"I just want to feel your nipple in my mouth," he whispered. "I want to slide my hand to your pretty thighs and see how wet and soft you are there. How much could you stand, baby, before you screamed again?"

Not much. She was weak. She was entranced by the pleasure tearing through her body and she could do nothing to stop it.

"I want you naked, Kelly," he breathed against her lips. "Will you be naked for me, baby?"

One hand moved to her hips, curling into the waistband of her sweatpants as he began to push them down her thighs.

"Rowdy . . ." Was she scared? She was terrified, but not of being hurt. She couldn't make sense of the sensations racing through her, pleasure and fear, confusion and dazed hunger. They were flooding her, drowning her with conflicting needs.

"We're just playing, Kelly." He moved back, sliding the pants down her legs before pulling them free of her body.

She was naked now, exposed if it hadn't been for the darkness of the room.

He lifted her hand again, kissing it before he surprised her by laying it over her lips.

"Shhh. We don't want anyone to hear."

She didn't think he really gave a damn if anyone did hear, but she pressed her fingers to her lips, certain she would die of embarrassment if her mother or Ray heard her pleasure.

She saw the flash of his teeth in a wicked grin before his head lowered.

It was a good thing she covered her mouth before his lips touched her aching nipple, before they surrounded the sensitive peak and drew it into his mouth. Because her cry was barely muffled with one hand as the other flew to his head.

Her back arched, and she swore flames burned over her body as he began to suckle at her. He wasn't slow and easy. He didn't ease her into it, he didn't tease her into it, he devoured her, and she was helpless beneath it.

"God. Baby." He buried his head between her breasts then, his breathing rough and hard as his hands moved down her waist, her hips. "You're going to my head faster than the whisky did."

She needed more. She pressed against him, certain she was going to scream for more if he didn't touch her again.

"Easy. Easy." His breathing was a rough groan as his lips moved along her chest, her collarbone. "Come here, baby. Let's ease this fire before I lose my sanity."

He pulled her to him as he moved her hand from her lips and covered them with his own. Then his other hand went between her thighs.

Kelly jerked against him, her hand latching onto his wrist as she felt his fingers part the wet folds.

"Oh God, you're bare." His voice was tortured as his fingers moved over flesh despite her hand gripping him. "Sweet heaven have mercy."

His thumb flicked over her clit as his fingers parted the swollen flesh.

"Easy. We're going to do this quick, baby. If we don't, I'm going to end up taking you here, in your bed, and then we'll both be screaming."

His lips covered hers again as his thumb moved along the outer edge of the sensitive bud of flesh as his fingers began to caress the greedy opening.

She was crying out beneath his lips. One arm latched around his neck as the nails of the other bit into his wrist. It didn't deter him. His thumb caressed, rotated, then pressed against her with diabolical results.

Stars exploded before her eyes as she jerked beneath him, shuddering violently as pleasure whipped over her nerve endings and devastatingly clashed through her senses.

She could feel her juices rushing from her sex, feel his fingers rubbing through them, intensifying her climax as a growl vibrated against her lips, covering her fractured scream.

And she was lost. She was distantly aware of his release, the movement of his free hand, the feel of his semen washing over thigh, which only intensified her own pleasure and egged at her fears. Not her fear of his touch, or the fear of being with him. But the overwhelming fear that there wasn't a chance in hell that she could handle him.

Kelly eased into sleep within minutes of Rowdy cleaning them both up and tucking the blankets around her. He felt her relax against him, felt the soft sigh that left her lips. Moving slowly, he eased the blanket further over her shoulders, feeling her head on his arm, her silky hair against his chest as he held her. It was killing him, the pain, the fear he knew she had to have endured. He could feel his heart breaking in his chest even as a killing rage burned in his soul.

She was his. She had been his as long as he had known her and by God he wasn't letting her go. She knew him, knew he would cut out his own heart before he'd hurt her—that trust was still within her. If it weren't, she would never have been able to climax so sweetly for him, or sleep in his arms, to allow him to hold her, her sweet body tucked so close against his own. Naked.

He stared into the dimly lit bedroom, his eyes narrowed, his mind working. Whoever dared to hurt her, to stalk her, wouldn't be breathing for long. He wouldn't be breathing two seconds past the time Rowdy learned who he was. And that was a silent promise, a vow he made to Kelly. She would never be hurt again.

SEVEN

Maria opened Kelly's door the next morning, not really expecting what she saw. Ray had warned her the night before, but he had been drunk, amorous, so she hadn't really taken him seriously. Perhaps she should have—the shock wouldn't have been so great.

She was used to coming in to find Kelly napping in the large wingback chair on the other side of the room, the television droning in the background. The room was silent now, and Rowdy was staring at her through slitted eyes from the bed.

He was wrapped around her sleeping daughter like a living vine. Kelly lay on her side, her back pressed against Rowdy's front, her head sheltered beneath his chin. One hard leg lay over her daughter's fragile ones beneath the blankets, his arms surrounding her as her hair tangled over them. He was bent over her, wrapped around her, and Kelly was sleeping peacefully.

It was more than obvious that they both were naked. Kelly was her baby; seeing her sleeping in a man's arms, especially Rowdy's, was disconcerting. She had expected the closeness they had before her marriage to Ray to develop, but not in this way. As siblings, very close friends, but never this. This terrified her.

The sexual tension that vibrated from the two whenever they were together had always worried her, deeply. She had been terrified for years that Rowdy would break her daughter's heart. What she saw now filled her with conflicting emotions. Rowdy would protect Kelly, and, ultimately, that was Maria's greatest wish. Her daughter's protection. But what he could do to her baby's heart was almost more than she could bear.

As she stared at the two, Rowdy's frown darkened, his gaze narrowing at her. "What?" he mouthed.

Ray had warned her, she had known herself what was coming.

"We're going to the marina." She mouthed the words back at him, hoping her daughter would continue to sleep.

He nodded with a subtle shift of his head, never really moving. Content. That was how he appeared. Content where he was, holding Kelly close.

She backed slowly from the room, her hand lingering on the door panel for a moment as she fought the worry building within her. Maybe Ray was right. Maybe Rowdy was all Kelly truly needed to get past the attack. Maria hoped so. The shadows in her daughter's eyes broke her heart, but even more the worry that whoever had attacked Kelly would return terrified her. Until they caught him, Maria knew she would never sleep easy.

Kelly came awake slowly, her senses alive, her skin tingling at the warmth that surrounded her. There was no momentary fear, no surprise. Rowdy was holding her. She could feel him wrapped around her, spooned against her as though she had been made for the position.

She was aware of something else as well as she lay there, her body tucked into his. He was hard. His erection pressed against the crevice of her buttocks, a thick intruder, waiting. She bit her lip, stiffening in his arms, her muscles tightening. Pleasure and fear combined inside her. And the pleasure was stronger. The culmination of what felt like a lifetime of fantasies and needs rose inside her, blocking the fear, pushing it back until nothing mattered except Rowdy.

"Easy, baby." His voice was drowsy, calm. "It's just a hard-on." He snuggled against her, tucking her closer to his chest as her hands gripped the bedspread and she fought to level her breathing.

"I hate to say this," she wheezed. "That's not a hard-on, Rowdy. That's a baseball bat."

His snorted chuckle vibrated against her back, and only pressed his erection closer against her rear. She stiffened further.

"Want me to move? I'm pretty comfortable right now."

Oh, she just bet he was. She forced herself to breathe deeply, to push back the panic threatening, building in her mind. This was Rowdy and he wouldn't hurt her now.

"You're thinking it to death," he murmured and he rubbed his chin against her hair. "Scared?"

"Of your baseball bat?" She fought for humor rather than hysteria. "I don't know, Rowdy, I hear you're pretty fond of it. Lots of practice and all."

She felt his hand move, his fingers running over hers, sending tingling spirals of heat to build beneath them.

"You're a little minx," he growled at her ear, a velvet-soft sound that rippled through her senses. "That wasn't very nice."

A grin tugged at her lips at his chastising tone. She relaxed against him, feeling her body conform to his, settling against hard muscle and aroused heat.

"I'm not nice, remember?" Her eyes closed as he chuckled at her back. It was an old argument going back years before. It usually occurred whenever she told him what lousy taste he had in women, and pointed out their faults in vivid detail.

"I do remember." His lips smoothed over the top of her head, the caress sending trailing fingers of pleasure to wash through her body. The slightest caress, no matter how subtle, had the power to make her tremble. "You have a mean wit sometimes, Kelly."

She gave an amused snort at that. "I just didn't care to tell you the truth, Rowdy."

His girlfriends weren't exactly the kind of woman he brought home to dinner. As a matter of fact, he had never brought a woman home to dinner. Kelly would never have been able to tolerate that. She wondered if he had known that.

"Do you remember when you were seventeen, and you bought that scrap of material you called a bathing suit?" he mused softly.

She remembered the bathing suit, bought specifically in the hope of teasing him past the control she always hated so much.

"I didn't think you noticed." She turned her head, staring up at him, close.

His eyes were darker, tiny pinpoints of emerald glittered in the sea green iris, mesmerizing her, filling her vision. And his lips. Her eyes darted to his lips, so close. And she knew how they felt rubbing against her own, firm and warm, stoking fires inside her she hadn't imagined existed.

"I noticed," he whispered, his voice rougher now. "All summer. I think my cock still has the imprint of my zipper on it."

His hand stroked up her arm, his palm creating a heated friction that had her nerves prickling with awareness. She could still feel his erection like heated iron resting against the crevice of her rear, but his lips drew her.

"Are you going to kiss me again, Rowdy? Anytime soon?"

"Maybe." The seductive croon had a shiver racing through her.

"When?" *Now would be a good time.*

"When do you want me to?" His hand slid from her arm to her stomach and rested there.

She felt his fingers, long, broad, resting against her, with nothing between them. And they were moving, slowly easing above her hips, passing her abdomen until his hand rested on the bare flesh of her midriff.

"Now." God, if he didn't kiss her she was going to die from the need of it. "You distracted me last night. I didn't get to feel it real good."

"My little Lolita." His lips lowered, brushed against hers. "How long have you been teasing me now?"

"Since I was nine?" She breathed a laugh against his lips.

The first day she had seen him. He had been as handsome as sin and a god in her eyes when he saved her from a bully in that park.

"Hmm. I was fifteen. You were the sweetest little girl. Staring up at me with those big gray eyes so full of tears because that bully had taken your hair bow."

"And you got my hair bow back." She was panting for breath, her lips brushing his with each word.

"I got your hair bow back."

He took her breath. His lips captured hers in an all too brief, fiery kiss. No tongue, no more than a taste of him on her lips before he drew back.

"Rowdy . . ." She reached for him, needing more, aching for more. "That's not fair."

His fingers played against her midriff, rubbing in slow sensual circles, creating little starbursts of sensation that exploded in her sex. Her nipples were on fire, begging to be touched, caressed. His hands were so close, the heat of them warming the tight, aching mounds.

She stilled against him as his hips shifted against her rear once again.

"I'm not scared of you," she whispered, staring into his eyes, fighting to keep her own open. "I've never been scared of you, Rowdy."

"Yeah, you are," he whispered, his eyes darkening. "I can see it in your eyes, in your face." A somber smile touched his lips. "But that's okay, baby, you won't be scared for long."

She opened her lips to speak, then stared at him in astonishment as he rolled from the bed and flashed her a wicked smile. A teasing smile, before bending over and picking up his discarded sweats. He pulled them over his legs, covering his nakedness and the full, engorged length of his erection.

Kelly rolled to her back, propping herself on her elbows and staring at him as he moved to the bottom of the bed. He was so obviously aroused it made her mouth water. His cock pressed against the sweatpants with implicit demand, a thick length of steel-hard flesh that she ached for.

"I don't like being teased like that," she pouted. "Come back here and kiss me properly."

"You don't deserve it yet." His voice was a dark croon, his expression arrogant, certain. Smug.

"I don't deserve it?" Disbelief warred with amusement. "I've been of age for at least six years now, Rowdy. Ready, willing and able. And"—she stretched her legs out slowly, looking at him from beneath lowered lids—"I think I've waited too long. You didn't give me a chance to fully enjoy it last night."

His eyes narrowed, a seductive droop of the eyelids, the exceptional green eyes glittering from between heavy black lashes.

"Oh, I agree." His voice lowered, his hands gripping the railed footboard of the bed, his fingers curling around it, clenching. "We've waited too long, Kelly. Now, let's see how bad you want it." He winked slowly. "Better shower, baby, I think you're due at the marina this afternoon. I'll take you in on the Harley."

And just as easily as that he turned and sauntered to the bedroom door. He didn't look back, didn't pause. He opened the door and left the bedroom, his broad, bare shoulders straight and strong. Too damned sexy for his own good.

Dammit.

Mackay's Marina was one of the smaller ones, specializing in rentals and mechanical servicing. Some berths were leased out, and the attached restaurant and convenience store added to the overall "one stop" friendly atmosphere of the landing.

Mackay's Marina had begun with Rowdy's grandfather, Joseph Mackay, and then under Ray Mackay's guidance had turned into a thriving, yearlong enterprise. One he wanted to turn over to Rowdy as soon as his son was willing.

The bait shop and sporting goods section of the main buildings were separated from the store and restaurant by the main office. Kelly's mother had put in the convenience store and additional gas pumps after their marriage on the condition that part of the enterprise go to Kelly once they retired. It was an agreement Ray and Rowdy had accepted easily.

Kelly was ringing up the variety of goods that old man Tanner and his son Ricky had picked up, when she saw Rowdy and Dawg walk into the main room. Natches had just left a few minutes ago after spending nearly an hour flirting and straightening the shelves at the side of the room.

She would have been a fool not to notice that the careful restraint in his demeanor toward her had changed. He watched her now with a subtle interest; a promise unique to the Mackay boys. She knew their moves, and knew the instant he walked in the room that he was no longer simply watching over her as he and Dawg had done in the past year. The additional element of desire was no longer hidden from her.

"Kelly girl, you need to put these fishing rods on sale." Ken Tanner's scowl was fierce, his brown eyes eagle-bright. Wisps of gray hair stood on end over his head, and his lined face was normally fierce, though he had a heart of gold.

"I'll tell Ray, Ken. But you know how he is. That will be $14.62."

She took the money from him, ignoring his son. Ricky was a shifty-eyed little prick who took pleasure in poking at others' weaknesses. Thankfully, he reined it in while his father was around.

As she counted out his change, she caught sight of Rowdy moving behind the counter while Dawg started straightening some of the higher shelves across the room. Dawg had spent his summers working at the marina before he left high school. For him, Rowdy, and Natches, it was almost automatic to work when they were hanging around.

"Hey, babe." She stiffened as Rowdy moved behind her, placing a hand on her shoulder as he leaned down to kiss the top of her head. "Tired yet?"

She felt the flush that suffused her face as Ricky's gaze became frankly assessing and old man Tanner grinned in delight.

"Rowdy Mackay. Boy, it's about time you came home. You just visiting or staying?" Ken's raspy voice boomed through the store.

"Hello, Ken. Ricky." He moved to the counter, shaking the

76

gnarled hand reaching out to him. The older man's hand was a pale, weak extension when clasped in Rowdy's strong, darkly tanned hands. "I'm home to stay this time."

"Well, it's about time." He nodded firmly, his knowing gaze shifting to Kelly for a long second, a hint of compassion entering his eyes. "You going to take care of our girl here?"

"Ken!" Her face flamed hotter at the question as she chastised him.

"Like all of us ain't watched you twitching around him since you were too young to know what a twitch was." He snorted, frowning back at her. "Don't you be playing dumb, girl. Just 'cause I'm old don't make me blind."

She ignored Rowdy's chuckle as she quickly bagged the items Ken had bought and handed them across the counter.

"I hope you catch lots of fish, Ken," she gritted out between her clenched teeth, pasting a facsimile of a smile on her face.

She was as fond as she could be of the old man, but he wasn't one to mince words.

His snicker was amused, kindly. "It's all in the bait, girl. It's all in the bait." He nodded to Rowdy with one of the few smiles Kelly had ever seen out of him. "Let's go, Ricky." He nudged at his son, heading toward the lake-side door. "See you later, Rowdy."

"Later, Ken." As he spoke, Kelly felt his hand settle in the small of her back, his fingers rubbing in tiny circles over the loose cotton shirt she wore.

"Stop that," she hissed, turning on him as Ken and Ricky left the building, the glass door whishing shut behind them.

She pushed his hand away, propped her hands on her hips, and glared up at his smiling face as he crossed his arms over his chest and smiled wickedly back at her.

"You're just going to make me pout if you start refusing my

pitiful advances, Kelly," he sighed. "And here I stayed awake all night last night with a numb arm just so you could sleep comfortable."

Dawg's snicker was clearly heard.

"Dumb and dumber," she muttered, though she couldn't keep the smile from her face as he reached out to run the backs of his fingers over the side of her neck. Shivers raced through her at the small caress. And it wasn't fear. She could feel the pleasure suffusing her body, dampening the flesh between her thighs.

It was disconcerting. She had spent months with the fear that she would never be able to enjoy Rowdy's touch again. That the desires he had filled her with, the needs and fantasies, would be swamped with the fear. The knowledge that they were coming back, perhaps stronger than ever was at once nerve-racking and comforting.

"It's almost closing time. I thought we'd help you close up. Then we take all that Chinese food I have out in the cycle's saddle-bag and have dinner before we head out on the lake." He pushed her hair back from her shoulder as he spoke, his fingers lingering on the shell of her ear for long seconds after he finished.

From the corner of her eye she saw Dawg locking the lake-side doors and hanging up the Closed sign.

"Ray will skin you alive." She shook her head, though she couldn't still the smile on her lips. "Summer hours are longer now, Rowdy. I still have an hour."

"I asked Dad first." He moved back, his expression intent, sexy. "Better yet, Dawg can finish up for you. Come on, Kelly, sneak away with me."

Sneak away with him? How many times had she dreamed of hearing him say those words? She would have snuck out with him, anytime, any place.

"Go on, Kelly." Dawg lent his approval to the idea. "I'll close up shop here and help Ray and your mom outside before I leave."

As Rowdy's first cousin, and the oldest by several months, Dawg had usually led the pranks the Nauti Boys had gotten into. The three men had been hell on wheels through their high school years.

She breathed in deeply, her hands sliding from her hips to her jeans pockets as she glanced up at Rowdy again.

"You know you want to," he whispered with a wink. "Come on, I even spent the day airing out the boat and getting her ready."

The *Nauti Buoy* was his pride and joy, not to mention his weekend home. He and his friends spent their summers on the water, normally in the houseboats they had acquired over the years. Their title, the Nauti Boys, had come as much from the names of their boats as from their sexual practices.

"Okay." She gripped her courage with both hands and gave him a short nod. "I haven't had Chinese in a while."

She hadn't eaten out much period, preferring to stay in the house when she was home rather than forcing herself to pretend a security she didn't feel. It terrified her, not knowing who her attacker was. If he was a friend or a stranger, someone she trusted or would have trusted.

"Good," he said, his voice warm, approving as she moved past him, tugging at the hem of her oversized shirt before one of his big hands caught one of hers.

Warmth surrounded her fingers, fed into her bloodstream, and sent heat surging through her system. Adrenaline spiked the wave of warmth, fed it into her tightening nipples, her swollen clit.

"We'll catch you on the lake later, Dawg."

"I'll give you a call before I head out." Dawg nodded as they moved past him, his eyes narrowed, the brilliant green glittering behind the spiked lashes surrounding them. They held the same teasing warmth and sensual promise that Natches's had earlier.

"Come on."

She followed Rowdy as he moved through the main marina office, waving to her mother as he opened the door and escorted her through it. She wondered if she looked as confused as she felt.

Stilling her emotions and her equilibrium after waking up with him that morning had been hard enough. She had been nervous, her fingers shaking, her stomach clenching each time she thought of waking up beside him, feeling him surrounding her, his erection pressing into her rear. That had been the most disconcerting part. She should have been frightened. The psychologist had told her she would likely be frightened the first time she tried intimate relations after the near-rape. That the intimacy of allowing a man to touch her, to hold her, might be difficult to get through.

It hadn't been. He had made her more aroused than frightened. And in ways, that was more frightening than the fear of his touch. Everyone had told her for months that being touched would be difficult for her, but being touched by Rowdy had been a dream come true.

"You think too much sometimes," Rowdy announced as he collected the bags of Chinese food from the steel saddlebags mounted to the side of the motorcycle.

"I can walk and chew gum at the same time too." She rolled her eyes at him, feeling his hand at the small of her back again.

In the past twenty-four hours he had touched her more than he had in the last ten years. Of course he hadn't been home for the better part of those ten years, but it wasn't as though the opportunity hadn't been there.

"Why didn't you go on to college?" he asked as they moved

onto the docks. "I expected you to head off right after high school."

She shrugged at the question. "I took business classes at the tech school. You might get the marina when Ray and Mom retire, but the store and fuel supply are mine," she reminded him. "They'll only grow as the traffic on the lake increases, and I wanted to be prepared for it."

"You say that as though you think I might want to get rid of you." They turned along the plank, heading for the *Nauti Buoy*, the fifty-foot sea green and white houseboat.

"Not get rid of me *maybe*." She stepped onto the wide porch, moving back as he slid open the glass sliding doors before heading into the dim, air-conditioned comfort of the living room/kitchen.

The shades were all drawn, the lights out. As he closed the door behind them, he pulled the heavy drapes closed over it, sealing them inside the intimate, cool comfort of his home away from home.

"Then what?" he asked as he moved to the small kitchen. "Do you think I wouldn't want you around, Kelly?"

The wheel column sat in the corner in front of the large shaded window beside the glass doors. A six-foot burgundy couch sat to her side, two matching chairs on the other side of the room, behind the wheel. The kitchen was equipped with a mini refrigerator, chest-type freezer, and narrow four-burner stove with an overhead microwave and oak cabinets. The double sink was narrow, but efficient. Across from the work area a circular table with four cushioned captain's chairs sat beneath a stained-glass chandelier. Farther along was a small bathroom and shower, berth bed, and a walkout to the back diving area.

She loved the *Nauti Buoy*. They had spent the summers on it when she was younger. Upstairs was another larger, opulent bedroom, as well as a master bathroom and deck. Before Ray had given it to Rowdy, there had been two bedrooms downstairs. Now, the second one was a drying/changing area for the back deck with a small washer/dryer combo.

"I wasn't sure," she finally answered, staring back at him, her fingers knotting in the hem of her shirt.

"Your mother helped build the marina." He turned to her after setting the food on the table. "I wouldn't take it from you, no matter what happened."

He hooked his thumbs in the pockets of his jeans, watching her with those eyes. Eyes that stripped her defenses, that sent butterflies crashing to and fro in the pit of her stomach.

She licked her lips, staring back at him. The last thing on her mind now was the business. Nerves clashed as her senses became more heightened; the air in the confines of the craft became heavier, dense with the seductive, subtle scent that was unique to Rowdy.

"I know you wouldn't, Rowdy." She cleared her throat, forcing herself to move to the cabinet and the kitchenware there.

As she pulled plates and silverware from where they were held and set the table, Rowdy warmed the food in the microwave, setting it on the table before pulling a bottle of cheap wine from the fridge.

At some point, he had turned on a CD, lowering the volume until the soft, intimate music flowed through the cabin.

"Let's eat." The dark throb in his voice was so sexual that the suggestion took on a whole new meaning.

"Eat." She breathed in slowly. "Okay. We eat."

EIGHT

As they ate, he told her about the Marines. She knew
he was glossing over the harder details, the blood and death he'd
seen overseas, the friends he had lost. She knew when he was talking about those friends who were no longer alive to laugh with
him. His eyes would darken, his expression becoming reflective.

He told her about the desert, made her laugh at some of the
pranks he and his buddies had played on their CO or other sol-
diers. She saw the beauty of the sun rising over a desert landscape,
or the calm tranquillity of the moon rising, with his deep voice and
reverent descriptions.

But he had missed home. She heard that in every word. How
beautiful the moon glistening off the sand could be, but it didn't com-
pare to the early morning fog that rose from the lake or the moon
slicing a path of golden light across the wet surface.

How he would miss the guys he'd fought with, but he dreamed

of slipping off into the mountains and making the homemade moonshine he, Natches, and Dawg often made.

The silence of the desert, the symphony of the forest. He saw the beauty of the land he'd been in, but he knew the treasures to be found in the land he'd grown up in.

"What about women?" She asked the question that plagued her most as he stacked the dishes in the tiny dishwasher and turned back to where she watched him from the table.

She propped her elbow on the table, cupping her chin in her hands as she watched him curiously.

"I wasn't a saint, baby." His lips quirked with that sexy little half smile that was trademark Rowdy. "But there was nothing serious. Hasn't been anyone in a while, actually. What about you?"

He was leaning against the counter, his muscular body relaxed. Well, mostly relaxed. He was hard. She could glimpse the bulge in the front of his jeans from the lower portion of her vision and was dying for a full look.

"No one for me," she answered with a self-mocking grimace. "I couldn't get over you. You left and broke my young heart."

"Better your young heart than my neck," he grunted. "I was twenty-two-years-old, Kelly. I should have been shot for even look-ing at you then." His eyelids lowered. "But it was damned hard not to look. You filled out a pair of shorts almost as good as you fill them out now."

She felt the flush that rose over her face, her gaze flickering away from him for long moments as she breathed in deeply.

"You know, those loose clothes are going to have to go," he sighed. "One of my favorite parts of coming home was watching you run around in those snug little shorts and tank tops. Made my dick harder than hell, but it was a sight I sure as hell miss, Kelly."

Her gaze slammed into his. The green was darker now, his expression heavy with hunger.

"I . . ." She swallowed tightly. "I'm more comfortable—"

"Bullshit." The whispered retort was delivered with a knowing smile. "You're scared. I'm home now, Kelly. Trust me."

He had promised her, so long ago, as long as he was around, no one would hurt her. It was the bully, she remembered. She was terrified of staying in the park after school while her mother worked, after the bullies had started picking on her. Unless Rowdy was there. He had taken care of her. And sometimes one of the others. If Rowdy couldn't be there, Dawg or Natches had been.

"Remember when I promised I'd always take care of you?" he whispered. "You were the littlest bit of thing I had ever laid my young eyes on. Those tears on your face when those bullies stole that frippery in your hair made me madder than hell."

"You saved my hair bows." She restrained her teasing smile. "And saved Mom a ton of extra money. I loved my hair bows."

"You still love your hair bows." He grinned. "I saw them scattered all over your bathroom last night when I got up for a drink. Damned things own your sink counter."

The style of those pretty hair trifles had changed now. Rather than actual bows there were silver barrettes, glittering little bobby pins, and stylish little doodads he had yet to identify.

She lifted her brows. "They're pretty though."

He pushed from the counter, moving with a predatory ease, a shift of bone, muscle, and sinew that had her breath catching in her throat as he walked to the table.

"No." He reached out, the backs of his fingers smoothing over the side of her face. "You're pretty. Too damned pretty for those loose clothes. Take them off for me."

Her eyes widened. "I didn't bring a change—"

"You have on a bra and panties, I presume?" His fingers wrapped around her wrist, drawing her to her feet. "I bet they cover you better than that damned bathing suit did when you were seventeen."

The air was suddenly too thick to breathe, her sight dazed, filled with the color of Rowdy's eyes and the desire she could see glowing in them. Her thighs tightened as she felt the tingle of response racing through her womb, rippling through her vagina.

"I'll head the boat for the cove," he whispered. "We could do some swimming, watch the moon rise over the lake. Would you like that, Kelly?"

"A bra and panties isn't exactly a bathing suit." She drew in a deep breath, moving away from him as she tugged at the large shirt.

"It's not exactly naked, either," he said as he moved to the wheel column. "Think about it. So do we go to the cove anyway?" He glanced back at her, lifting a black brow suggestively.

Kelly breathed in deeply.

"The cove sounds like fun." She finally nodded firmly.

"And the clothes?" His gaze dropped over her body before coming back to her eyes.

She lifted her brow mockingly. "You haven't done anything to deserve it yet, Rowdy," she purred sweetly. "I guess I'll just have to think about it."

She was going to have to think about it?

As he maneuvered the *Nauti Buoy* toward the hidden cove, Rowdy found a smile tugging at his lips. He might not deserve to see those loose clothes coming over her perky little body, but he was going to. The long, thin, denim shirt fell to her thighs and draped over her slender shoulders. Even her jeans were loose, a protective shell to cover herself with.

His jaw clenched at the thought. Kelly had never had a problem wearing clothes that emphasized her slender body, until now. The attack had changed that; she was nervous now, where before she had been confident of herself as a desirable, pretty young woman.

She didn't tease him like she had for far too many years. She was more contained, quieter. And he realized he missed the spitfire she had been. By now, they should have been arguing loud enough to draw attention, while she drove him crazy with a combination of lust and exasperation.

Instead, she was standing at the glass sliding doors, staring into the distance reflectively as her fingers gripped the drapes at the side.

"I think you're wrong, Kelly." He leaned into the back of the barstool he was sitting in, one hand gripping the wheel as the boat plowed through the water toward the cove.

"About what?" She turned back to him with a frown, her gray eyes twinkling with good humor.

"I think I deserve to see you stripped down to something decent." He scowled. "Stop letting that bastard win."

She rolled her eyes before turning back to the scenery outside the boat.

"You don't know everything, Rowdy," she retorted, but there was no conviction in her voice.

"I know you." He began unbuttoning his own shirt as he glanced at her, his cock throbbing in delight as she glanced back at him, her eyes shadowed with interest.

Within seconds he'd stripped the shirt, tossing it back on the chair behind him as he flashed her a wicked grin.

She turned to him then, crossing her arms over her breasts as she lifted her brow.

"You could at least lose the jeans," he pointed out. "That shirt is big enough to cover two of you. No one would know."

Four years ago she had worn that tiny little bikini all damned day, flipping around him like a wood nymph intent on driving mortal men insane. Now, he couldn't even get her out of her pants.

"You're pushing," she warned, her voice holding a subtle snap.

"You haven't seen me push yet, baby," he growled in return. "Do you think I didn't take the time to find out just how much you've been hiding since that bastard attacked you? You stopped dressing like the girl I knew and started dressing like your damned grandmother instead. You're scared."

"Well, duh!" she mocked him. "Go figure. Maybe I should just prance around naked for you, Rowdy." She wasn't really angry, yet. Her eyes were sparkling though, her cheeks flushing with irritation.

"That would work for me." He grinned wolfishly. "Let's try it and see if it will work for you. Take yours off and I'll take mine off."

"You would take yours off anyway." Her laughter was soft, knowing.

"For you, baby, anytime." He winked.

"A far cry from your answer in the past years." The shade of mockery in her voice wasn't lost on him. "Why now? You come back and suddenly can't wait to get into bed with me? It's enough to make a girl suspicious."

"No doubt," he agreed, grinning back at her. "There's no secret there, sweetheart. I wasn't about to take a kid to my bed. Being a virgin will be hard enough for you, I at least wanted you to be mature enough to know what the hell you were getting into. But I had no intentions of not coming back for you."

Surprise reflected in her eyes.

"And if I decided I wanted someone else?" Her eyes narrowed, her lips thinning at the confidence he knew she was reading in his tone.

"Then Dawg or Natches would have taken care of it until I made it back on leave." He shrugged easily. "I put a claim on you a long time ago, Kelly. You just didn't realize it."

"Somewhere between the little sex games that your buddies shared in?"

Ohhh, now was that just a little shade of jealousy there? He watched her closely from the corner of his eye as he kept the teasing grin in place.

"Sex games are for adults." He scratched at his chin as he glanced back at her. "You couldn't handle them."

"Who says I couldn't handle them?" She frowned back at him as she straightened and placed her hands on her hips. "You never gave me the chance to try."

He snorted. "Don't let your mouth write checks your body can't cash, baby. Don't dare me."

He gave her a dark, warning look, one she immediately recognized. He wasn't playing here. Not yet. And before he started, he wanted her aware of the rules.

"I'm not stupid." She pushed her hands into her jeans pockets, staring back at him with an edge of anger, of arousal. "I paid attention to your reputation a long time ago."

She wasn't shying away from him. That was good. He didn't want her shying away from him; he wanted her curious, interested. He wanted her horny.

"Did you now?" He ran his hand over his chest as he guided the houseboat into a turn that would take it off the main section of the lake and into a more narrow waterway leading to the cove. "And you still teased me every chance you had. You've stopped teasing me. Maybe you decided you can't handle it."

She rolled her eyes. "You're being a prick."

"I'm being honest, Kelly." He gave his head a quick, negative jerk. "You listened to the rumors, you say. Evidently you didn't listen close enough."

"What does that mean?"

"Exactly what I said," he answered, narrowing his eyes as he glanced back at her. "I'm fine with having the princess. I'll take you to my bed, treat you like crystal, and love you with everything I have to give you, for as long as you can put up with me. But don't tempt the beast, sugar, because when he gets hungry, you might get more than you've bargained for."

He watched her expression go blank.

"You love me?" She blinked back at him, so damned innocent it made his guts clench.

"Kelly, I've always loved you," he told her, meaning it. Knowing he meant it. "In one way or the other, you've always been a part of me. You're old enough to decide if you want to settle in with one man, forever, or not. I figure I can give you this summer to decide for sure if I'm that man. If not, then I'll let you go. It wouldn't be easy, but I'd do it—"

"But, Rowdy, I've always loved you." She watched him in confusion now, hope and fear in equal parts shadowing her eyes.

He tapped his fingers against the wheel, turning it until it swung into another waterway leading to the private cove. Natches's family owned the small property that bordered the bay. It was on the back side of undeveloped land, and completely private.

"Yeah, I know you have," he finally answered as he pulled along the tree-shaded bank and cut the engine.

He didn't say anything more as he moved beyond the sliding doors, throwing out the heavy front anchor weight before moving to the back and doing the same. As he returned to the living area, he paused by the table.

"I came back for you," he said, leaning against the small bar, forcing himself to stand away from her. "That's why Dad was so worried. He knew I came back for you. And the rumors are fact, baby. So don't push me where the games are concerned."

"I don't need you or your dad making decisions for me," she snapped, her gray eyes flaring in defiance. "If we're going to try for a relationship, then we'll meet in the middle. Somehow. But not if you think you can plan my life for me."

His lips twitched. She was a bundle of fire, that was for damned sure.

"Take off the pants," he whispered. "Let's go one step at a time, Kelly. See what your limits are together."

"Our limits," she retorted. "Not just mine."

His lips curled into a frankly sexual, wicked smile.

Kelly licked her lips nervously. The action had the head of his erection pounding with need. Damn, he wanted that little tongue there laving the thick crest, licking around it as though it were a favorite treat.

She bit her lower lip and glanced away before breathing in deeply. Her hands moved, pulling out of the jeans pockets before moving beneath the shirt to unsnap the pants. She kicked off her sandals then pushed the jeans over her hips and down her legs.

Within seconds she was laying them over the chair with his shirt before turning back to him.

"You used to tease me like a brazen little hussy," he whispered, staring at her legs, dying to feel them around his hips. "It was one of the things I looked forward to most when I thought of coming home." He watched her move toward him, her eyes becoming cloudy with passion as he kept his voice low, carefully teasing.

"You didn't act as though you enjoyed it," she murmured as she drew up to him. He jerked as she placed her small hand on his bare chest and ran it slowly down to his tight abdomen. "You stayed away from me."

He lifted his hand, moving it to her arm, feeling the softness of her skin as he ran his fingers to her elbow and back again.

"If you knew the things I wanted to do to you over the years, you would have run screaming." He stared down at her uplifted face, his gaze on her lips. The soft, candy pink perfection of those full curves had him aching. "You're still too damned young for the things I want to do to you. With you."

"What did you want to do to me, Rowdy?" Her hand slid from his abdomen to his chest again as she stared at him, her eyes reflecting the same hungry need she had shown for years, but it also showed a shadow of fear, of hesitation.

"Everything." He wasn't going to lie to her. Now wasn't the time to hide any part of who or what he was, or the hungers he could unleash on her. If there was a time to be honest with her, it was now. Before the emotional connection that had bonded them for so many years deepened, before there was a chance she could be hurt.

Arousal flashed in her eyes as her breathing became heavier, jerkier. "Give me an example."

He ran his fingers down her arm until he found her hand, lifted it, pulling her fingers to his lips as he watched her through narrowed eyes. Her gaze flickered to his lips as he licked over the pad of two fingers, her eyelids drooping, pleasure rather than fear filling her gaze.

"You know what I want," he whispered. "Exactly what I suspect you're most frightened of now." He lifted his other hand, smoothing back her hair from her face, his thumb caressing her cheek. "I want to strip you down, love you from head to toe as often as possible, and sometimes . . . we might not be alone."

Her breath caught in a hard hitch a second before she jerked away from him, moving across the room, her shoulders stiff and straight as he forced himself to relax, to wait.

"And if we weren't alone?" Her voice was thin, breathy. He couldn't tell if it was arousal or fear that inspired it.

"If we weren't alone, you know the only men I'd ever allow around you," he told her softly.

"And if it's not what I want?" She asked, her gray eyes dark, shadowed with indecision.

"Then I won't press you for it." He crossed his arms over his chest again as he leaned against the counter. "That doesn't mean I won't think about it, that I won't fantasize the hell out of it. I won't lie to you, Kelly. Ever. And I won't have things between us that don't need to be there."

"And how do they feel about this?" Arousal lay thick in her voice, as did the fear. "Have the three of you already been making plans to seduce me?"

"There are times when men don't have to make plans, Kelly." He kept his voice smooth, even. "They know me, just as well as I know them. No plans will ever be made outside of your presence."

She breathed in slowly, her nostrils flaring as she watched him closely.

"Which brings me to another point," he continued. "Whether you want to do it or not, you're going to at least have to fake it. Until I catch that bastard who attacked you, I'll let him think it's going on. I'll torture him with the knowledge of it. Because I'll be damned if I'll let him threaten you any longer. So you might want to think about at least enjoying some of the pretense."

As he spoke, he watched her pale, then flush as fury contorted her features with lightning swiftness. A spark was all it took, and he had known he was taking that risk.

"You think you're going to play with me?" she threw back at him, her voice rising in fury. "That I'm going to let you play head games with that sick bastard until he comes after me again?"

Betrayal flashed in her eyes, in her voice.

"Think again, damn you." She stalked over to the chair, yanking her pants from the seat and jerking them over her legs as she cast him a heated glare. "You're a son of a bitch, Rowdy. I can't believe you'd do this." Emotion clogged her throat, the pain in her voice tearing at his chest.

"Hell yes, I'll do it," he snarled, stalking to her as she struggled to snap and zip her jeans. He gripped her arms, staring down at her, rage eating him alive at the thought of that perverted bastard holding her down, cutting her with that knife. "I'll do whatever it takes, Kelly, do you understand me? He's a threat to you. A danger. And that I will not tolerate. If we don't catch him, he's going to rape again, and the next woman might not live to regret it. Is that what you want?"

"You want to use me." She slapped at his arms, breaking away from him as she screamed the accusation in his face, her gray eyes swimming with tears. "You want to pervert what I feel for you, what I've needed for years, and turn it into some kind of damned war game."

"I want you until I can't breathe, dammit," he growled back at her. "I haven't taken a comfortable breath since you developed breasts. But he's going to come after you again, sooner or later. You know it and I know it. What happens if he catches me off guard? If he gets to you again?"

"You can't know that. And I'm careful now."

"I snuck up on you yesterday morning," he snapped. "Do you have any idea how easy it is to get past even Dad's security system? Do you think you could have stopped him even if that window had been closed and locked?" He saw the truth in her eyes. "Forget that, Kelly. The other girls he raped couldn't stop him. He raped one of them while her parents slept only rooms away from her. You can't hide from him, and you can't run."

"Stop yelling at me!" She pushed him back furiously, her hands cracking against his stomach as she slapped against it to forcibly put distance between them.

"You aren't listening to me," he snarled.

"And I *won't* listen to you," she screamed, the tears falling from her eyes, her face pale, her eyes raging with fury and the sense of betrayal he could see tearing through her. "You call this love? Setting me up? Oh God, Rowdy, how could you do this to me?"

A sob tore through her body as she stared up at him, her fists clenched at her side, tears wetting her cheeks and breaking his heart.

"Do what, Kelly?" he finally asked wearily, shaking his head. "Want you safe? Well? I'm telling you who and what I am, and what I am endangers you with this bastard anyway if he's even heard of me. Dawg, Natches, and I have been sharing our women since we were old enough to understand what our dicks were made for. You know that as well as anyone else does. Loving me doesn't mean you have to do shit about it. Loving you doesn't mean it's something I have to have. But we're talking about more than that now. We're talking about your life, and I'll do whatever the hell it takes to keep that bastard from ever touching you again. Ever, Kelly."

"And how do you know it wasn't one of them?" she threw in his face. "It could have been either of them. He tried to rape me anally, Rowdy. And the three of you are considered the ass-fucking kings, so tell me how you know it's not one of them."

"Because they know me," he snapped back. "And they've

watched you twitch that little ass at me since you were a teenager. Trust me, baby, if it was one of them, they would have never made the mistake of believing that good girl persona you project to every other man close enough to watch you. You're a good girl to the world, but you, baby, are bad to the bone when it comes to me. I know it, and you know it. You just have to accept it."

"Get fucked!" she screamed back, enraged, her face flushed red, her eyes glittering now with a fury he'd rarely seen in her.

He smiled. A slow, teasing, wicked grin that only fueled her rage as his gaze dropped down her body then back up.

"But, darlin', ain't that what we were talking about?"

Before she could do more than gasp he had her in his arms again, his lips covering hers, his tongue slipping past her lips to taste the wild anger and arousal pumping through her.

She didn't think. She didn't fear. He felt her hands grip his shoulders, her little nails pricking against his flesh as his hand moved beneath her shirt, to her thighs.

"Damn you," he growled, lifting his head to stare into her dazed, stormy eyes as his palm cupped the hot flesh between her thighs, the heat of his flesh searing her even through her jeans. "I bet you're wet, Kelly. So fucking wet it's seeping through your panties."

He pressed closer, feeling her hips buck at the pressure against her clit.

God, he wanted to strip her. He wanted to tear those clothes off her and lay her down on the closest available surface and devour her. He wanted to bury his lips between those perfect thighs, send his tongue searching through the silken folds of her pussy.

And she wanted it, too. She was pressing against his hand, her hips bucking into it as the heat of her filled his palm.

"Feel good?"

"I hate you," she snapped, her breathing rough as a low whimper left her throat.

"No, you don't." He rotated his hand, watching her eyes flare, feeling the heat intensify against his palm. "You love me, Kelly, just like you love this. And you want more. Admit it, baby."

Her thighs parted further as his fingers curved, massaging the sensitive flesh through her clothes.

"I want you, not a game," she cried out, arching to her tiptoes, helpless against him. He liked her helpless against his touch, loved feeling the heat of her against his hand.

"And if the game comes with it?" He watched her intently, his eyes narrowed. "I'll do whatever it takes to keep you safe. And this is what it takes. I won't let him catch us unprepared. I won't let him touch you again."

He released her slowly, hating letting her go as she stared back at him miserably.

"Think about that," he whispered, keeping his voice gentle. "I hate it like hell, and no one wishes I could have seduced you more than I do. I would have loved seducing you, baby. But your safety is more important."

"My safety?" she asked mockingly. "Or your desires?"

Anger flared inside him. "You know me better than that, Kelly." He kept his jaw tensed, his tone of voice low. "Nothing matters as much as keeping you safe."

"But only on your terms," she pointed out, furious, causing him to pause. "On your terms and by your rules. Well, you know what, Rowdy, your rules suck. Maybe I need to decide if playing your game is worth the risk to my heart and to my safety."

NINE

He watched as the *Nauti Buoy* pulled into her berth, *fifty feet and gleaming beneath the summer moon, her lights giving the craft a soft, romantic look. How he had dreamed of having such a craft, a place he could use to hide, to take his good girls and fulfill the promises he made to them.*

He thought he had chosen so wisely. His perfect girls, pure in heart and in nature, and they loved him. He was their love, but it had taken so long to find the one he wanted for all time. The perfect good girl. So sweet-natured and pure, never dirtying herself or her good name. Despite the brother.

His fists clenched at the thought of the brother. He was depraved, perverted, and he was going to dirty her. Rowdy Mackay was going to shame Kelly, and he knew it. He had seen them today, in the store, his hands on her, his eyes raking over her as though he owned her.

Rowdy Mackay didn't own her. She belonged to the man who

loved her, who respected her. And she was going to love him. Just like the others did. They hadn't loved anyone else either. He watched them sometimes, making certain they didn't allow anyone else to touch what belonged to him. Sometimes he called them, reminded them of who they were waiting for. They had promised to wait on him to find his one true love.

Kelly could be his true love. He thought it was possible. Until Rowdy came home.

The Nauti Boys. They were depraved. Perverts. But they had never fooled with the good girls. They left the perfect ones alone, always preferring the tramps, the little whores willing to spread their legs not just for one of them, but sometimes for all three at once. They shared their women all the time, watching and listening to their nasty screams as they begged for more.

His fists clenched, his gut rolling in sick suspicion. Rowdy had taken Kelly away on the houseboat. He had never done that by himself before. In the past, it had always been with her and her friends, never alone.

He shook at the fear that the bastard had dirtied her. He couldn't let that happen. Kelly was sweet and clean, she had never been dirtied by another man's seed, by another's possession of her.

She had screamed for him when he touched her, though. He hadn't had time to hear her beg for him, or to hear her promise to remain true to him. No sooner had he attempted to possess her than that big dumb hick visiting his whore girlfriend had started yelling outside the door. He couldn't get caught. His sweet Kelly couldn't be seen with a man in her bed. It would ruin her reputation and she wouldn't be clean anymore. Her reputation meant everything.

Bastard Rowdy. *Rowdy Mackay thought he was perfect, thought all the girls were his. He was going to hurt sweet Kelly, his sister. She was his sister, he had no business touching her. Sisters shouldn't be touched, his father had warned him of that.*

His eyes narrowed as Kelly moved from the boat and jumped onto the narrow floating dock. She was angry. He could see it in her face, in the stiff set of her body beneath the bright lights of the dock.

She said something as Rowdy locked the doors, causing the man to stiffen, to turn to her slowly. He didn't like the smile Rowdy gave her. It was carnal. Dirty.

He watched as she stalked ahead of the other man, her loose clothing demure, hiding the body that belonged to him alone. How perfect she was. His good girl. He had to finish his claim on her. He had to make certain she belonged to him. Not Rowdy. Never Rowdy and his perverted friends.

He watched as Rowdy walked her to her car. He was too close to her, even though she was angry. Rowdy was standing too close. He was crowding her.

She unlocked the door and opened it, then Rowdy touched her. Don't touch her. *He clenched his fists, sniffing miserably, fighting the tears that fell from his eyes. Rowdy shouldn't be touching her.*

But he was. The depraved bastard was touching her hair, her cheek, smiling down at her. Rage shattered in his head, filling his vision with a red haze as he watched another move from the shadows of the dock. Dawg. The bastard couldn't even use his real name—he used the nickname of the animal he was.

Kelly started as the other men called out to them, flashed Rowdy a furious look, then got into her car. The car door closed and within seconds she was pulling from the parking lot. She was going home. But she wouldn't be going alone. Rowdy would go as well. He lived in the house with her. His bedroom would be close to hers, he could hear her, smell her, maybe touch her as she slept.

Oh God, don't let him touch her, *he prayed.* Don't let him dirty the good girl. *She was his good girl. And, she just might be his perfect love.*

Kelly forcibly restrained the anger pounding through her bloodstream as she stepped into the house with Rowdy close behind her.

"It's about time you two found your way home." Ray and Maria stepped into the entryway.

Kelly breathed in deeply before turning to them, pasting a smile on her face as she met their concerned gazes.

"Rowdy has a habit of poking along on the way back from the docks." She kept her voice flat and even. "You know how he is."

They weren't convinced.

"She's a lousy liar, isn't she?" Rowdy drawled, his deep baritone still sending shivers up her spine despite her anger.

She glanced over at him. His thumbs were hooked in the pockets of his jeans, long legs stiff and straight as he smiled in open amusement back at their parents. She drew in a deep, hard breath.

"I'm going up to bed." She smiled stiffly. "Rowdy can be a butt by himself. I don't feel like dealing with it."

She raced up the stairs, fearing Rowdy would follow her, grateful he didn't. She slammed the door to her bedroom, twisting the lock on the handle before she stomped to her window and jerked the heavy curtains closed.

"Beg me for it," he panted at her ear, holding her down. "You're my good girl, Kelly. You're mine, it's okay to let me in. Let me in . . ."

She shook her head at the intrusive memory. She had managed to hold back the fear while she was with Rowdy, but now that she was alone, it was sneaking in, attacking her. The feeling of being watched was overwhelming, her skin crawling as her stomach churned with panic.

She had, as Rowdy had argued, essentially been the one who got away. She had escaped the full rape, suffering only some cuts made to weaken her, and a terror that still brought her awake with a cry on her lips.

She didn't wear the clothes she used to because the marks were still there. Shorts and tank tops might reveal the nearly imperceptible white scars that still marred her arms, shoulders, and legs. Nakedness would reveal the ones on her buttocks. Deeper slices had been made there as he held her down, cutting her panties from her.

Her mother swore they weren't noticeable. But to Kelly, they were.

She still remembered the feel of that knife biting into her, razor-sharp, the skin parting as cold pain streaked through her nervous system, and the feel of hot blood as it began to pour from the wounds. The doctor had assured her that within a few years they would be gone entirely. She wondered if the memories would fade as well.

She paced through the dark room to the wide recliner that sat on the far wall, beneath the standing lamp she used to read by. Collapsing into it, she propped her elbows on her knees and dropped her head in her hands. She didn't need Rowdy's arguments earlier to understand that she wasn't out of danger. She knew she wasn't, just as she knew that it was only a matter of time before her attacker made his next move.

She felt stalked. There was no proof, nothing but her own suspicions and her own fears. Shaking her head, she moved to her dresser. She pulled free one of the long sleeveless gowns she slept in and headed for the shower. *A cold shower maybe*, she thought as she adjusted the water. If she didn't get the memory of his kiss, his teasing out of her head, she would go crazy.

But even the cool water did nothing to still the idea he had planted in her head earlier. She was furious that Rowdy would play games to draw the stalker out, but she was smart enough to realize she wasn't safe.

She dried her hair, staring at the thin white scars on her shoulders and upper arms. There were four on one, three on the other. They showed clearly in the bright light of the bathroom, the dark blue gown emphasizing the marks.

At times she swore she could feel the ones on her buttocks.

She shook her head as she turned from the mirror, moving to the bedroom, her hand reaching out to flip off the light. She paused at the switch, her eyes narrowing on the man in her bedroom.

Rowdy had obviously showered as well. Dressed in gray sweatpants, he was propped against her pillows, waiting on her, a scowl creasing his handsome face.

"That expression freezes on your face and you'll be terrifying little kids on the streets," she informed him as she flipped off the light and walked into the bedroom.

"I'm not leaving you alone at night, Kelly—"

"Windows were locked and so was the door," she informed him as she stood by the side of the bed, her arms crossed over her breasts.

"And I got in the door anyway."

She inhaled slowly, her gaze sliding to the shadowed outline of the door as Rowdy reached over and clicked on the dim lamp on the small table beside him.

The lock was in the standing position, still locked.

"How did you do that?" She turned back to him, pretending to ignore the fact that he was mouthwateringly sexy as he lay on the flowered comforter of her bed.

"It's a piece of cake," he grunted. "The window locks aren't a lot harder to release. Until I can get the contractor out here to add to the security, you're stuck with me."

His expression was determined, stubborn. It was easy to tell when Rowdy had made up his mind. His expression went completely bland and his sea green eyes turned as cool as the arctic.

"Fine." She shrugged. "You sleep here and I'll sleep in your bed. No biggie." She moved for the door.

"Open that door, Kelly, and your mom and my dad are going to get dragged into this little disagreement we're having. Is that really what you want?"

Damn.

She stopped halfway to the door before turning back to him.

"Whose side would they take?" She opened her eyes wide, with mocking innocence. "Now I wonder, what will they think about the little proposal you put to me earlier?"

He tilted his head, his eyes glittering with lust, with amused hunger.

"Dad would probably kick my ass out of the house," he growled good-naturedly. "Is that what you really want?"

She turned away from him, restraining the urge to kick his butt herself. He was right. Ray would likely skin his hide if he ever learned of his son's proposal.

It wasn't that she hadn't expected it. She had. She had looked forward to it. How was that for some sick shit? She had actually looked forward to the day Rowdy would return and make good on the promise his kiss had made years ago.

And she had known if he did, the possibility of just such a

proposal would come. She had been ready for it. Prepared for it. What she hadn't expected was the cold-blooded intention he had of using it to catch her would-be rapist. As though the act no longer had anything to do with the two of them. As though the desire, the need, and the hunger were a means to an end and nothing more. It was without feeling, without emotion. And God help her, whenever she was around Rowdy, she felt nothing but emotion. Swirls of it. Lava-hot, lightning forks of sensation that rippled over her nerve endings, rendering even the air itself a caress against her sensitive flesh.

And emotions? Oh, she didn't even want to go there. Except she was already there. Arousal, uncertainty, fear of the unknown, and a fear of losing the dream in the face of reality.

He was asking her to choose. She had wanted to be seduced.

She turned back to him, drawing in a slow, deep breath, her head lifting as she stared at the confident, cool countenance he presented to her.

"Get out of my bedroom." She crossed her arms over her breasts, pressing her lips together as she glared at him. "I'm not one of the Nauti Boys' playthings. And I'm not in the mood for games. Not yours or anyone else's."

She watched the surprise gleam in his eyes for just a second. For the first time in all the years she had known him, she had never surprised him, until now.

With a ripple of muscle, he moved from the bed, his gaze never leaving hers as he rose, coming to his feet and walking around the bed.

He was aroused. The thick length of his erection tented his sweatpants, drew her eyes and made her mouth water. She had fantasized about that erection. About all the things a woman could do with such a prime piece of flesh.

She let her eyes linger on the proof of that arousal before lifting them to his face again. He was close. So close she could smell the clean, male scent of him. Dial soap and heated male arousal.

She stood still as he stalked around her, the movements deliberate, predatory. Suddenly he wasn't the laid-back, patiently amused Rowdy she had always known. She could feel the purpose, the male intent that poured from him.

Her breath caught as he paused behind her, his hand reaching up to allow his fingers to smooth her hair back over her shoulder, to bare the shell of her ear.

"You're mine." She jumped at his whispered response. "And, baby, I do like to play." His hands ran down her arms, creating a friction of heat as she felt his lips at her shoulders. "I guess that makes you my playmate, if not my plaything."

Her eyes widened a second before she jerked out of his hold, turning back to him furiously.

"I don't think so." She gave him a tight, angry smile.

Stupid male confidence, she fumed.

He tilted his head, the beginnings of a smile twitching at the corners of his lips.

"I could convince you."

No doubt.

She snorted as though it weren't possible. Unfortunately, he probably could convince her, but at what cost to her soul?

"Go get in your own bed, Rowdy. Don't make me cause a scene. Ray wouldn't like it." She walked to hers, flipping back the blankets and moving into the comfort of the mattress, ignoring him as though he didn't matter. "Good night."

He chuckled. "You've changed," he murmured as he paced to the other side of the bed, staring down at her, aroused, determined.

"I haven't changed at all, Rowdy." She pulled the blankets to her waist as she sat propped against the pillows. "Perhaps you just never really knew me." She raised her brows in emphasis. "That's always a possibility."

"You enjoyed waking up with me," he accused. "You don't want to throw me out."

That one was a no-brainer. No, she didn't want to throw him out. She wanted to curl against him and sleep as fearlessly as she had the night before and awaken as warm and protected as she had that morning.

She lifted her chin, refusing to answer him, fighting to hold his knowing stare as he watched her from beneath the veil of his thick, black lashes.

"Go play with someone else." She might have to kill him if he tried. "I'm not interested in the games."

"And you think this is a game?" He scowled down at her, his hands bracing on his powerful hips as his eyes began to simmer with irritation.

"I think it is for you," she answered somberly. "And I'm not a game. Don't play games with me, Rowdy. Not now, not ever."

TEN

Rowdy leaned forward, muscular arms propping him up on the mattress as he stared into her eyes. Kelly fought the need to glance away from him, to deny the hold he had on her. There was no turning away from him. He mesmerized her, made her hungry, made her need.

"I'm not scared of you, Rowdy," she tried to smirk back at him. "Don't try to intimidate me."

"If you don't like the games, then don't play them." His voice was dangerously, warningly soft. "You want something from me, then tell me what you want."

Her teeth clenched in anger.

"Fine," she snapped. "I want you out of my bedroom and out of my face. Go away." She made a shooing motion with her hand then stared at him in shock as his hand whipped out, catching her wrist.

Her heart jumped to her throat as he brought her fingers to his mouth, rubbed them against the velvet roughness of his lips before opening them and licking over the pads with a subtle flick of his tongue.

She was helpless. Struck dumb by the sheer sensuality of watching him caress nothing but her fingertips. Feeling the warmth of his lips, the flickering heat of his tongue, the sensual nip of his teeth.

Each caress sent flares of heat exploding with sensual devastation throughout her body. Her nipples were so hard, the nerves there so sensitized, that they were sending rippling flares of response straight to her womb, convulsing it with an erotic punch of pleasure.

"Rowdy . . ." She was shocked at the whimper in her voice, at her inability to pull away from him.

He came closer. Kneeling on the bed, still holding her hand, he pulled her to him until she was on her knees facing him.

He took her other wrist, placing her palms against his chest before his hands smoothed up her arms, over her shoulders, down her back to her hips. She trembled, shuddering at the light caress; it could have been firmer, could have been more destructive. It was subtle instead. Soft. Giving her the chance to break away, knowing she couldn't. That she wouldn't.

"You're mine," he whispered again as his head lowered.

She stared back at him, fighting to breathe, fighting against the desires raging inside her. She was helpless against his touch, against the hunger that gleamed in his eyes.

Just as she became helpless against his kiss.

His lips covered hers, slowly at first. So slowly, too slowly. They stroked over hers, his tongue flickering out to lave them a second before his teeth caught the lower curve, nipping at it as he watched her.

Her breathing hitched as she felt his hands bunch in the material of the gown at her hips. It drew slowly up her thighs, working over her flesh, baring her to his hands.

"Easy," he whispered against her lips. "Just feel, Kelly. Feel for me. Burn for me . . ."

She felt cool air caress her thighs, then his hands against her naked flesh, callused, heated, as his lips slanted over hers and he stole her mind with his kiss.

Deep, drugging kisses. Pleasure tore through her system, consumed her to the point that the knowledge that she was being lowered, laid beneath him, barely registered in her mind. All she knew was the pleasure. The feel of his hard body above her, his hands smoothing over her bare thighs, her hips, then working on the tiny buttons at the bodice while his kisses ravished her lips.

She was drowning in him. The taste of him. His touch. The muted male sounds of hunger and pleasure as she began to touch him. She needed to touch him. To immerse herself in every sensual sensation she could consume. Her nervous system was rioting with the chaotic impulses rushing through them. The air around them became heated, steamy with the desperation that infused each kiss, each touch.

"God, you taste sweet." His lips tore from hers, his breathing heavy, hard, as they moved to her neck.

She tilted her neck, panting for air as she felt his teeth rake down the sensitive column, then felt the brush of cool air over her naked breasts.

As his head lifted, she opened her eyes, staring back at him in dazed fascination as his gaze dropped. He had pulled apart the unbuttoned edges of her gown, displaying the swollen, hard-tipped mounds of her breasts.

The expression on his face was pure, carnal hunger. His eyes heavy-lidded, his lips moist and swollen from their kisses, his cheekbones flushed a brick red.

As though suspended between dream and reality, she watched as his head lowered, her eyes widening, a strangled groan leaving her lips as his tongue covered one spiked, aroused nipple.

Reaction shot through her, jerking at her body as her hands tightened on his neck, her back arching. This was heaven. It was ecstasy. The most pleasure she had ever known in her life.

His tongue lashed at the hard point as he sucked the flesh into his mouth, drawing on her deeply, creating a pleasure–pain sensation that had a startled cry leaving her lips.

Lips he immediately covered, stilling the aroused cries as his fingers replaced his mouth. Tweaking at the tender tips, causing her to writhe beneath him as she fought to get closer, to still the ache burning between her thighs.

"Shh. Easy." His groan was whispered against her lips, his voice dark, desperate. "Damn, Kelly. I can't take you here. Dad will kill me."

"I'll kill you if you don't." His chest pressed against her breasts, rasped her nipples so she fought to breathe. "Don't stop, Rowdy, please."

His hand smoothed down to her thigh, his fingers close, so close to where she needed them. She gazed back at him pleadingly, feeling her vagina ripple with need, the muscles clenching in desperation.

"If I take you, you're going to scream," he whispered, his eyes darkening, a ravenous lust filling his expression. "I want to hear every cry that leaves your lips, Kelly. Every scream as you come around me. I can't do that here. We can't do that here. You know that."

She shook her head, a weak whimper passing her lips.

"I've waited too long, Rowdy."

"Shh." His kiss was gentle and much too short as he eased her gown over her thighs and then covered her breasts once again. "Tomorrow. We'll go out on the boat," he whispered, pushing her hair back before moving slowly to her side and pulling her into his arms.

She laid her head against his chest, fighting to regulate her breathing, to tear herself back from the endless spiral of heat he had thrown her into.

"That wasn't fair," she whispered as he lifted the sheet over them. "You're supposed to be sleeping in your own bed."

She was too weak to make him move now, too desperate for his touch, any touch, to force him from her bed.

"Go to sleep." His arms contracted around her. "I'd be fighting shadows if I slept away from you, Kelly. Let me hold you. Know you're okay."

She pressed her lips to his chest. "It wasn't your fault, Rowdy," she told him softly, wondering at the edge of remorse she heard in his voice.

He was silent, but his hands still stroked her back, soothing now, where seconds before they had been arousing.

"Just let me hold you," he repeated. "Sleep beside me, Kelly. We'll argue out the rest of it later."

"You want me to sleep?" She sighed, shaking her head. "Rowdy, I'm never going to sleep with your hard-on poking at my belly all night."

"Sure you can," he chuckled at her ear. "You need your rest, baby. Because tomorrow night, I really wouldn't bet on you getting any sleep at all."

She was silent then, lying against him, feeling his arms surrounding her, protecting her. God, what was she doing? She had lived and breathed for the day Rowdy would return and see her as more than just a pesky little girl. That he would see her as a woman, as his woman. And here he was, ready to claim her, and she was fighting it, fighting him. Or was she fighting herself?

"This isn't a game, Kelly." His voice was soft, surrounding her, causing her eyelids to flutter in pleasure as it stroked over her senses. "I'm deadly serious about this. About us. I wasn't joking when I said you were mine. I came home to claim you, if that's what you still want."

"Maybe it doesn't work that way, Rowdy. I want you until I can't think, can't breathe. But you're different now."

"I'm no different than I've ever been and you know it." His voice hardened. "You don't like the fact that I'm willing to do whatever it takes to protect you. You want everything tied up in roses and sweet promises. I can give you that, to a point. But I won't ignore the danger. And you have to accept that. This will be taken care of."

He wasn't angry; he wasn't trying to convince her. He was telling her.

"You're talking about using me. Me and whatever we share between us sexually, flaunting it in front of him to provoke him." That terrified her more than she wanted to admit.

"It's the quickest way to finish this."

"Maybe the quickest way isn't always the best." She didn't know if she wanted to take that step, if she wanted to force a madman's hand.

"Or maybe you think you can hide whatever this relationship brings." His voice hardened. "Do you believe that's possible, Kelly? Whether you make the choice to immerse yourself in everything I can give you, or not, doesn't make a difference. Everyone is going to believe you are. He'll believe you are. My plan will just flush him out quicker, that's all. But we'll play it however you choose."

She didn't like the easy, matter-of-fact way he said that. She could feel a "but" in there somewhere, she just had to find it.

"You could have at least tried to hide that part of your sex life from the world," she finally sighed with an edge of irritation.

"Why?" He sounded genuinely curious now. "Kelly, I'm who I am. I don't hide that, from anyone. I don't flaunt it. I don't advertise it. Others have. What happens between you and me I expect will stay between you and me. You don't advertise yourself, and you won't advertise our relationship. Why should we do without something we might enjoy because of what others suspect, or think?"

She hated it when he pulled logic into his arguments with her. He had always done that.

"Because I'm scared," she whispered, rolling away from him to sit on the side of the bed.

"Of me?"

"Of myself. Of what could happen." She moved to her feet, pacing away from the bed as she rubbed at the chill that rushed over her arms. "You're talking about pushing someone who isn't sane. And in the same breath . . ." She shook her head.

"I'm asking you to make a decision," he finished for her. "Not about your safety but about something much more important to you. Your sexuality."

"I'm still a virgin." Her laughter was self-mocking. "I expected something a little more romantic, Rowdy."

"And you deserved something a hell of a lot more romantic, Kelly." He sighed. "But catching this stalker is more important than romance. And I'm not going to play games with you. From the beginning, we won't be alone. If it doesn't happen for you with Dawg and Natches, then we have to at least give the impression of it. We can't afford to let this guy catch us unawares, I can't afford to let him hurt you again, because God as my witness, my sanity won't survive it, Kelly."

"God!" She pushed her fingers through her hair, turning from him, trying to ignore the fact that she wasn't insulted, wasn't offended or furious. "You're not talking about this thing with your cousins being a one-time deal, are you?" She kept her back to him, kept her expression hidden.

"No. I'm not."

The rumors had started when they were in their teens. Three young men with charisma and sexuality, who had been the downfall of a local divorcée. It had begun then, at an age that none of the three men would reveal. Too young, Rowdy knew. But damn, it had been hot that summer, and not just from the sun. Loren Barnes had been a quiet, schoolmarmish lady on the outside, but inside she had been hotter than fireworks in July.

She had taken three uncertain virgin boys and, in a few short months, taught them to be men well before their time. All together. All at once. One soft female body, her approval and cries of pleasure penetrating their lust-hazed minds as they took her lessons and drove her to the brink of passion with them.

She taught them how to romance, how to tease, how to cajole, how to subtly drive a woman crazy and make her so wet the slick essence of her would dampen her thighs. She had taught them how much more pleasure they could bring together than alone. And to the Mackay boys, that was what it was all about.

Women were treasures, precious gifts of never-ending excitement, sweetly scented flesh, and mysterious motives. They were a challenge and a comfort, a balm to the soul, and an adventure like nothing else ever created. They were infinitely strong, and yet infinitely vulnerable. Rowdy, Dawg, and Natches had realized years before that alone they couldn't give the pleasure they could together, but also, they couldn't protect as well.

Ironically, it was Kelly who taught them that lesson. As a kid, keeping up with her had been practically impossible for just one of them. It took the three of them to keep her safe, to keep her happy as she grew up. Watching for the bullies who liked to pick on her because she was poor, because she was pretty as a picture and sweetly gentle. And they wanted to keep her that way.

She was also impetuous, defiant, and smart as a whip. There had been nothing sexual involved. She amused them, made them laugh, and challenged them to keep up with her with an innocent thirst for life and adventure that appealed to the teenagers. After her mother married Ray, she was then "family," as well.

As she grew older, as they grew older, things had slowly shifted for all of them. Four years ago it had come to a head. She had just turned twenty, hotter than fireworks and as tempting as sin itself. The three of them had been a little too drunk, a little too wild that night. And she had been there.

"Make up your mind, Rowdy. You don't put a claim on her, one of us is going to." Natches's eyes followed her as she laughed and danced beneath the brilliance of the full summer moon.

"She's still too young." He denied the need, as well as the challenge.

"Keeping the local boys off her ass is getting harder," Dawg muttered. "I'm tired of bruising my knuckles on their thick skulls. Make up your mind. If you don't intend to keep her, one of us will."

Rowdy grimaced, finished his beer, then crumpled the can as he fought to hold onto his control. It was getting harder each time he came home, to stay the hell away from her.

"*She's too fucking young and the two of you know it,*" he snapped. "*She's not ready for it.*"

"*She's old enough to make the choice,*" Natches drawled. "*You're going back to the Marines and that's fine. But if she's not willing to wait on you, then we aren't either. Claim her man, or one of us will.*"

She had been like a fire at midnight. He had to make her want to wait on him. He had to ensure her need for him. And he had done that. But in doing it, he had cemented his need for her.

As he held her in the darkness of the night, the soft warmth of her pressed into his chest, he knew her earlier protest was the key to her soul. The romance. She needed the romance, she deserved it, but God knew he had no idea how to make it romantic. He could give her pleasure. Enough pleasure to leave her screaming in orgasm, begging for more. But the heart of the woman needed more. A lesson Loren had taught them, but one they had forgotten over the years.

The women they had drawn to them hadn't been ones to need the romance, or even want it.

For the first time in his life Rowdy felt helpless. Eliminating the threat to her was imperative. And he wasn't going to lie to her. Not Kelly. She deserved more than that.

"You're not asleep." Her whisper was as soft as a breath.

"Neither are you." He sighed, knowing her mind had been running as fast as his.

They hadn't said much since that final question. She had drawn in a deep, hard breath, informed him she was going to sleep then curled into his arms, and turned out the lights. But she hadn't gone to sleep anymore than he had.

"Why do you do it?" she finally asked. He didn't have to ask what she was talking about. It was a question he had hoped she wouldn't ask. Yet he had known she would.

He slid his hand from her hip to her stomach, feeling the muscles flutter beneath his palm.

"A man's pleasure comes from his woman's," he whispered. "Because we learned how much better it can be for a woman when no part of her body is neglected. Because we learned as young men how much easier it is to protect what's ours when we work together. Hell, Kelly, I could give you a thousand reasons and none of them would really make sense. Because it's who we are, what we are."

"Will it end?" He knew where she was going, what she would eventually ask.

"Only if you want it to. My needs aren't more important than yours. It won't be every time. It won't be an either-or."

She was silent for long moments. He closed his eyes, grimacing in painful awareness of the can of worms he had opened.

"And when they find the women they want for their own? What then?"

"It's not an either-or," he repeated. "I'll do nothing you can't live with, Kelly. Ever."

"But you'll want to." Her voice lowered further. "If Dawg or Natches found a woman they wanted for their own, then you'd want to be a part of it, wouldn't you, Rowdy?"

"I wouldn't miss being a part of it, anymore than you would miss their touch after having had it." There was no way to reassure her, and God knew he wanted to.

He felt her flinch against him.

"You would touch another woman?"

"I would never do anything that would jeopardize us." That wasn't acceptable. "Ever. Not at any time."

As he stared into the darkness, he thought of her touch, her kiss. Could he touch another woman? At any time?

"So it would be my choice?"

"It would be your choice."

"But you would still want to." It wasn't a question.

"I don't know." He couldn't lie to her. He wouldn't lie to her, even though he was terrified of losing her.

He caressed her abdomen as he held her, as silence filled the room once again.

"This might not work." Her voice trembled with an awareness of what she might be looking at. "I don't know if I can do that. I don't know if I could handle your need to do it."

He sighed heavily into her hair, drawing her closer, knowing he could be risking both their hearts with the hungers that tormented him. It was the reason he had left four years before, the reason he couldn't begin this relationship with anything less than the truth.

"I can live without it," he told her softly. "I don't know if I could live without you, Kelly. Not now. Not after the years I've spent needing you. I'll give you everything I am, as much as you want. That's all I can do."

She turned to him then, her soft gray eyes dark in the dim light of the room as he stared into the shadowed expanse of her face.

"The first time . . ."

He closed his eyes. "However you want it."

Bonding came in so many ways. He would have had Dawg and Natches there, but he wouldn't push her. He couldn't push her. Not now.

"You want them there."

His eyes flew open at the soft statement.

"I want them there," he affirmed, knowing her safety demanded nothing less. He ignored the possessiveness raging inside him. "Kelly, I want everything for you, and I know that's hard to understand. The first time, it's special for a woman. It begins a bonding with her lover, one that never really dies. It's why I've never taken a virgin, never fooled with a woman who didn't know the score, until you."

He felt the shiver that raced over her, the little tremor of fear, or response, he wasn't certain.

"You want me to have that, with them?" The uncertainty in her voice, the edge of hurt broke his heart.

"Kelly, listen to me." He framed the side of her face with his hand, his thumb smoothing over her cheek. "I'm not going to do a damned thing that's going to hurt you or make you uncomfortable. Baby, it won't be good for me, or for Dawg and Natches, if it isn't something you want with everything inside you. This is your choice. The perception of it isn't."

"But you want it," she said fiercely.

"Don't make excuses." He could feel it in her then, the need to have the choice taken from her, to be seduced. "I'm not making them and I won't let you. Think about it, Kelly. Decide what you want, what you need. I'm not a kid, and you've known me too long to be able to fool yourself about me. You've known, you wanted to sugarcoat it, pretend it wasn't real, but you knew. Now decide what you want, because I won't make that decision for you. Not now, not ever. I love you, baby, but I can't love you enough for both of us."

He felt her then, her fingers moving against his chest, leaving a path of fire in their wake as they smoothed over his chest.

"Can you do anything without your cousins?" she asked. "Or do you need their help all the time, Rowdy? Maybe you're the one making excuses."

Damn. Her fingers were at his abdomen now, her nails raking

121

over his flesh, tracing the skin above the waistband of his sweat-pants.

Impetuous. Defiant. An adventure. That was Kelly.

His hand trapped hers, holding it still against him, his eyes narrowing on her in the darkness.

"Anywhere but here," he growled. "Now go to sleep, minx. I'll be damned if I'll have our parents hearing us in here screwing our brains out. I'm right fond of keeping my private parts intact if it's all the same to you."

She chuckled, flipped around, then horror of all horrors, because his control was edging toward nonexistence, that curvy little ass tucked into his hips, cushioning the raging fullness of his cock. *Son of a bitch.*

"Good night, Rowdy." Her husky little purr nearly had him coming in his pants. "Maybe tomorrow we'll see what you can actually do without your cousins around to approve of it."

A grin tilted his lips. Oh, he'd show her all right, in ways she could never imagine.

ELEVEN

Kelly stared at the bed as she came from the shower the next morning. It was perfectly made, the flowered comforter smoothed out, the pillows neatly stacked at the headboard. And lying at the bottom of the mattress was clothing she hadn't worn since the attack.

The low-rise jeans were patched and faded, and she new exactly how low they were. The waistband barely reached her hipbones, with the snap in the front dipping lower nearly an inch.

The white vest-style summer shirt rose above her navel, and would reveal the belly ring that lay glittering on top of the shirt. The brilliant green emerald twinkled and gleamed beneath a shaft of sunlight coming in from the window. She had chosen that particular gem because of its resemblance to Rowdy's eyes.

Kelly drew in a deep breath before turning her head to stare at Rowdy where he sat in the recliner. Leaning forward, his arms resting on his knees, he watched her silently, emotion swirling in his gaze. Compassion, understanding, determination.

She stepped closer to the bed, turning back to stare at the clothes. She had been too scared to wear them before, terrified that how she dressed had somehow caused the attack.

She was still scared, but as she stood there, she realized that the terror that had often filled her before Rowdy's return wasn't there now. Just as he had protected her from those bullies years before, she knew he would protect her now.

She cleared her throat before speaking.

"You're certain you can catch him? That he's watching me? Waiting?" She picked up the belly ring, staring down at it intently.

"I'm certain, Kelly." His voice was dark, deep, confident.

"Do you know who it is?" She knew Rowdy, and his cousins. And she knew Dawg and Natches had been investigating the attack since it happened.

"Not yet. But we will. He's not sane enough to hide for long."

Could she be a woman again, rather than a child hiding? Kelly admitted, if only silently, that the woman had been protesting the baggy clothes and the lack of adventure for a year now. She was ready to return, just as the psychologist had warned her she would be.

She nodded slowly. "I need to go to town today. To the spa." The intimate waxing had been put off too long.

Tension began to sizzle in the room. She knew he would know what it meant. Rowdy was an expert on a woman's body and all the various procedures they used to tempt a man.

"I'd like to drive you in." His voice was hoarse. "We could pick up dinner later and go out on the lake."

She inhaled roughly before nodding. She could feel her insides quivering with the knowledge that once he got her out on the lake, she would be in his bed.

"That sounds good," she said as she turned back to him slowly.

She dropped the towel that covered her, watched his eyes flame, his face flush, and his body come to immediate attention as she stood before him.

"It's hard to put in." She held the belly ring out to him. "Would you help me?"

"Good God!" His gaze moved to hers slowly. "Dad's home, Kelly. If I fuck you here, he'll kill me."

"I didn't ask you to fuck me, Rowdy." She kept her voice low, intimate as she moved to him. "I asked you to put the ring in." She extended her arm, her fingers holding the glittering gem.

She loved teasing Rowdy, always had. The look in his eyes made her breathless, showed his hunger. It was the reason she had always waited on him, always known she belonged to him. For years, every time he looked at her, he ate her with his eyes, consumed her with the hunger in them. Just as he did now.

Without speaking, he moved forward on the chair, spreading his legs before his hand gripped her hips, pulling her to him. His hands were hot on her flesh, sending sizzling impulses of pleasure raking over her nerve endings.

"Give me the ring." His expression was heavy with sensual intent as he took the ring from her fingers.

Kelly stood still, silent as he inserted the curved metal into the tiny hole before snapping the ball end in place. But he didn't stop touching her there. He positioned the emerald teardrop in place over the entrance to her navel before his fingertips skimmed over her lower belly.

Her womb convulsed beneath his fingers as pleasure tore

through her. Lower, she felt the curves of her pussy dampen further than they already were as her vagina pulsed in heavy need.

"Look how pretty," he whispered, his eyes centering between her thighs as her fingers gripped his shoulders and her knees trembled. "You're wet for me, Kelly."

"I'm always wet for you. I've been wet for you for years, Rowdy," she informed him, her voice almost a whimper of hunger.

She realized then the mistake she had made in teasing him. She was too hungry, needed him too much to tempt what she knew she couldn't have beneath Ray's roof.

She stared down at Rowdy in a haze of need as he shifted, his head coming closer, his lips pressing into her lower belly as she gasped at the contact. Long-fingered hands smoothed down her hips to her thighs, nudging them apart gently before raising his head. He stared at the flushed folds of her mound. His thumb caressed over the tattoo just above her pussy. The eagle in flight, one wing dipping toward her damp flesh.

"I want to taste you, Kelly," he groaned, his voice roughening further. "I want to lay you down, spread those pretty legs, and lick all that soft syrup from you."

Weakness flooded her, taking her breath, her senses, and turning them into one hard ache for just that.

"You're so wet." The fingers of one hand trailed around her thigh, then slid slowly, so slowly, but with destructive results, through the thick wetness that lay between the soft folds of flesh.

"Rowdy," she breathed, her fingers sliding to his hair as his head dipped to her belly again. "Please touch me. Please."

She had waited so long, dreamed so desperately of his touch that now that it was happening, she feared it was just another dream.

"I'm going to do more than touch you, baby," he whispered as his lips moved closer to the pounding ache of her clit. "I'm going to touch you, taste you, I'm going to make you scream for me, Kelly. Beg for more."

Okay. She could handle that.

"Now."

She felt his chuckle, the sound rasping, filled with hunger as his fingers circled her clit. Her hips arched forward as a low cry left her lips. Need flamed inside her with an intensity that drove anything else from her mind.

"Shhh, baby," he groaned, his fingers parting her. "Remember Ray."

Ray who?

His breath whispered over the damp, throbbing bud, sending her senses reeling as a knock sounded at the door. Kelly jerked in Rowdy's grip as she felt him tense beneath her hold.

"Rowdy, I'm heading out. I need to talk to you before I leave," Ray called through the thick panel. "Get out here, boy, so I can get to work."

She heard his footsteps retreating as Rowdy's fingers slowly slid from her flesh.

"Damn," he breathed out, moving her back as he lifted his head to stare back at her. "You're dangerous, darlin'."

"Don't stop." Kelly shook her head as he rose from the chair, his hands smoothing up her back, yet holding her from him.

"I'll take you to the spa," he whispered. "And later, I'll show you how much I love having your sweet pussy bare to me. Get dressed, baby, so we can escape for awhile."

His lips whispered over hers, ignoring her silent plea for more as her lips parted.

"Get dressed," he told her again, moving back. "Stop driving me crazy, baby. Let's get out of here."

Okay, two could play this game, Kelly was certain. With

narrowed eyes she watched as Rowdy stalked from the bedroom, his body tight with tension and the bulge in his pants so apparent he had pulled the tail of his white cotton shirt free of his pants to cover it. She was sure there was no way Ray wouldn't be aware of his son's problem.

She snickered at the thought of the tough Rowdy squirming beneath his father's gaze. Ray was a good guy, but she knew how he was. He hadn't wanted this relationship to develop between her and Rowdy, neither had her mother, though she wasn't certain why. She had loved Rowdy forever, and despite Ray and her mother's marriage, she had never understood the reasons for their disapproval.

Twenty minutes later, dressed and feeling more feminine and less afraid than she had in months, Kelly picked up her phone and called the spa. Marla Reiner, her favorite technician, was available and eager to see Kelly returning to her regular visits. With a little maneuvering, Marla managed to schedule her right in and disconnected the call with a cheery good-bye.

Drawing in a deep breath, Kelly placed her hand on her stomach to still the butterflies racing through her system before she moved to her bedroom door and headed downstairs.

In the back of her mind was the knowledge that nothing would ever be the same from this day on. Once Rowdy had her, she knew what would happen. Questions still plagued her, as did an instinctive discomfort regarding the idea that Rowdy could ever want to touch another woman, no matter the relationship that developed between her and his cousins.

God, it was so strange having that thought in her mind. It had always stayed distant, an awareness of what could happen if she ever got into Rowdy's bed. There wouldn't be just one man, but three pleasuring her. Now that it could be reality, she found herself both curious and hesitant. Aroused and frightened. But Kelly knew she wasn't willing to draw back. Maybe she was different, maybe she wasn't.

For years rumors had abounded of the Mackay cousins. Women whispered their names with naughty pleasure at the thought of them. Her friends had jokingly informed her that she was insane for not moving into Dawg's or Natches's bed while Rowdy was in the service.

She could have. But deep inside she knew that who her heart belonged to made a difference. Alone, Dawg and Natches held no appeal for her. But with Rowdy . . .

She stepped into the kitchen, watching as he turned to face her, his deep green eyes approving, and hungry.

She belonged to Rowdy.

God, she was gorgeous. Rowdy couldn't keep his eyes off her as he drove the truck into Somerset, listening to her soft voice relating the local gossip.

Johnny Flowers traded wives with his worst enemy, Buck Layne. Crista Jansen was back home and had moved into her parents' home place outside of town. No one knew why she had returned to town after years away, but everyone was gossiping about it. Rowdy bet Dawg was interested in that one. He had been hot as hell for Crista before she ran off to college eight years before.

One of Rowdy's old girlfriends now owned the café he and Dawg and Natches had frequented before Rowdy left, and for the most part, for all the things that had changed, everything was pretty much the same. It was one of the things Rowdy loved about home. It was familiar, endearing.

Lake Cumberland was a place of mystery and beauty, and the small towns that surrounded it were filled with friends and family and memories that had gotten him through the last eight years in the service.

And memories of Kelly.

He glanced at her again, the light reflecting off the emerald at her pretty belly drawing his gaze again. It made his dick hard. Damn, he was dying for her, his cock was throbbing in his jeans and his mouth watering for the taste of her.

He entered the city limits, navigating the summer traffic as he drove to the popular spa the women in town seemed to flock to.

"Here you go." He pulled into an empty space in front of the entrance and turned to her. "I programmed my number into your cell phone; call me before you leave. I'm meeting Dawg and Natches at the café up the street, so I won't be far."

Those kissable lips curved into a slow, promising smile as she leaned close.

"I bet I could walk down the street all by myself, Rowdy," she whispered teasingly, sending a jolt of fear to slice through his soul.

"No!" He hadn't meant his voice to be so harsh, but the slight flinch and the spark of fear and anger that filled her eyes assured him he was much harsher than he intended to be.

Rowdy drew in a quick, hard breath before pushing his fingers through his hair, frustration eating him alive.

"I'm sorry, baby," he growled, his voice still rougher than he wanted. "Don't scare me like that. Give me a while, okay?" He gave her a quick, comforting smile. "Let me protect you, Kelly."

She sat against the door now, her gray eyes quiet, her expression closed until she glanced away and lowered her head.

"I understand, Rowdy," she finally sighed. "But I'm tired of hiding." She turned back to him, a frown edging at her brows. "I'm tired of letting him win."

"Kelly, promise me you'll call me before you leave." He reached out to her, his fingers running down her cheek, feeling the small quiver of response that ran through her. "Don't fight me on this, please. He's a madman—"

"I'm not crazy." She brushed his hand away as she glared back at him. "I'll call you, Rowdy. But I don't think he's going to try anything in broad daylight. It would be too risky."

"Point taken." He nodded. "But we can't be certain, either. Until I know what we're dealing with, we're going to be careful."

"So says the man who wants to poke at the crazy person by letting him think I'm taking on the Mackay cousins all at once," she reminded him. "I think walking down the street is a hell of a lot safer."

"Exactly why you shouldn't be walking down the street alone," he pointed out softly. "He knows I have you now, Kelly. Which means Dawg and Natches aren't far behind, in his eyes. From here on out, we can't underestimate him; we take nothing for granted."

Rowdy forcibly tamped down the violence rising inside him. He knew if he ever managed to get hold of the bastard who dared to touch her, then he would kill him. There would be nothing left for justice to convict.

"Fine. I'll call you before I leave," she snapped with a spark of anger he couldn't blame her for. "But don't take forever to pick me up, if you don't mind. I have a few other things I'd like to do while I'm in town. And I'd appreciate a little less paranoia until he actually shows that he *is* stalking me."

She reached out to grip the door handle. Just as fast Rowdy caught her arm, causing her to turn back to him. His hand moved, his fingers threading through her hair as he drew her head back and captured her lips quickly with his.

Summer heat, lightning, and the sweet taste of a woman's passion met his hunger, tightening his gut with lust. He couldn't wait to get her beneath him. At that moment, nothing mattered except getting through the rest of the day until he could get her to the houseboat and the large bed awaiting them there.

He forced himself to release her seconds later, staring into her dazed features with a satisfaction so intense it caused his balls to tighten.

"That wasn't fair." She smiled despite the chastisement, her cheeks flushed with warmth and her breathing ragged.

"Sure it was," he whispered, pulling back from her, despite the need to wrap her in his arms and run away with her. He wanted to hide her. To make certain no one could ever touch her again. "I need to touch you, babe. That's always fair considering how long I've waited to do it."

She snorted at that before pushing her fingers through her hair and flashing him a disgruntled look. "No one made you wait."

She was out of the truck before he could stop her, tossing him a cheery smile before crossing the sidewalk and entering the spa.

Rowdy breathed out roughly. She was going to be the death of him, there was just no other way around it. With her shining innocence, tempting eyes, and sweetly rounded body, he knew she was capable of making him curse as often as he sighed in need.

He gave his head a quick jerk before reversing from the parking spot and driving farther down the street to the café he had told Dawg and Natches to meet him in.

Reginald's Café was newly remodeled, the inside cool and welcoming as he entered. Dawg and Natches were waiting at one of the back tables, steaming cups of coffee sitting in front of them.

"'Bout time you got here, cuz," Dawg grunted as he slid into the chair across from him. "I thought we were gonna have to come down there and rescue Kelly from your clutches ourselves."

Natches chuckled as Rowdy leaned back in his chair and

watched his cousin curiously. Dawg had changed over the years, more than any of them, Rowdy sometimes thought. He was darker, despite the joviality, quieter than he used to be.

Rowdy didn't know what had happened during the years he spent in the Marines, but it had affected his cousin. Natches was just as lazy as always, his smile quiet, his eyes watchful. Of course, none of them were as relaxed, as carefree as they used to be.

There was a darkness in them that had always lurked just beneath the surface. A difference that separated them from other men, made them appear wilder, more dangerous. And in ways they were more dangerous. They had proved that overseas.

"What's up?" Rowdy could tell there was more going on than a general bad mood.

Dawg leaned forward, his eyes narrowed.

"You had company outside the house last night." Dawg's voice was low. "On that little knob above the house that looks into Kelly's room. I was checking it out this morning before heading here. He must have been there all night. The grass was indented where he sat, with claw marks at the side where the bastard dug his fingers into the ground. He's getting pissed."

Hell. Rowdy had known Kelly's attacker was watching, waiting. He just hadn't been certain where, or how.

"Where do we go from here, Rowdy?" Natches watched him with a spark of excitement in his eyes that Rowdy knew was as much to the thought of a good fight as to the chance of touching Kelly.

"I'm taking her back to the boat this evening," he answered. "We'll head out to the cove. We should be staying the night. We'll see how brave he wants to get. We'll have dinner on the boat. Let the bastard think we're all having a fine time. After dark the two of you can slip on shore and I'll pull farther out into the water. We'll see what happens."

Dawg and Natches nodded somberly. They were waiting, watchful, their bodies now on high alert. Not that anyone else would have noticed the change.

They paused as the waitress moved toward them, her steps slow, her head down, waves of burnished chestnut curls pulled into a low ponytail, her classically pretty features stiff and tense.

Rowdy cocked his head at the woman. Crista Jensen kept her head carefully lowered as she refilled the coffee cups before turning to leave.

"You didn't ask me if I wanted anything to eat, Crista." Dawg surprised them all with his mocking drawl. "Didn't Jenny warn you to look after us good?"

"Shut up, Dawg," Natches muttered, his voice low but easy to hear.

Rowdy watched as Crista pulled the ordering pad from the back pocket of her jeans, a pencil from behind her ear and watched Dawg with a spark of anger. Dawg stared back at her expectantly.

"What would you like to order, Dawg?" Her words were gritted, her voice raspy.

"Eh. Nothing right now, but be sure to check back in a few minutes." Dawg's smile was all teeth, a predatory snarl if Rowdy had ever seen one.

"I'll be sure to do that." Crista's smile was no less antagonistic as she returned the order pad to the back pocket of her jeans, picked up the coffeepot, and stalked away.

The minute her back turned, Dawg's eyes narrowed and a flash of anger seared the depths as he rose to his feet, dug into his pocket, and slapped a few dollars to the table.

"I'll see you at the marina," he snapped before stalking from the café.

Rowdy watched, perplexed, before turning to Natches.

"What the hell was that?"

"Dawg in heat," Natches snickered. "She won't give him the time of day."

Rowdy glanced to the woman in question and restrained his smile as he noticed her gaze, centered squarely on Dawg as he stormed from the café. Sad, weary, her expression marked with indecision. Yeah, she was giving him the time of day, perhaps more than the big lug deserved.

Now this was an interesting development.

"So, how are we playing tonight? One on one or is she ready for all of us?"

"Kelly will let us know what she wants." Rowdy shifted his shoulders, a primitive surge of something akin to possessiveness rising inside him as Natches watched him curiously.

That was strange. He was one second from baring his teeth and daring Natches to touch Kelly. He knew the pleasure the three of them could bring her, versus the pleasure he alone could bestow. So what the fuck was his problem all of a sudden?

Shit. He could feel the back of his neck prickling as irritation began to surge inside him.

"Waiting on her has been a bitch," Natches grimaced, his light green eyes gleaming with lustful determination. "She's going to go up in flames—"

"Shut up, Natches." Rowdy lifted his coffee cup to his lips, glaring at his cousin across the table as Crista moved to a table close to them.

Natches watched the woman, his expression considering.

"Something's up with that one," he sighed. "Dawg has been like a bear with a sore tail ever since she arrived back in town. She didn't even let the family know she was coming."

"What about her husband? Didn't she marry some guy from Virginia?"

Natches shook his head. "She was engaged for awhile. Guess it fell through."

Rowdy almost breathed a sigh of relief that the conversation had moved from Kelly. He was going to have to figure this out. Now wasn't a time to be hedging between desires, dammit. But he was hedging, and he knew it.

He glanced at Crista Jansen again, narrowing his eyes. Dawg had had a thing for the other woman for years. She had always managed to resist his charms, his attempts to talk to her, to seduce here.

Rowdy and Natches had watched him attempt to bargain for a single date from her for nearly a year before they joined the Marines, and Natches had related that the first thing Dawg had gone looking for when he came home from the service was Crista. Only to learn she had left Somerset.

Could he fuck her? Rowdy turned his gaze back to the Formica-topped table and sipped from his coffee again. A year ago, he could have, easily. The thought of having her between himself and his two cousins would have had his dick perking in interest.

His dick wasn't interested. He frowned. Hell, there was no excitement, period. He stared back at her.

She was pretty enough. Nicely rounded. She moved a little self-consciously, as though not quite comfortable with what she was doing.

Her face was a rounded oval, her skin clear and silky-looking. Nice hair. But he wasn't interested. He wasn't aroused. As a matter of fact, the urge to get up and leave the café was so damned strong it was all he could do to stay in place.

He should have been practically drooling at the thought of

helping Dawg and Natches fuck her to oblivion. They were sure as hell hot enough at the thought of fucking Kelly.

"Can I get you two anything else?" Crista refilled the coffee cup, her expression resigned for some reason as she glanced at Dawg's chair.

"An explanation would be nice." Rowdy lifted his head, watching her closely as she seemed to pale.

"Excuse me?"

"Dawg's been chasing you for years, Crista. What's up?"

Crista's eyes burned with anger as she slowly tucked the ordering pad into her back pocket and glared at him furiously.

"I'm not a plaything for the three of you," she snarled then, surprising him and Natches. "If you cared for anything past yourselves then you damned well wouldn't expect it. You'd grow the hell up and get over it."

Her voice was hoarse as tears sheened her eyes before she blinked them back furiously.

"Forget it," she snapped. "The three of you might as well be clones of each other. You can't even breathe alone."

Turning, she stalked back to the register where two customers waited, her fingers stabbing at the input keys as she flicked a scornful glance back at them.

"Have I been gone too long?" Rowdy turned back to Natches, gratified to see the same surprise reflecting in his face.

"Damn, and she used to be such a nice, quiet little girl," Natches grumped as he scratched at his chin.

Rowdy snorted at the description. Crista had been anything but nice and quiet and they all knew it.

"I don't have a problem breathing without your help." Rowdy grinned as he finished his coffee.

"Damned good thing." Natches shook his head as he peeked another look back at the little waitress, a frown pulling at his brow. "Hell, you've been gone eight years, Rowdy, and other than a few times you were home, me and Dawg's been pretty damned tame. What the hell has her by the ear anyway?"

Rowdy shook his head as he glanced at his empty coffee cup.

"Do you think she's going to bring us more coffee?" he asked ruefully.

Both men looked back at the woman, estimating their chances for caffeine.

"If she knows what's good for her." Natches's grin was wicked. "Or else, I might have to call Dawg back to sweet-talk her for us."

Rowdy chuckled, though when he glanced back at Crista he could feel the frown tugging at his brow again. The fact that Dawg wanted her should have been all it took to produce a raging hard-on and more than a surfeit of interest. Instead, all he felt was an edge of sadness. Their lifestyle, the very truth of their sexuality stood between Dawg and a woman Rowdy knew had to be more than interested in the other man.

Women didn't get that upset if they weren't interested. If they didn't care. Crista Jansen cared—it had been there in her eyes, in her anger. But he had to agree with one thing. She wasn't the type of woman who would willingly share her man, anymore than Kelly was. And that was the clincher. She was a woman worth keeping, a one-man woman. And she needed a one-woman man.

TWELVE

Kelly waited at the door of the spa, watching as Rowdy pulled into the parking area in the pickup. She felt naughty as she waited for him, her body waxed and buffed, smoothed and lotioned.

As he stepped out of the pickup she pushed open the door and moved out to meet him, returning his smile as she felt the flush across her cheeks.

"Ready?" He opened the passenger-side door as she neared the truck, his green eyes intent as he watched her closely.

"All ready." Her voice trembled, dammit. Then she trembled all over as his hands gripped her hips and he lifted her into the seat of the truck.

She could feel the blush deepening in her face.

"Damn, that blush is pretty." Rowdy cupped her face, turning her face to him for a quick kiss and a wicked grin.

"And you're bad," she laughed as he moved back, winking at her before closing the door and heading back to the driver's side.

Within seconds, the interior of the truck was once again filled with his scent. Male. No cologne. Just the scent of primal heat teasing her senses.

"Hungry?" he asked as he slid the vehicle into reverse and pulled out of the parking spot.

"Starved." Her stomach was convinced she hadn't eaten in weeks.

"Why don't we pick up a few greasy cheeseburgers and fries and head out to the boat for awhile?" He suggested smoothly, glancing at her from the corner of his eye as she felt her heart race.

Alone on the boat with Rowdy? And he had to ask?

"Sounds good." She nodded as her thighs clenched and her breasts suddenly felt heavier, more sensitive.

There was something in his expression that warned her he was tired of waiting. A ready stillness, a tension. Rowdy had shown amazing restraint to this point. She had a feeling that patience had come to an abrupt end.

"Will we be taking the boat out?"

"No. The marina is pretty empty today," he said as he made a quick turn into a local fast-food restaurant. "I thought we'd eat, laze around, drink a few beers, and talk."

"Talk," she repeated slowly.

"And other things." There was no smile this time, no teasing, no edging around what they both wanted as he stared back at her. "Still want to go?"

"Yes." Kelly stared back at him, trying to regulate her breathing, to still the excitement climbing inside her.

He nodded slowly before turning his gaze back to the drive-thru he was pulling up beside.

Good to his word, he ordered greasy cheeseburgers, several of them, and masses of fries.

They were silent as he pulled forward, paid for the food, and collected the bag before driving back onto the road. Kelly watched the miles pass, staying quiet. She had waited for this, for too long she sometimes thought. And now, knowing that the waiting was nearly at an end, she could feel her nerves rocketing.

She was a virgin. There wasn't a chance in hell she knew near enough about the male body to please him the first time. Suddenly, she almost regretted waiting. Maybe she should have gone for some kind of experience, but there had been no desire to become intimate with the men she had dated.

Not that she normally dated them long. Dawg and Natches were always too close, always butting their noses into her dates. She had found it amusing over the years, but now she wondered if she should have put a stop to it. Should have at least tried to learn how to please a man.

She wanted to please Rowdy. She wanted to know how to touch him, how to excite him.

"Stop worrying so much," he chastised gently as they neared the marina.

"I'm not worrying." She forced a smile to her face. She was not going to act like a nervous teenager.

He snorted at her denial, his gaze knowing as he glanced at her again. "I know you, Kelly. You're sitting over there biting a hole in your lip. That means you're worrying."

Damn. Busted.

"You don't know everything, Rowdy Mackay." She stuck her tongue out at him as she tossed her head defiantly. "You just think you do."

"I know damned near everything about you," he argued, his lips pulling into a sensual smile as he turned the truck along the lakefront road. "When you're biting your lip like that, you're worrying. And there's nothing that's going to happen between us that

141

you need to worry about. Anticipate maybe." There was that wicked smile again. "But nothing to worry about."

Her face heated again. Damn him. Blushing was not her favorite thing to do.

"What are you going to do if Ray comes out to the boat to check on us?" She leaned back in her seat and regarded him in amusement now. "You know how overprotective he gets."

"Dad had to drive to Louisville this morning." Satisfaction filled his voice. "Your mom went with him. They have the Colberts minding the store and pumps while they're gone."

"So while the cat's away the mouse gets to play, huh?" she asked with a laugh.

"Mouse?" He frowned back playfully. "Sweetheart, trust me here, there ain't no mice on my boat. But the big bad wolf might end up devouring a certain little lamb for sure."

Kelly couldn't help the laugh that bubbled from her throat as Rowdy pulled into the parking slot nearest the entrance to the upper end of the docks. The locked gate was normally for maintenance only, but the Mackay cousins used it rather than walking the distance along the docks to the main entrance.

He laid his forearms over the steering wheel as he turned to look at her then, his green eyes capturing hers as all amusement fled his expression. "Are you ready?"

Kelly inhaled slowly. "I've been ready for years, Rowdy. You're the one that took his own sweet time."

He was dying for her. Rowdy clenched his teeth as he placed his hand at Kelly's back and led her along the floating dock to the *Nauti Buoy*. At this rate, his cock was going to permanently carry the imprint of his zipper. Every step he took the scent of her filled his head; beneath his hand the silken feel of her flesh tortured his senses.

In his other hand he carried the food, which meant he was going to wait to consume Kelly. And waiting wasn't high on his list of priorities today.

The knowledge that the bastard who had attacked her was watching her burned at him. *The son of a bitch*. Rowdy had known he was watching, could feel it, but the proof of it sent fury surging through his veins.

Just five minutes with the bastard, he thought, that was all he needed. *Hell five seconds. Just long enough to relish hearing the son of a bitch's neck break*. Rowdy swore if he got his hands on the man who dared to hurt her, he would die. Never, not ever, would he threaten Kelly again.

"Where are your cousins?" Kelly asked as they neared the *Nauti Dawg*. Rowdy's boat was now sitting between Dawg's and Natches's.

"I didn't ask their schedule." He grinned.

They were around, watching. Seeing who was paying attention to the three boats now parked off to themselves in the temporary docks normally reserved for those boats waiting transporting out of the lake. Later tonight they would be positioned on the hill above the house instead. It was time to catch this bastard, before he went completely off the deep end.

He swore he felt a shiver race up her spine and hid his smile. Kelly was curious, but wary. Until he let her know Dawg and Natches wouldn't be there, she hadn't totally relaxed with him.

"Do you think I would push them on you, Kelly?" He asked softly as they stepped onto the *Nauti Buoy* and he unlocked the glass sliding doors.

"No, I didn't." She shrugged as he glanced over at her. "And I do know how to say 'no,' Rowdy."

But would she say 'no'? It was something he hadn't wanted to think about. He deliberately didn't think about it simply because each time the subject came up he got heartburn. He'd never had heartburn a day in his life, but lately, it was becoming a daily malady.

"Yeah, I know you know how to say no," he grunted as he sat the food on the table and turned back to her. "That's what you told me every time I tried to get you to help me in the yard when you were younger."

"Tried to con me into doing the yard myself." She gave him a knowing look. "Try another one hotshot. I knew your tricks. You would leave me to it and disappear with your buddies without worrying about me following you."

He sighed heavily, but he wasn't fooling her.

"I'm so misunderstood." He shook his head as he neared her, his lashes lowered, his expression just sexy as hell as he passed her.

"Ouch!" She jumped as the palm of his hand landed on her butt before he locked the doors then pulled the heavy drapes over the glass.

"That's what you get for being sassy." He laughed at her frown. "Get over here and eat, woman, then you can show me your wax job."

"I'm not a car, Rowdy." She rolled her eyes despite the flaming awareness sizzling through her body.

She tried not to stare at him, tried not to sink into the brilliance of those green eyes, glittering with hunger and emotion. But it was damned hard not to.

The jeans he was wearing conformed to his hard thighs and emphasized the mouthwatering bulge between them. The shirt he wore stretched across his broad chest and molded to his hard abs. If there was an ounce of fat on his body she couldn't see it.

"Come on, sugar girl." His voice lowered as he moved to the

table, turning on the small light hanging overhead. "You empty the bag and I'll get the beer."

Beer and cheeseburgers. Kelly couldn't remember a meal she had enjoyed more as she sat across from Rowdy and talked. They argued. They always argued. Over the weather signs, the best fishing holes, and life in general.

"I think you disagree with me just to have something to do," Rowdy finally laughed as she tossed a French fry at his head.

"Probably. I'd hate for you to confuse me with all those women who swoon at your feet and beg for your attention," she pointed out before finishing her beer and setting the bottle aside. "You're spoiled, Rowdy."

"I *wish* I was spoiled." He sat back in his chair and looked at her. He just looked at her, his gaze intent now rather than teasing or flirting. "I remember the day I realized you were turning into a woman," he finally said softly, his voice deepening. "You were going out with that little prick Charlie Dayne. Your skirt was too short, your legs too tanned and you wearing the necklace I had bought you that Christmas. That damned little heart was laying right on the upper curve of your breast because that shirt was cut too low."

"You tried to get Mom to make me change clothes." She remembered. She remembered seeing his eyes that day, seeing the wild fire in them that nearly stole her breath.

"You were sixteen fucking years old," he whispered. "And all I could think about"—he shook his head—"I should have been shot for what I was thinking, Kelly."

"I thought about you then too." She was mesmerized by the fire in his eyes now. "I only went out with Charlie because I knew you didn't like him."

His eyes narrowed. "Donnie Winters?"

145

She leaned forward with a little snicker. "He liked you more than he liked me. He thought you were hot, Rowdy."

He blinked back at her before realization dawned in his eyes. "You little minx." He shuddered.

"I had six months of free hand washes for my car at his parents' car detailing shop simply because he got to see you without your shirt on." She laughed, moving cautiously from the table as he leaned forward in his chair, obviously remembering the fact that he had been outside working on his car that day. Shirtless. And the date had been unexpected, a spur of the moment decision Kelly had made.

"You sold my body for a few car washes?" He asked slowly.

Kelly giggled. "A few? Hey stud, one a week for six months. I told you, you were hot."

"I'm going to paddle your ass." He came out of his chair, watching carefully as she backed away from him, trying not to laugh at the outrage in his expression.

"He went on all evening about the sweat dripping down your chest, Rowdy," she snickered. "I think he was more impressed than I was." She shrieked as he bounded over the table, turned, and tried to run.

There was no place to run, and controlling her laughter enough to actually fend him off was impossible, especially once his fingers found the ultrasensitive ticklish areas in her sides and sent her to the floor as she fought his attacking fingers.

"Oh, God. Don't you tickle me," she cried breathlessly, rolling, bucking against him as he came over her, his teeth bared in a laughing growl as he caught her hands, stretching them over her head, and stared her down with mocking retribution.

"You'll pay for that, Kelly," he promised wickedly.

"What are you going to do, stud?" She blew him an air kiss before collapsing in giggles again as he tickled down her side.

"I surrender," she laughed breathlessly, twisting beneath him, desperate to escape the fingers. "I promise. I promise. I surrender."

His fingers stilled, but he didn't move. Her eyes opened, the laughter dying on her lips at the hunger in his face. He was doing nothing to hide it now, nothing to dilute it. And it stole her breath.

"Rowdy," she whispered his name, her heart suddenly slamming against her ribs as his gaze dropped to the buttons of her blouse.

"You were sixteen years old," he whispered. "And all I could think about was doing this."

His head lowered, his lips pressing to the upper swell of one breast as his tongue licked over it. Velvet flames rasped over her flesh as a shock of sensation slammed into her womb.

"And this." His head lifted. "Open your lips for me baby, let me show you why I had to run has hard and as fast as I could run."

He kept hold of her arms, keeping them stretched above her head, helpless beneath him, restrained as his lips lowered and stole her breath.

Heat flamed through her, ripping across nerve endings and destroying any sense of control as his lips slanted across hers in a kiss guaranteed to wipe every thought from her mind except for thoughts of him.

Kelly arched to him, a broken moan leaving her lips as his tongue laved the lower curve, slipped in to tease hers then retreated as he bestowed a series of deep, short kisses that had her begging for more.

"God, the taste of you," he whispered before licking at her lips again. "You make me hungrier than I've ever been in my life, Kelly. You make me lose my mind with my need for you."

"I can handle that," she panted, breathless, on fire for him now. "Lose your mind some more now."

She arched her neck as his lips slid down it, his free hand moving to the small buttons of her blouse and slowly, too slowly, pushing them through the buttonholes as his lips followed the path he was revealing.

"Oh God, Rowdy," she moaned as his teeth raked over the sensitive chord in her neck as her blouse parted, revealing the white lace bra she had worn beneath it.

Sexy and silky, the bra was bought with Rowdy in mind during his last trip home.

"Sweet Kelly," he groaned as his lips traveled to the valley of her breasts, his tongue licking at the curves as he then flicked open the little closure at the front of the bra.

She was going to explode. She was going to melt. Kelly could feel the perspiration gathering on her body as tension tightened her and arousal prepared her.

"Such pretty breasts. And sweet, sweet hard little nipples." His fingers pulled back the cup of her bra to reveal one swollen curve, peaked with a tight, reddened nipple. "Like perfect ripe little berries."

When his tongue curled around the peak and drew it in his mouth, Kelly was certain she lost her mind. Stars exploded behind her closed eyelids and a whimpering moan tore from her throat as he began to suckle.

It was so good it was killing her. Her head twisted against the carpet as she strained beneath him, desperate to be free as the pleasure began to tear through her body.

She didn't just feel the draw of his mouth on that nipple, but an echo of it in the other nipple. Fingers of sensation trailed to her womb, then ricocheted to her clit and beyond. The slow, sweet suction erupted in pinpoints of flames throughout her body and left her gasping, nearly incoherent beneath the caress.

"God, you're sweet." Rough. Hoarse. The obvious hunger and need in his voice left her weak even as her nerve endings sizzled with unbearable heat.

This was what she had dreamed of, waited on. Rowdy holding her, his voice husky, his desire for her obvious in each touch, each kiss.

"Don't stop," she begged as he stroked his cheek over the sensitized nipple. "Not yet." She would hate to have to kill him.

"Never," he growled. "Not ever. But I won't take you here."

Before she could catch him, pull him back to her, he was on his feet and lifting her body against his. The room seemed to tilt, the world around her shaking as his lips covered hers again and his hard arms lifted her against him.

Tension radiated in the air around them as she realized the world was tilting because he was lifting her in his arms. It was shaking because he was moving quickly to the steps that led to the bedroom upstairs. Then it stilled, and only the fireworks remained as she felt the mattress beneath her back and Rowdy coming over her.

Her breath caught at the feel of his big, heavy body above her, sheltering her, protecting her. As long as Rowdy was near, then she would always be safe. And warm. Hot even.

She arched against him as he drew the blouse and the strap of her bra from one shoulder, his lips caressing her skin with heated strokes as he undressed her.

"The thought of your soft, waxed flesh has tormented me today," he growled as he lifted her, his hands pulling the clothing from her body as her head fell back on her shoulders to allow his lips to caress her neck.

"Do you have any idea how bad I want to bury my lips between your legs?" He nipped at the rounded curve of her breast as he

149

tossed the shirt and bra to the side and lowered her back to the mattress. "So bad, Kelly, that I stay hard thinking about the taste of you."

His voice was rough, deep. The dark timbre sent shivers racing over her body as she trembled beneath him, her hands reaching up to touch his bare shoulders while his fingers went to the button of her jeans.

Sharp explosions of sensation began to vibrate through her clit, her vagina, as a maelstrom of pleasure whipped through her body.

Finally. God, finally he was touching her as she needed to be touched, holding her, sliding the jeans and thong from her to bare the sensitive, damp folds of her pussy.

"God. Oh hell, Kelly."

Her eyes opened at the serrated sound of his voice, her lashes fluttering over her eyes as she focused on his face. His expression was primal, intent as he stared between her thighs before lifting his gaze to hers.

"You're wet for me." His hand reached out, his fingers running through the drenched slit as she arched, a broken cry leaving her lips at the wake of fire that trailed with his touch.

Then she lost her breath entirely as he brought those fingers to his lips, tasting her, his gaze deepening, his eyes growing brighter as he suddenly moved from the bed, his hands going to his own jeans.

Within seconds he was naked, his hard body gleaming with sweat, the engorged crest of his erection glistening with pre-come.

"I want to taste you," she whispered then, lifting up, reaching for him, desperate for him.

He was hard. Heavy. Her fingers wrapped around the base of his cock and her head lowered, her tongue swiping over the engorged head.

Oh he liked that. The mushroomed head pulsed and spilled a glistening droplet of pre-come. Which she had to lick off. Taste.

"Put it in your mouth." His hands were in her hair now, his green eyes glittering with lust. "Suck it, baby."

Her lips opened slowly as he pressed the thickly flared head against them, cupping over it as it slid into the warmth of her mouth.

A tight grimace pulled at his lips. "Fuck yeah. God, you look pretty. So sweet and pretty."

Kelly swiped her tongue over the throbbing crest, moaning at the dark, erotic taste of his flesh as he began to move, to thrust in small, easy movements against her lips as she began to suck delicately.

It was so good. So sexy. Her gaze was locked on his, her mouth filled with his erection as her hands stroked the straining shaft.

It was the stuff of fantasies. His hands pulling at her hair, burying his cock almost to her throat while his muscles strained from hunger. Hunger for her. For her touch. For her body.

"Not yet, baby. I can't come yet. Oh, God, not yet." He held her back, controlling her needy denial as he pulled his cock from her lips. One hand pressed her back to the bed as he moved between her thighs once again. "Let me have you first, Kelly. Just this once, baby."

His hands restrained her gently, pressing her back to the bed as his head lowered to the wet folds between her thighs, and her senses ignited.

His tongue rasped over the bare, tender flesh with the softest stroke, licking at her, burning her with each touch as she fought to get closer.

It wasn't enough. She needed more.

"Rowdy . . ." Her wail of need tore from her throat as his

tongue flickered around her clit, sending pulsating, fiery fingers of sensation wrapping around the tight bundle of nerves. Kelly strained closer, her head thrashing on the bed as her hands dug into his hair and she fought to hold him to her.

Just another second. She knew if he would linger right there, right where the pleasure burned deeper, then the agonizing need tearing through her would ease.

Just another second.

She cried out again as he hummed against her flesh, his hands parting her legs further before she felt the slightest pressure at the entrance to her vagina. A parting, a caress that sent her senses spinning.

"Rowdy, please . . . please . . ." She couldn't hold back the pleas, the need for release.

"So sweet," he crooned against her clit, causing her to jerk, to arch, the terrible need tormenting her only growing by the second now.

Wicked electric arcs of pleasure whipped over her flesh as perspiration began to cover her body and the hunger straining in every cell drove her closer to the brink. She needed. She ached.

She screamed as his lips covered her clit, his tongue flickering as he suckled at her flesh and stars exploded before her closed eyes.

Release was cataclysmic; it erupted inside her, drawing her muscles tight, pulling her upper body forward as she fought for something to hold onto, to find a sense of balance. A balance that couldn't exist within the fiery ecstasy overtaking her.

"Jesus! Kelly." Rowdy rose fiercely between her thighs, a hazy image invading her senses as she stared back at him, dazed, uncomprehending until she felt the sudden, thick pressure parting her, pressing against the convulsing entrance to her vagina.

"Now." She couldn't scream, she could barely speak. "Please. Please . . ."

Her hands gripped his wrists now, her upper body still tense, tight, lifting to him as her gaze dropped between her thighs. There, straining, thick, his cock pressed against her as his hips began to press closer.

"Rowdy." The thin, pleading sound of her own voice was unfamiliar to her ears.

"Easy. Easy, baby." He was panting, his hard abs flexing, thighs tightening.

"No." She couldn't help watching, seeing the thick length of his erection, the heavy veins throbbing, the tight flesh steel hard and iron hot. "Now." She lifted closer, moaning in painful need as her flesh began to stretch.

"Kelly. Baby." His cock slid in deeper, the dark crest disappearing inside her and causing the untouched muscles to convulse as the dampness increased, easing his way.

Her eyes lifted to his, seeing the color blazing from within his dark face, his expression a grimace of painful pleasure.

"Don't wait." She couldn't bear the waiting. "Please."

The sudden jolt of his hips buried him deeper as Kelly shuddered at the tight penetration, her head hitting the mattress as her hips lifted closer.

She was consumed with pleasure. It burned through her nerve endings, clenched her womb, convulsed her vagina, and demanded satisfaction.

"Now." Her hips lifted in a sharp, quick move as he fought to penetrate her slowly, to ease inside her. She didn't want ease. She wanted the burn, the destructive, flaming pleasure she could feel building inside her.

And it came. The sudden upthrust buried his flesh deeper inside her, breaking through her virginity, sending a burst of rapture, sharp and much too short, through her system.

"Fuck! Kelly."

"Oh God. Oh God . . . yes. Please, Rowdy." She twisted beneath him, fighting the tighter hold on her hips, the sudden restraint as he paused above her. "Please. Fuck me. Fuck me now . . ."

She couldn't scream; all she could do was lose her breath as he drew back then filled her, impaled her. Buried the full length of his cock inside her before he came over her, gripping her hair in his fingers as his lips covered hers.

Mindless, rapturous. The sensations blazed deeper, higher; they filled her senses, overcame reality, and sent her spiraling through a star-studded night as he gave her what she begged for.

His cock was a hard, blistering length of iron thrusting inside her, stroking tender tissue, building the tension, the pleasure, to a height that Kelly swore she couldn't bear.

Writhing beneath him, she fought for release, gasping, begging, her hands buried in his hair, her lips open against his, every cell possessed by him, stroked by him, enflamed by him, until she was certain only death could await, because there was no way to survive such pleasure.

"Fuck! There, baby."

She was trying to scream as his lips lifted, one hand gripping her hip, the other her hair as her lashes raised and she fought to plead silently, desperately for release.

"There sweet Kelly," he groaned, the strokes suddenly intensifying, the rapid-fire thrusts pulling the tension tighter. Deeper. "Just like that, baby."

She shook her head as she felt the sudden contractions in her womb.

"There it is sweetheart." His voice was tight, encouraging. "Let it have you, baby. I'll hold you. I promise."

Rowdy would hold her. She wasn't really going to die. She was going to disintegrate.

"Come for me, Kelly. Let it go, sweetheart. I have you. Forever, baby." His voice was guttural, desperate, carnal. It was like black velvet, rasping over her senses, surrounding her, stroking her, filling her.

Her release slammed into her. Kelly felt the sudden implosion, then a heavy gathering, a second before ecstasy exploded violently inside her.

Convulsive spasms of release erupted around his hard flesh, a heavy, wet warmth washing over his cock as her release spilled through her.

Her muscles locked around him, attempting to hold him, to capture forever the rapture radiating through her with such brilliant force.

And she did die, she thought with hazy perception. All preconceived notions of loving Rowdy, died. All her fantasies of what pleasure could be, they died. And they were reborn.

His voice wrapped around her, his arms surrounded her, and he was driving deep, burying himself inside her before she felt the white-hot flames of his release as he began to fill her, spurting inside her with a force that stole any remaining sanity she may have possessed.

Kelly collapsed beneath him, exhausted, fighting to breathe, her strength exhausted as she shuddered in the aftershocks of a pleasure she could have never imagined existed.

This was why women crowded around Rowdy. Why they vied for his attention and begged for his touch. Why she had waited, prayed, and saved herself for him alone.

"I love you." She could barely force the words from her lips as she let exhaustion take her. "Just love you."

THIRTEEN

Rowdy ordered pizza at midnight and brought it to bed. He fed her bites of pepperoni and cheese and let her drink from his beer. He propped himself behind her, naked, and let her use his chest for a pillow as she acclimated herself from being a virgin to being his woman.

"When were the parents getting home?" The moon had risen hours ago, somewhere around the time that Rowdy was making her scream in the shower.

"They were staying overnight." His voice was low, lazy. It soothed now, reaching into that part of her soul that had been stripped bare by his loving. "I thought we would stay the night on the boat."

Kelly stilled against him. She could feel the tension slowly invading his body now, and it wasn't sexual.

"Why?" Not that she cared to spend the night on the boat, but she knew he worried about vulnerabilities the boat presented if someone were watching it.

His arms came around her, snug, sheltering, and she knew immediately that something was wrong. Rowdy sighed behind her, his muscular arms flexing as he rubbed his cheek against her hair.

"You may as well tell me, Rowdy."

"Someone was watching the house last night," he said softly. "On the hill in front of your bedroom window. They were there for most of the night."

Kelly swallowed tightly as she stared across the room. "He's been watching me." She had sensed it. A part of her had known she was being watched, she just hadn't wanted to admit it.

"It's okay, Kelly." Rowdy's voice lowered as his lips pressed against the top of her head. "It might not even be him. I just want to be certain."

"And how are you going to be certain?" she asked, feeling the fear invade her in a slow, insidious crawl. "Where are Dawg and Natches?"

"They're watching the boat. The sheriff is going to check out the hill tonight. He's ex-Army, he knows how to do it. Besides, there's no way I can make love to you in Dad's house. Every time I think about it, Kelly, my balls shrivel."

He was trying to lighten the mood. She could hear it in his voice. Kelly shook her head as she pulled herself from his arms and moved from the bed, swiping the shirt he had worn earlier from the floor and pulling it on.

"Kelly," he protested softly. "Baby, I'll fix this. I promise."

She held her hand up without turning back to him, hiding her desperate attempt to hold back her screams with sheer force. Shaking her head she moved quickly to the doorway then down the steps that led to the first floor of the houseboat.

Where she was going to go, she didn't know. There was no place to hide, no way to escape.

You're my good girl, Kelly. My good little girl. Tell me you love me. You love me, don't you?

Kelly stumbled at the last step as the words whispered through her mind, the memory of his hissing voice, his hands holding her down, parting the cheeks of her rear as he spread the lubrication there and attempted to rape her.

She had felt him trying to enter her.

She wrapped her arms over her stomach, determined not to throw up, not to scream in rage.

"Don't do this to yourself!" Rowdy's voice was dark, angry, as his arms came around her again, turning her to his chest, pulling her against him as he surrounded her, sharing the heat of his body as she felt ice building in her soul. "Kelly, I swear. We'll catch him."

She shook her head desperately, realizing tears were washing down her cheeks as the sobs clawed at her chest.

She could still feel the cuts the attacker had sliced into her flesh, the blood running over her skin, hot, slick.

"I can't do this," she cried, her fingers curling into fists as he held her to him, refusing to let her go. "I can't do it again." She would never survive another attack and she knew it. "Oh, God, Rowdy. Oh, God. I can't . . ."

Rowdy picked Kelly up in his arms, moving to the sofa, cradling her against his naked body as he held her head to his chest and fought back the intense, primal violence threatening within him.

The bastard had scarred her. Not just her mind with his attempted rape, but her soul. The attack had instilled a fear inside her that he knew she would never fully recover from, and it destroyed him.

"It's okay, Kelly," he crooned at her ear. "I have you, baby. No one can hurt you here, sweetheart. I swear it."

She shuddered against him. The cries had eased, but the trembling in her body hadn't.

"Kelly, baby, you have to trust me." He cupped her chin, forcing her to look up at him, his heart breaking at the sight of her eyes drenched in tears, her face pale from fear. "It's going to be okay, baby."

"It won't be." Husky, filled with fear, her voice sliced open his heart. "I knew he was watching me. I could feel him. God, Rowdy."

She jumped from his lap before he could stop her, stumbling across the floor. She turned on him, her eyes blazing with cloudy fury as she stared across the distance.

"He won't stop. He won't stop until he hurts someone again, and next time, he might hurt you."

What he thought was fury in her eyes was actually horror. He saw it swamp her features, leeching the rest of the color from her face.

Rowdy straightened from the couch, aware he was naked, aware his body was responding to the sight of her, the smell of her. He saw her gaze flicker down, then jerk back up.

"God, Rowdy now is not the time for that." The look of complete female irritation on her face shouldn't have been amusing—he was certain.

He made sure his look was completely wicked. He couldn't bear to see the fear in her eyes; if he had to replace it with irritation or even anger, than so be it.

"Sweetheart, anytime is the perfect for this when you're around," he chuckled.

"No." She shook her head, pacing back. "We have to talk about this, Rowdy. I have to figure this out."

"Figure what out?" His eyes narrowed at the purpose that began to fill her face.

"I have to leave." Her voice was laden with sorrow, with grief. "I have relatives on Dad's side in Montana. It's a nice little town. I can go there. For awhile." Her voice roughened with the threat of tears.

"No."

"Don't be stubborn, Rowdy." She faced him, determination and grief filling her eyes. "I can't stay here. He could strike at Mom or your dad. Or—you." Her voice trembled.

What the hell was he going to do with her? Rowdy stared back at her somberly, feeling his chest ache with an emotion that so out-distanced love that he couldn't describe it.

"Forget it." He crossed his arms over his chest and frowned back at her. "I'll only follow you, Kelly."

"You can't follow me," she snapped. "This is your home. The marina. The lake. All of it."

"There's lakes in Montana." He shrugged. Arguing over her leaving would only make her more determined to go. He knew Kelly. Once she decided she was right, that was it. It took blood, sweat, and tears, on her part, before she would realize how wrong she was.

She was stubborn, defiant, soft, and loving, but she could drive him crazy in two hours flat if he let her. But he would never be bored with her. Frustrated, yes. Bored? Never.

"You can't leave." She glared back at him. "Your friends are here. Your cousins, your family."

"So are yours." He shrugged. "If you want to leave, fine. Pack. We'll go to Montana. Hell, we'll go to fucking Fiji if you want to and become beach bums, but you aren't leaving without me."

She propped her fists on her hips as her lips flattened.

"So I'm supposed to just sit here and wait on that bastard to attack again? Wait on him to hurt someone else? Maybe you?"

"I can take him." His smile was tight, hard. He would relish it.

"You can't fight a bullet, Rowdy," she argued desperately. "What if he doesn't fight fair?"

"What if you try dropping any idea you have of leaving me," he growled. "It's not going to happen. I didn't go through hell for the past eight years to give you a chance to be certain you want me, just to have some sick bastard fuck it up. You're mine, Kelly."

And if his words didn't convince her, then his cock better, because it was stiff as steel and throbbing with a life of its own.

Her gaze flickered down again, a bit of color flushing her pale cheeks as she licked her lips nervously.

"Put your pants on."

"Why? I'll just have to take them right back off," he promised her. "Take the shirt off."

"No." She crossed her arms over her breasts again. "We're not finished talking."

"Of course we are." He moved closer. "The only thing left is your decision. Do we stay or do we leave? Because whichever, Kelly, we do together."

Before she could evade him he had her in his arms again, ignoring the sharp little nails that pressed into his shoulders as he pulled her hips in against his and pressed his cock against her lower stomach.

"Feel how hard I am, Kelly." He nipped at her ear as she trembled in his arms. "Do you really want to leave me like this? Hot and hard for you? Aching for you every night that you're gone? Like I've ached for the past eight years."

"You survived," she moaned.

"But I hadn't had you then." He licked the shell of her ear before trailing his lips to her throat. "I hadn't felt your hot little pussy wrapped around my cock, milking me dry. I've had that now. I don't think I can live without it."

He watched as heat began to fill her eyes, as the anger in her expression softened, just a little.

"I don't want you hurt," she whispered breathlessly. "He's crazy—"

"Damn right he is," Rowdy bit off the fury that would have filled his voice, barely managing just anger. "He touched you, Kelly. He made the mistake of taking from you, of hurting you. Do you think I'll ever forget that? That he won't pay for it if I ever manage to find out who he is? The son of a bitch would have served himself better to run as hard and as far as he could from me, rather than stalking you. Because I won't rest until I find him."

Kelly opened her lips to speak, to argue he was certain, only to be interrupted by a less than polite pounding on the side of the houseboat.

"Open up, cuz," Dawg called through the sliding doors. "We have trouble, man."

Kelly's eyes widened in alarm as Rowdy stalked to the back of the houseboat, grabbed a pair of shorts, and jerked them on before stalking back to the door.

Dawg and Natches stepped into the room seconds later, their expressions dark, cold.

"He hit the house while we were on the hill, Rowdy," Dawg growled as he glanced over at Kelly. "Kelly's room. He trashed it."

He was going to kill the motherfucker. The minute Rowdy walked into Kelly's room, he made that vow. This wasn't like the promises he had made before to kill a son of a bitch. This was a vow, a soul-deep pledge to kill the sleazy, fucking bastard crazy enough to do this to his woman.

Her room was destroyed. Everything she had was destroyed.

Bits of lace and silk that had once been a treasure trove of frilly feminine panties and bras were scattered on the floor. Her hair bows were broken, ripped, cut. Her bedspread was slashed to ribbons as were her clothes.

Rowdy knelt in front of the closet and picked up the tatters of what had once been a pretty scarlet sundress. Beside it lay a shoe, the heel broken off, the red leather hacked at.

Makeup was smeared, swiped, and dumped over her dresser. Jeans were shredded, frothy nightgowns were unrecognizable, and more than a dozen pair of lace and silk stockings were destroyed.

The feathers from the pillows drifted along the floor, the dresser mirror was smashed, and the padding in the chair had been ripped out.

Kelly was still waiting downstairs to come up and see if anything was missing. The sheriff and his boys had finished dusting for prints, but nothing had been found.

"Someone was pissed." Deputy Carlyle stood in the doorway, his expression curious as he stared around the wreckage.

Rowdy lifted his gaze and stared back at the younger man. Carlyle was new on the force. An unfamiliar face and therefore suspicious as far as Rowdy was concerned.

And Rowdy didn't like the way he was staring around Kelly's room. Curious. A little too interested in the bits of fluff that had once been her clothes.

Carlyle was young, maybe in his early twenties, definitely not long out of the Police Academy, with an ego that showed clearly on his handsome face.

"Did you get any prints?" Rowdy raised slowly, his eyes narrowed as he stared at the deputy.

"Nothin'." Carlyle leaned against the door, his too lean body rangy, his brown eyes surveying the room again. "No prints on the door either. He slid right by the security system, came straight up here, and sliced and diced. Good thing Kelly wasn't here."

Rowdy restrained a growl. Bastard had no right to act so familiar with Kelly.

"Yeah. Good thing," he retorted instead.

"Sheriff contacted your parents, they'll be here soon." Carlyle smiled. "They were upset of course."

His parents? Rowdy frowned at the hint of condemnation in the deputy's voice. As if Kelly were his sister, or some blood relation. The judgment set his teeth on edge.

"Are you finished here?" Rowdy asked tightly. "Anything else you need, Deputy?"

Carlyle lifted a brow. "Nothing, Mr. Mackay. We have everything." He smiled confidently.

"Then maybe you should leave." Rowdy smiled back, all teeth.

"I will." Carlyle nodded. "As soon as we get Kelly up here to see if anything is missing. I need that before I leave. The sheriff insisted."

Assaulting an officer of the law was a very bad thing, Rowdy reminded himself. Kelly would be upset. She wouldn't be happy with him at all.

"She can give her statement tomorrow afternoon, Deputy," he all but barked. "She won't be able to tell you shit tonight."

Carlyle smiled again as he lowered his head and shook it slowly.

"I heard you were a real tough guy," he commented, his voice on the wrong side of mocking. "I'd rein that in if I were you, boy."

Boy? Rowdy narrowed his eyes slowly.

"Get the fuck out of my house," Rowdy growled. "Don't piss me off any further, *boy*. And before you get on your high horse maybe you should call your boss and ask him just how far back we go together. You're risking more than my fist in that smirking face of yours."

Beating around the bush wasn't his style, and he'd just had enough of this little dweeb's sneer.

"Dawg and Natches are still downstairs, Mackay," the deputy said.

"So?" Rowdy snapped.

"Last I heard, there isn't much you boys don't do together. Don't tell me you'd actually fight without them."

Rowdy smiled at that one. The kid was a punk, and he was about to learn a lesson he didn't want right now. "I managed to kill just fine without them for four years, Deputy. Want to test it?"

Carlyle's smirk was going to get him killed for sure.

"I'll just leave you to your business here then," he chuckled. "Bring Kelly into the office in the morning. I'm looking forward to talking to her."

Carlyle turned then and ambled down the hall as Rowdy reminded himself that killing outside the Marines was a bad thing. Very bad. Especially smart-mouthed deputies.

Son of a bitch, when had kids like that decided the job was a power trip? Rowdy had half a mind to follow him outside and show him what real power was. The kind of power that slipped up on you in the dark and left you bleeding.

And he could have, hell, he would have taken him out while he was standing there in the doorway with that sneer, but all he saw was Kelly. She would have been horrified if he had actually hurt that little punk while she was around.

Shaking his head he moved downstairs, mentally gearing himself up to face Kelly. Every little treasure she possessed had been in that room. The teddy bear he won for her at a fair when she was just a kid. The porcelain doll one of her friends had gotten her for a birthday. Her frilly hair bows and her silky clothes.

He stepped into the living room, his gaze connecting with Dawg and Natches as Kelly jumped to her feet from the chair she had been sitting in.

"How bad is it?" Her fingers were twisting together in front of her, her face pale.

Damn, he hated this.

"It's pretty bad, baby," he sighed, moving to her and pulling her into his arms.

She fit against him perfectly. A warm weight he hadn't known was missing in his life until now.

"I'm okay." She shook her head against his chest. "I need to go up there, though. I have to see what's left. The sheriff wants a statement."

And he couldn't keep her from going up there, despite the fact that it was killing him.

He stared at Dawg and Natches over her head and with a small movement of his head indicated that he wanted the area outside of the house checked. The sheriff's boys could have missed something. Something his cousins might identify quicker than the investigative team that had come out could have.

Dawg nodded as he and Natches moved from the room.

"Come on," Rowdy sighed, keeping his arm around her. "Let's go check it out."

There was nothing left, just as Rowdy had warned her. Kelly stared at the mess silently from the doorway and fought back her tears. Even the jewelry box had been destroyed.

"How am I supposed to tell if anything is missing?" The destruction was complete.

"We'll get it cleaned up." Rowdy's arms were wrapped around her from behind, his presence sheltering her. "I'm sorry, baby."

"It's not your fault." Kelly shook her head, trying to hold back the fear growing inside her. "He's angry now, isn't he?"

Always be my good girl. You'll always be my good girl.

"Yeah, he's angry now," Rowdy admitted. "But he's not the only one. Do you want to go through the room now or wait till morning? It might be better to wait."

She had been violated again. Kelly could feel the pervasive knowledge that even though the attacker hadn't touched her again, he had still violated her. He had taken something else from her.

She shook her head. "I need to get this cleaned up. I can't stand knowing it's destroyed like this."

She had to force back her tears. It broke her heart, seeing her treasures destroyed as they were, knowing there was nothing she could do to bring them back. But wasn't that the purpose behind this sort of attack? To take her mementos, the things she loved away from her?

She moved into the bedroom, staring around at the destruction, and wanted to scream. This was her room. She had had all her treasures here. Her jewelry, her stuffed animals, her dolls. And her hair bows. For once Rowdy hadn't been able to save her hair bows.

She bent down and picked up the pieces of a hair comb. The small fake pearls were crushed, the little crystals shattered. It had been one of her favorites.

"We'll replace them, Kelly," Rowdy promised behind her. "All of them."

She cradled the bit of plastic that was left in her palm. They could replace the hair bows, but nothing could replace the sense of security that had been stolen from her.

FOURTEEN

Rowdy had finally managed to convince Kelly and her mother to leave the bedroom alone until morning. They were both exhausted when he and his father walked into the bedroom at three a.m. to find the two women crying in each other's arms.

Rowdy had taken Kelly to his bedroom where he held her as she slept, and Ray had taken her mother to their bed. Rowdy was certain his father had gotten no more sleep than he had though, despite the fact that Dawg and Natches had slept downstairs until the security system could be repaired.

At eight, Rowdy met Ray in the hallway heading downstairs.

"Kelly still asleep?" Ray kept his voice low.

Rowdy nodded sharply.

"Coffee?" His father's eyes glittered with anger.

"If I know Dawg, it's already on." Rowdy was certain he had smelled it moments before he left his bedroom.

Ray tugged at the band of his jeans and sniffed sharply, his jaw bunching. "Let's go get some. I've had about all I can take of sitting around and thinking."

Rowdy knew exactly what he was talking about.

They met Dawg and Natches in the kitchen. Both men were hunched over steaming cups of coffee, talking quietly as Rowdy and Ray entered the room.

"It's fresh." Dawg nodded to the pot on the counter.

"Did you manage to find anything this morning?" Rowdy asked as he moved to the cabinet and pulled two cups down.

"Nothing." Dawg sighed. "Me and Natches went over this place with a fine-toothed comb. Whoever it was slipped in like a damned ghost and back out the same way."

"Bastard!" Ray snapped. "I'm about tired of this, Rowdy. Maria and Kelly are losing enough sleep. They don't need this."

"I know, Dad." Hell, he didn't need it. He was having nightmares the way it was.

"He was just watching her until you came back, Rowdy," Dawg informed him. "We found several places where he's been watching the house from. The rains have wiped out most of the evidence of someone watching, but he likes to snack while he's watching. A few candy papers, a couple of soda bottles. No prints though. We checked for that. He's watching from points above the house, several different areas."

"She said she knew she was being watched," Rowdy sighed. "She felt it."

"We'll find him." Natches's eyes were flinty, cold. "He'll make the wrong move soon."

Rowdy rubbed the back of his neck as he pulled out a chair and sat. His cup smacked the table as he sat it down.

"He destroyed every fucking piece of clothes she owns. Every goddamned hair bow and frilly girly thing she possessed. He destroyed her."

And Rowdy would destroy him, it was that simple. Once Rowdy got his hands on the bastard, he was dead. Painfully dead. The hurting, screaming kind of dead.

"How do you catch a damned ghost?" Ray snarled as he sat at the other end of the table. "The sheriff has been looking for him, I've been watching out for anyone suspicious, and no one has seen shit."

Rowdy's gaze connected with Dawg's and Natches's. The bastard had come after Kelly again because he knew she was on the boat with Rowdy. He was pissed. He would make a mistake soon enough.

"Don't you three think you're going to keep me out of this," Ray warned knowingly. "You're not as good at those sneaking little looks as you think you are. Tell me what you're up to."

"We're not up to anything, Dad." Rowdy pushed his fingers wearily through his still damp hair. "He's mad. He had to have known Kelly was on the boat with me last night. He considers her his *good girl*. She's not waiting for him, so he's punishing her. He'll make a mistake soon enough."

"Especially if you have your way?" Ray growled. "Be careful, Rowdy. Don't try to play games with this bastard."

"No games." Rowdy lifted his cup to sip at the coffee as he stared back at his father. "I won't have to play any games. He won't be able to stand her being with me. He's trying to scare her away from me with this. When it doesn't work, he'll come after me."

"Or Kelly?" Ray snapped. "What if he goes after Kelly?"

Dawg shook his head at that one. "He'll come after Rowdy. And when he does, we'll all be waiting."

Ray stared at the three of them harshly. "Don't play with Kelly's reputation, Dawg," he warned him. "I won't like that."

Dawg glanced at Rowdy.

"The three of you are going to piss me off," Ray snapped.

Hell, just what he needed, his father getting in on this. If Ray was suspicious, then Maria would be too and then she would start working on Kelly. Rowdy knew what it was going to take to bring Kelly's attacker out of the woodwork. If they didn't push him, then he would strike when none of them expected it. They couldn't take that chance.

"I'll take care of this." He stared back at his father firmly. He wasn't arguing over it. He wasn't debating it. One way or the other, he would make certain Kelly was safe.

"Without hurting Kelly further?" Ray's expression was suspicious.

"There's no way to keep Kelly out of this," Rowdy warned him. "She's the one he's after."

"And she's the one that needs to know how we're going to stop him," Kelly's voice stated from the doorway.

All eyes turned to her. She was dressed in one of her mother's gowns and a robe, her long hair flowing around her, her gray eyes stormy.

She was scared and fighting to be strong. Enduring. Kelly was enduring. He had known that years ago, but he was learning it more now. She wouldn't go down easy. She might have her weak moments, but she would come back fighting. And what he needed her to do now was fight.

He watched as she moved to the coffeepot, filled her cup, then turned back to stare at the four of them in determination.

"Whatever happens, Ray, it's my decision," she stated. "You and Mom can't protect me forever."

Ray's jaw bunched with the anger that acknowledgment brought.

Turning back to Rowdy, his eyes narrowed warningly as he rose from the table. "She better not get hurt," he snapped. "Or the three of you will answer to me."

He stalked from the kitchen then and stomped up the stairs, obviously heading for the bedroom he shared with Maria.

Silent, Rowdy watched as Kelly moved to Ray's chair and sat down gingerly, placing her cup carefully on the table before asking, "What's the quickest way to draw him out?"

FIFTEEN

Knowing what Rowdy had planned and actually seeing it being put into effect were two different things. Kelly found that watching the men converge on a project was almost scary.

The Nauti Boys weren't known for playing nice, in any way. But seeing the hard, cold men studying the banks as they maneuvered into the wide, deserted cove two days later, reminded her that they had been warriors for years, Marines who had survived a long, bloody war.

The men gathered in the living room. Dawg stood at the sliding glass doors that led to the deck, while Natches watched the back, and Rowdy kept a check on the bank along the side of the river.

Their eyes were narrowed, bodies tense and prepared, and all Kelly could do was worry. And try to stem the butterflies rising in her stomach.

She knew the plan was to make her stalker believe she was playing with all the Nauti Boys at once while protecting her from the three of them. They believed he was unbalanced enough, angry enough to show himself. But there was more. She could feel the tension between the three men, the knowledge that they were waiting on her. Wondering if she would give to the three of them together as she had given to Rowdy.

"You're too quiet, baby." Rowdy's voice was soft, filled with hidden depths as he glanced back at where she sat on the couch, staring back at him.

"There doesn't seem to be much to say," she responded quietly, seeing the shadows that filled his eyes.

She wished he wasn't so handsome, wished he wasn't so male. And she wished his cousins didn't draw her almost as much as Rowdy himself did. It was one of the issues she had struggled with since the attack. Her rapist had called her a good girl, but she knew she wasn't, not really, and that scared her. No woman had ever held even one of the Mackay cousins' hearts—what made her think she could? What made her think she could hold all three?

"I told you, Kelly, whatever happens, it will be just you and me."

Yes, he had. On the way to the marina, his voice quiet and throbbing with lust, but she had heard the tinge of regret as well. As though he were torn in his needs, in his wants.

She was aware of Dawg listening, his back to them, his body tense.

"The Nauti Boys playing separately." She arched her brow at the comment. "That's just about unheard of, Rowdy."

Dawg snorted. Rowdy shook his head, his green eyes chastising.

"Your tongue has grown sharper over the years, darlin'," he growled. "I'm a hungry man right now. It's not nice to tempt hungry men."

She settled into the corner of the couch, lifting her legs to the cushions and stretching them to the side. Rowdy's gaze followed the movement with a spark of interest.

"My tongue has always been sharp, you just haven't been around enough to notice." She shrugged. "Dawg and Natches should have warned you of that. Wasn't that part of their job description?"

Knowing they had been watching her and running off potential lovers hadn't suited her well. It was a damned good thing she hadn't known before Rowdy came home.

"The job was hard enough as it was, brat." Dawg turned his head, flashing her a mock frown over his shoulder. "There was no sense in making it more complicated."

Rowdy chuckled as Kelly glanced back at Dawg archly. He winked with a slow, sensual lowering of one thickly lashed eyelid. And she knew that move shouldn't have affected her; unfortunately, it always did. Dawg was a natural-born flirt.

"You make it sound like I was hard to watch." The pretend pout was aimed at Rowdy. "And here I thought I was being a . . ." The words trailed off as she caught what she was about to say.

She thought she had been a *good girl*.

She jerked from the couch, ignoring Rowdy's soft protest as she stalked through the cabin of the houseboat to the back deck.

For a moment, she wasn't certain she could keep her dinner in her stomach as fear lurched through her. A cold sweat covered her skin and she felt naked, exposed in the tiny bathing suit she had managed to let Rowdy convince her to wear.

Ignoring Natches, she moved to the rail, staring down at the water churning at the hull, and swallowed tightly. She had been a good girl. She had waited for Rowdy, instinctively knowing she belonged to him. She may have moments of insecurity in holding his heart, but she had always known she loved him. Always known that he would be her first. She gripped the rail, forcing back her fears as the remembered sound of her own screams echoed through her head.

"He's won."

The sound of Natches's voice had her breathing in roughly as she shook her head.

"I bet you feel like you're naked, on display," he continued.

"Don't, Natches." She fought back the fears rolling through her. "Please."

"Is your skin crawling, Kelly?"

It was. The feel of him behind her, knowing he could see her bare skin, that he wanted to touch her, was suddenly terrifying.

This was Natches. He was almost an extension of Rowdy, a protector, a friend.

"I don't want this," she whispered. "I don't want to be scared because I'm about to say the wrong thing. I don't want to forget every dream I ever had, or lose the man I've loved forever because I can't control the nightmares."

"You'll never lose Rowdy, Kelly," he spoke behind her, far enough away that she wasn't jumping out of her own skin, but close enough that she could clearly hear him. "He's waited on you for eight years now. You're not going to get rid of him easily."

Her breathing hitched.

"If it doesn't happen tonight, Kelly, then he'll wait until you're ready." His voice was soothing, gentle.

Kelly turned to him, staring into his compassionate expression, ignoring the flame of fury that burned behind the sympathy in his eyes.

"And you and Dawg?"

His lips tugged into a crooked smile as his pale green eyes seemed to darken with a hungry cast.

"You belong to Rowdy, Kelly, and vice versa. If that's what you want, then Rowdy will let us know. Until then, nothing has changed with us. We're no different than we've always been to you, and our feelings for you haven't changed."

His gaze flickered over her quickly, and Kelly remembered that he had looked at her the same way for years. With a tinge of teasing lust that he never allowed free. Dawg had always done the same thing, knowing the day would come that Rowdy would claim her, and possibly they would as well.

She glanced at the doorway as Rowdy suddenly filled it, his green eyes bright as they went over her body. He paused at her thighs, centering his gaze on the black material of the bikini bottom she wore before lifting to the fabric that stretched over her breasts.

"I never mistook you for a good girl," he murmured, his voice deep, rough. "You were *my* girl, Kelly. Always."

His girl. Her breath caught in her throat as she stared back at him. Not his good girl, his bad girl, or his naughty girl. Just his.

"I bet you fantasized about it." Rowdy's voice sent curls of heat whipping through her womb before they struck at her clit, her nipples.

She had fantasized about it. Of Rowdy holding her, whispering in her ear, watching. . . . She bit back her moan at the thought of those fantasies.

"Come back in, Kelly." His voice was a rough growl now, his expression heavy with lust as his eyes darkened to an emerald depth.

She stared at the hand he extended to her before her gaze flickered to Natches. He was watchful, tense, but rather than the driving hunger, his eyes held warmth and desire.

"I'm scared, Rowdy," she whispered.

"We're just going to go in and pilot the boat to the cove, babe. We're going to relax, nothing heavy, no decisions to be made, I promise."

Kelly reached out to his outstretched hand, feeling his heat and strength. Then he was pulling her to him, flush against his body, his hand carrying hers until her arm curved behind her back and she was arched into him. The length of his cock pressed into her belly, a thick wedge of heat and hardness that left her knees trembling.

"Just let me touch you, Kelly. Just me. That's all." His head was lowered until his lips caressed the shell of her ear, sending shivers racing down her spine.

He was seducing her. She lifted her free hand to his biceps, holding on tight as his lips traveled to her neck, smoothing over her sensitive flesh, sending sparks of intense need slicing through every nerve ending.

He lifted his head, a sensual smile curving his lips as he drew her back into the cabin, retaining his hold on her hand as he returned to the wheel.

Dawg moved aside, returning to his post at the balcony doors as Kelly glimpsed the narrow opening into the sheltered cove ahead.

They were staying the night, she knew that. The first step in drawing out a madman. Kelly allowed Rowdy to pull her in front of him, between him and the wheel. Her breath caught as his hand settled on her bare stomach, just over the butterflies beating violently within.

He stood behind her, flush against her, his erection resting in the small of her back, covered only by the thin material of his cutoffs.

"Do you think he knows where we're going?" She could barely force the words from her lips.

"He studies his victims," Rowdy sighed. "He'll know about

me, about Dawg and Natches. If he doesn't follow, he'll at least be aware of where you are."

Rowdy's plans were targeted at someone who would be watching, waiting. Which meant her rapist had been watching her more closely than she had ever imagined.

"Kelly, we'll catch him." His hold tightened on her. "I promise you, baby, we'll take care of this. We'll take care of you. I swear it."

"I should have listened," she whispered. "Everyone warned me about the window. I should have listened."

"It wouldn't have stopped him, baby. It didn't help the other women he raped. Women alone, who did everything right. He still got to them. This isn't your fault."

She knew that, in her head. Her fears and her shame told her otherwise.

No. No. No. He crouched on the cliff overlooking the cove, *sheltered by the pines and brush that surrounded him, rocking back and forth on his heels as he fought the pain inside his chest.*

They were all there. All three of them were there with her. Tears coursed down his face as he watched Dawg and Natches Mackay lower the anchor weights on each side of the boat before returning to the cabin.

The curtains were pulled. Thick, heavy curtains that wouldn't show so much as a shadow once night fell. There would be no way of knowing how far Kelly was allowing those bastards to debase her.

He sniffed, holding back his sobs, and let the rage building inside him burn. He had thought she was such a good girl. A sweet, pure angel who deserved his gentleness and his love.

She was a whore. Just like the other whores who had allowed

the Mackay cousins to touch them in the past. There was nothing
innocent about her. Nothing good. Nothing pure.

But she was his one true love.

And she was breaking his heart. He had refused to dirty her,
had given her his heart, and this was his repayment.

He had treasured her. Had shown her his caring, his respect and
consideration.

No more.

A small sob escaped him as he realized what had to be done. She
had stolen his heart. The only way to rid himself of the torment was
to rid himself of Kelly. She would have to die, but first . . . first he
would show her how bad girls were really treated.

She was nervous, frightened. Rowdy wasn't unaware
of how warily Kelly watched Dawg and Natches. Equal parts cu-
riosity and fear raged in her eyes. For as long as he could remember he had never had a problem sharing a woman with his cousins.
But something made him hesitate now. Held him back from seducing her into the acts that he and his cousins had seduced their
women into before.

The more he thought of Kelly's innocence, and the fact that she
had saved not just her body, but her heart for him as well, caused
something to clench in his chest. An emotion he couldn't name, a
hunger, a desire he couldn't define.

But Kelly had always engendered such emotions inside him. She
could turn his heart when no one else could, and bring out protective instincts he didn't think he possessed.

As they sat watching one of the latest action-adventure DVDs,
he felt her move against his side, drawing closer to him, her mostly
bare body tucking closer to his.

Neither Natches nor Dawg were watching her. They had joked through the evening, drank a few beers, and seemed as enthralled with the movie as any man should be. But the tension was rising. Kelly's tension as well as theirs.

He tightened his arm around her, drawing her closer to his chest, and felt the heat rising from her. Her hand flattened on his muscular abdomen, her fingers curling into the flesh as he stared down at her bent head.

He was hard, hurting, his cock throbbing beneath his cutoffs with raging demand.

His breath caught with a shocked hiss as he felt her hand caress the tight muscles of his abdomen. Inquisitive fingers ran along the band of his shorts, sending imperative signals to his overly tight cock.

"You're going to get in trouble," he whispered against her hair as the head of his dick began to throb in demand. If he didn't ease the constriction against his cock, then permanent zipper tracks were a definite threat.

"I'm naughty, remember?" She turned her head, her lips pressing against his breastbone as his hand lifted, his fingers tangling in her hair.

"Don't tease, Kelly," he growled. "I'm riding a very fine edge right now."

She licked him. *Son of a bitch*. He nearly jumped out of his skin as he felt the slow, savoring lick of her hot little tongue.

"Really? Strange, I could say the same thing about myself. Spending the last two nights sleeping with you, without being with you wasn't easy, Rowdy."

No shit. After having her, the hunger for her had only grown.

He wasn't unaware of Dawg and Natches listening closely, or the careful readiness of their bodies. They were as aroused as he was, as hungry.

She lifted her head, her slender, lithe body moving, rising as he watched, entranced. She stood in front of him before gracefully straddling his thighs and lowering herself into his lap.

"Son of a bitch!" His head fell back on the couch, his hands catching her hips as he jerked her flush with the tortured length of his cock.

Her pussy was hot, the heat of it burning through her scanty bathing suit bottom as well as the threadbare material of his denim cutoffs.

"We're not alone, baby." He tilted his head as her lips moved to his neck. Each touch reminded him of her inexperience, or her daring.

She knew Dawg and Natches could hear every move, every passionate sigh.

"I dreamed of you," she whispered in his ear a second later, her soft breath sending pleasure racing over his flesh. "While you were gone, I dreamed of touching you, kissing you, of all the things I knew you enjoyed. That I knew I would enjoy." The hesitant admission had his body tightening further.

He felt the tremor that quivered through her, the hint of fear and of arousal. The soft weight of her body against his was driving him crazy. The need to throw her to her back on the couch and devour her was making him sweat. The feel of her straddling his lap, her hands moving over his chest, her lips at his neck was too much.

She had initiated the contact, had known that Dawg and Natches were in the room. He should leave it at that, he thought. He should seduce her, as he knew she wanted to be seduced. But seduction and the acts he wanted to see her involved in did not go hand in hand. Rowdy knew Kelly's innocence, knew the demons that rode her, and he swore to himself he wouldn't add to them.

If this were her choice, then she would face it. And she would face it from the beginning.

• • •

Kelly felt her head spinning as pleasure washed through her with the force of a sensual tidal wave. She could feel Rowdy's hands roaming over her back, her buttocks, bringing a sense of heat and overwhelming pleasure rather than pain and fear.

One hand moved up her spine, threaded in her hair, and before she could guess his intention he was pulling her head back as he turned, lifting her, pushing her to the couch.

Before she could do more than gasp, he stole her breath with his kiss. Her lips parted beneath his, her tongue meeting his in a duel of exquisite ecstasy. She couldn't help curling her fingers into his broad shoulders, feeling the muscles flex beneath her touch, bunch with power as he buried her smaller body beneath his much larger one.

There was no fear here. There wasn't even the thought of fear. There was only Rowdy's touch, his lips covering hers, one hand tangled in her hair, the other moving inexorably to the rounded curve of one breast.

She fought to breathe, certain there had been enough oxygen in the air before his kiss. And she would have broken away to breathe, but it was so good, so hot, so filled with liquid, carnal delight that she couldn't draw away from him. But she could touch him. God, how she had dreamed of touching him over the years, feeling him against her, possessing her.

"Rowdy . . ." Her cry was instinctive as he pulled his lips from her, her eyes opening to stare into his expression in dazed fascination as he pressed his jeans-clad erection tight between her thighs.

"Be sure." His voice was guttural. "Look around you, Kelly. Be certain of what you're doing. There's no turning back. Ever."

Dark erotic power filled his expression. His brilliant green eyes were moss-dark, his face flushed, his lips heavy with greedy hunger.

"Kiss me, Rowdy." She didn't want to think about what could or would be. She wanted to feel the dreams she had known for so long. Rowdy taking her, his cousins pleasuring her.

"No," he growled, his voice rough, his hands clamping on her wrists as her hands moved for the snap of his cutoffs. "Look around, Kelly. Look at them. Let them know they're welcome or they leave. That simple. Your choice."

"That cold-blooded?" she asked nervously.

"No, dammit." He lifted her from him before she could do more than gasp, striding across the room before turning back to her.

"Rowdy, man, let this go," Dawg muttered warningly as Kelly sat up on the couch.

"You make the choice," he growled, his eyes tormented with need, with demand. "I won't do it for you."

Kelly rose jerkily from the couch, her body on fire, her face flaming with anger and embarrassment, and an instinctive demand that she deny them all. She stared at the three of them, all aroused, all awaiting her decision. A decision that had nothing to do with emotion and everything to do with hunger and their dominance. They wanted her surrender, a complete surrender, and she wasn't certain she could give it.

"All or nothing?" she questioned in reply.

"You know better than that, Kelly." Rowdy sliced his hand through the air with frustrated fury. "Don't play games."

"So I have to say the words instead?" she asked, challenging him, facing him with the same determination that glittered in his eyes.

"Words work." He crossed his arms over his chest as Dawg and Natches slouched in their chairs and watched him, each wearing dark, disapproving frowns.

"Oh, I just bet they would." She flipped her hair from her face before propping her hands on her hips. "Should I just ask you all to screw me, Rowdy? Why don't I just bare it now and let you take turns with me. Hell yeah, make it damned easy on you, wouldn't it? That way, you don't have to feel like shit later because you let another man take what was yours?"

"Do you think for one fucking minute that they don't know exactly who you belong to?" he questioned her with dark intent. "If I didn't care, baby, you wouldn't have been a virgin the other night."

"Says who?" she argued in amazement. "Do you really believe that all it takes is a touch from a Nauti Boy to turn any woman's crank?" She waved her hand mockingly. "Your ego is becoming more swollen than your dick, Rowdy."

Wrong word. All three men seemed to tighten, straighten at the explicit word that left her lips.

"Yeah, just look at the three of you." She rolled her eyes in mocking amusement. "Like little boys waiting for a treat. Well, fuck that. Find someplace else to treat, because I'll be damned if I'm still in the mood."

She stomped across the room, determined to reach the curving staircase that led to the upper bedroom and peace. She passed Rowdy with a disdainful little hiss, so irked and frustrated with his male, redneck attitude that she could have kicked him.

"Oh, no, you don't."

She hadn't expected him to reach for her. But even if she had, she wouldn't have expected him to lift her so quickly into his arms before his lips slammed down on hers.

It wasn't a romantic kiss. It wasn't soft and delving, or deep and passionate. It was hungry demand, carnal intent. It stole resistance and replaced it with pure fiery need, and nothing less.

Before she could protest, before she even processed the information, she found her rear braced on the counter, her thighs spread, and Rowdy devouring her.

She was lost in him, helpless in his arms as usual and loving it. Her fingers speared into his hair as his lips moved over hers, his tongue a restless marauder that conquered hers with inordinate ease.

And his hands weren't still either. Within seconds, the bikini top she wore was tossed aside, the hard tips of her breasts pressing into the fine layer of hair that covered his broad chest.

She shifted against him, her fingernails digging into his scalp as the tender, spike-hard tips burned in pleasure.

Kelly moaned at the loss as his lips pulled from hers, moving to her neck as her head fell back, the whiplash of sensations jerking her against him as his broad palms framed the tender mounds when he pulled back.

"So pretty." His lips were swollen, his eyes heavy-lidded and intense as they focused on the swollen curves. "You have the prettiest nipples, Kelly. As pretty pink as cotton candy. And they taste just as sweet."

Her gaze fell to her breasts. The light pink nipples were straining toward him, diamond-hard and desperate for his touch. No other man had touched her there. No one but Rowdy. She ached for him, needed him, belonged to him.

"I won't stop here," he whispered, his gaze lifting to hers. "Once I sate myself on these pretty nipples, I'm going to go lower, Kelly. I'm going to strip those damned bottoms off and spread your pretty legs. Then I'm going to lap at every sweet drop of syrup running between your thighs. Are you ready for that? And I won't care who's watching."

"God, Rowdy, I've dreamed of it." She had tossed in her lonely bed as the hunger for it kept her awake night after night.

A primal growl left his throat as his head lowered, his tongue swiping over one tender nipple before he enveloped it in his hot mouth.

His lips closed over the peak, sucking it into his mouth as his tongue curled around it. Kelly jerked violently, the pleasure so strong, so fiery that she could do nothing but cry out in response. Rowdy's hard hands held her in place as his lips devoured her, sending her senses reeling, her pulse rocketing as sensuality wrapped around her.

She heard a male groan, but whose it was she wasn't certain.

"They'll just watch," he whispered as his head lifted. "Watch me eat every perfect inch of your body this time. That's all. No pressure, Kelly."

She arched toward him. She didn't want to hear about it, she didn't want to analyze it. She wanted to feel. She wanted each sensation to rip through her, wanted the pleasure to never end.

And he took the offering. His lips closed on the opposite peak, drawing it into his mouth and setting it aflame as he surrounded the other with his thumb and forefinger. Then, his fingers tightened.

"Rowdy!" The surprised exclamation echoed around her as the fiery lance of sensation tore through her. Not quite pain. Almost, but a fiery kind of hurt that made the pleasure hotter, sweeter.

"God, Kelly . . ." The rough moan was whispered between her breasts as his head moved. He was fighting for breath, his fingers working her nipple, causing her to shudder with each tug at the eager tip. She could feel the hunger blazing out of control now, the need ripping through her, hard, bright, and hotter than a living flame. And she needed more. So much more.

Kelly could feel Dawg and Natches watching as she burned in Rowdy's arms. His lips and hands were never still, caressing over her, filling her senses with the dark taste of passion and the stinging need growing within her.

She was desperate for him. Her legs wrapped around his hips as she pressed her mound tighter against the rock-hard length of his cock. Her swollen clit was screaming for relief even as her tormented nipples begged for more.

"Come here, baby." Rowdy's voice was a rough growl as he lifted her from the counter, his hands curving beneath her bottom to hold her in place against the straining length of his erection. "I'm not taking you on this counter."

She didn't care where he took her, as long as he did.

"I need you." A whimpering cry whispered from her lips as her arms circled his shoulders, her lips moving to the corded strength of his neck. "Don't make me wait again, Rowdy. I can't wait any longer."

"No more waiting, baby." She felt him moving up the curving steps that led to the upper deck and the large bedroom. She had no idea if Dawg and Natches were following. She didn't care if they were, or if they weren't. Nothing mattered except Rowdy's touch. Except touching Rowdy.

As he lowered her to the wide bed that dominated the center of the room, Kelly twisted, pressing against his broad shoulders until he lowered himself beside her, stretching out beneath her gaze.

Finesse be damned. She wasn't experienced, he knew it and she knew it. But she was desperate to touch him, to taste him. Without thought she scrambled to his side, one hand gripping his shoulder, the other smoothing down his hard chest as her head lowered to the flat male nipples that drew her attention.

If his mouth on hers could make her weak, could she do the same to him?

"Shit! Kelly. Baby . . ." Maybe she could.

His hands buried in her hair, his body jerking against her as she nipped at the little discs before laving them with her tongue.

Hard, growling moans came from his chest as her hand lowered to the band of his cutoffs, her fingers tearing at the snap before he brushed her fingers away to release the material himself.

Kelly contented herself with tasting him. Both nipples, licking and nipping at them with rising pleasure before she began to move lower.

"God, Kelly." Rowdy tightened further as her tongue licked around his navel before heading to the length of hard flesh still covered by his cutoffs.

"I need to touch you, Rowdy," she whispered. "Let me touch you." She parted the fabric, then watched as he gripped the material of the waistband in his hands and shed it with easy grace.

And there he was. Hard, thick, his cock rising along his abdomen, pulsing with life as a small bead of semen collected at the tip. Kelly licked her lips, remembering the taste of him.

She bent, reaching out with her tongue to swipe over the bulging head as she tasted him. A bit salty, bold, wild, like Rowdy. And she wanted more.

A rumbled groan came from his throat as her fingers trailed down the ridged length of his erection, curiously exploring each shift of the bulging veins until she reached the hair-roughened sac below.

"Easy, baby." One hand clenched in her hair as the other cupped her cheek now. "Come down slow and easy. Take me in that pretty mouth of yours."

The hand moved from her cheek as her lips parted. It gripped the base of the hard stalk, lifting it until the head pressed against the damp curves. Kelly whimpered at the heat and hardness before her lips opened, stretching to surround him, to take him into her mouth as her tongue flickered over the expanse of skin that she was able to reach.

"God, yes!" His hips bucked against her mouth, driving his cock in deeper as she tried to lick at each new expanse of flesh.

It stretched her lips, filled her mouth with the taste of sexual intent, a wicked, intoxicating male taste that inflamed her senses. She felt his fingers bunching in her hair as she began to slowly suck at the engorged crest.

"Oh yes, baby," he crooned. "Your mouth is like liquid silk."

The sound of his voice was rough, erotic.

"That's it, baby," he encouraged her as she followed the lead of his hands in her hair, her lips moving up, then down, filling her mouth with as much of his erection as possible as she suckled at the rising flesh, her tongue flickering over it.

He took one hand and caught hers, wrapping her fingers around him, high enough to keep it from going too deep into her mouth before he returned his fingers to her hair. He sifted through the strands before tangling within them and moving more firmly against her, his cock thrusting with slow, easy strokes inside her mouth.

"Damn. You're stealing my sanity, baby," he growled as she felt the bloated crest throb in her mouth. "There you go. Suck it nice and hard. Oh hell . . ." Her lips tightened on him as she lifted her eyes to see the carnal expression on his dark face.

She had never realized how hungry she was for him, until now. Until his cock filled her mouth, the wild taste of aroused male consuming her, driving her past shame to a realm where nothing mattered but touch, taste, desire.

As her mouth moved on him, her hand began to stroke the strong shaft, moving up and down, pumping the hard column as he fucked her mouth with increasingly strong strokes.

At the same time, she felt a touch behind her. Male hands sliding her bikini bottoms from her, smoothing over the rounded curves of her ass. Was it Dawg or Natches? She didn't know, she didn't care.

She watched Rowdy's gaze flare, though, as he stared over her head for a long second. When his eyes returned to hers, they were wild with lust.

Then she felt it. A slow, reverent kiss on one buttock, then the next. A tongue, wicked and alluring, flickering along the top of the narrow crevice that separated the rounded cheeks.

Her head jerked up as a keening moan left her lips, her eyes widening in shocked pleasure. An insidiously wicked caress nearly had her collapsing against Rowdy. Only his hands held her upright, his gaze holding her sanity as she felt the probing tongue gently rimming the ultrasensitive entrance to her anus.

She should be screaming in fear, instead, she was panting with pleasure.

"Oh God, Rowdy . . ." Her voice was weak, questioning. Should it feel so good? Should she be so desperate for more?

"Shh, baby," he whispered gently. "Let it feel good. Just for a minute. Just for another minute."

She cried out as she felt that knowing tongue press against the entrance again. Her head whipped from side to side as she fought to breathe, fought to make sense of the blinding pleasure. When it breached the small hole with a slight pinching sensation, only to pull back, then probe inside again, she shuddered at the intensity of the carnal caress, suddenly terrified. Not of the touch or the man, but of herself.

"It's okay, Kelly . . . easy, baby." The touch was suddenly gone as Rowdy pulled her to him, his lips covering hers as he bore her to her back.

He kissed her with ruthless demand, leaning over her and

working his lips over hers with experienced lust. He ate her kiss, consumed her, and taught her to consume in return.

Rowdy lifted his head from the kiss, his senses drunk with the taste of the woman beneath him, his body aching to possess her.

The soft, dim glow spread over Kelly, clearly revealing bare silken flesh between her thighs, devoid of any sign of feminine hair. He had expected it, had known what awaited him, but the sight of it was a punch of lust to his gut anyway.

He blinked down at the pink, flushed curves as they gleamed with a layer of soft, silky syrup, licking his lips in hunger.

"Baby, you're pushing a man already hanging on the edge," he growled as he watched his fingers move, smoothing over the swollen flesh until they could delve into the rich, dewy slit below.

"Oh God. Rowdy . . ." Her cry pierced through him as he parted her, his gaze drinking in the flushed flesh covered in slick honey as her hips arched to him, her thighs spreading further.

He pressed the pad of his palm over her clit as his fingers found the tender entrance to her pussy and circled it slowly, his mouth watering to taste her. Lifting his fingers he turned his gaze to her again, narrowing his eyes as he moved his fingers to her pouty lips and painted them with her own juices.

Shock widened her eyes as she gasped. His other hand moved to her head, lacing his fingers through her hair as he spread the sweetness over her lush lips.

"Lick it off," he growled. "Come on, baby, see how sweet and hot you're going to taste when I get my tongue inside that hot little pussy."

"Rowdy . . ." He could hear the protest of her innocence, the dark hungers filling her, urged on by his own needs as she hesitated in the face of the unfamiliar intensity of their combined lust.

"Lick your lips," he ordered her again, his voice rough, the need to see her completely immersed in the needs building between them overwhelming.

Her tongue peeked out as the flush deepened on her face. A grimace twisted his lips as she licked at her own sweetness, tasting what he craved so desperately for himself. Then, her tongue curled around his finger, drawing a hoarse moan from his chest as she sucked it into her mouth.

The feel of her drawing the remaining taste from her fingers broke his control. He pulled from her, moving between her thighs, spreading them further as he lifted her to his descending mouth and buried his lips in the liquid heat flowing from her.

She was more intoxicating than moonshine, sweeter, hotter than life itself, and all his.

Kelly heard her own cries flowing through the night around her and could do nothing to still them, to smother them. Rowdy's mouth was burning through inhibitions, through shyness, and igniting a fire inside her pussy that threatened to consume her. He held her legs wide, his mouth eating her decadently, his whispering murmurs of pleasure and hunger fueling the flames burning through her.

His tongue was voracious. It licked, spread fire through the burning flesh and caressed her with a knowledge and experience that had her gasping. Small, flickering strokes against her clit caused her to arch to him, her hips jerking as sensation raked like talons of need through her nervous system. The pleasure, oh God, the pleasure was too much to bear. Each circular stroke around the hard, pulsing knot of her clit stole her breath. Her womb convulsed with the need for orgasm as the pleasure tore through it before spreading throughout her system.

His fingers weren't still either. One circled the sensitive opening to her vagina, spreading the juices that wept from her aching center before his tongue stroked lower, moving to lap at her, to draw the taste of her into his mouth as she screamed out from the precipice he kept her teetering on.

She was so close. Too close to be held back in such a way. She could feel the sensation burning throughout her body, igniting a firestorm that raced through her bloodstream.

Finally. She writhed beneath him, her head tossing as all the fantasies she had known in the past five years were finally coming to life. Rowdy was touching her, tasting her, loving her.

"Fuck, I could get drunk on your taste." His voice was a hoarse growl a second before his tongue plunged inside the gripping entrance to her cunt, fucking into her with licking strokes that had a strangled scream leaving her throat.

The tension building inside her was frightening. Control was a thing of the past, as Rowdy was causing the gathering tightness in her belly to deepen, to convulse with each inward thrust of his wicked tongue. Her hands tightened in his hair as she shuddered and the wet heat flowing from her vagina increased.

She was panting for air, sensation racing across her flesh, sensitizing her, leaving her gasping amid the inferno he was creating. His hands weren't still anymore than his tongue was. They smoothed over her thighs, his thumb flicked at her clit, sending sharp sensations of agonizing need tearing through her a moment before it retreated. His hands curled along the cheeks of her ass, and as his tongue plunged inside her again, he parted the soft curves, tugging at the entrance to her ass and sending sharp flares of heat whipping through her system.

"Rowdy . . ." She writhed, beneath him, her head tossing on the blankets as she felt perspiration gathering along her body, trickling down her breasts, her tummy, even as her juices flowed from her pussy. "I can't . . . I can't stand it. . . ."

It was different than the first time. The sensations were harder, fiercer, driving her further from herself as she fought to hold onto reality.

"Make it stop!" She tried to scream, to demand an ease to the pressure building in her womb, her thighs, deep inside her cunt.

He didn't answer. If anything, his mouth became more voracious, his fingers exploring further, pressing deeper against the untouched entrance he was massaging.

"Rowdy . . . I swear . . . I can't stand . . ." She lost her breath as she felt his finger breach her ass, felt it slide slowly inside her as his lips covered her clit, his thumb slipping into the entrance of her pussy and destroying her.

"Oh God!" She fought the lightning surge of almost painful sensation that shot through her.

"The hell you can't. You will come for me, Kelly. Now," he snarled, his finger retreating, gathering more of the silky liquid flowing from her before sliding in deeper, stronger, his thumb pumping into her pussy before his lips covered her clit again. He suckled at the tender bud, his tongue flickering over it as his finger bit into her ass, his thumb fucking her cunt until she felt herself erupt.

Her scream filled the night as she dissolved, saw lights exploding behind her clenched eyes and heard Rowdy's roar of pleasure a second before he was rising between her thighs and throwing her higher.

"Hang on, baby." He gripped her hands, moving them to his shoulders as she felt a thick pressure against the sensitized entrance to her pussy.

She stared up at him, dazed, awash in cascading waves of ecstasy.

"Sweet baby," he groaned, his green eyes darkening as his hands clasped her face. "Hold on to me, sweet thing. I can't wait. Not even another minute."

Her eye widened, fluttered, fought to stay open as she felt his cock stretching her, invading her. Better than the first time, stroking sensitive nerve endings, caressing delicate tissue until she wept with need. And it didn't stop. It went on and on, as though in slow motion, stretching her until she was certain she could hold no more before she found she could.

She jerked in his grip, her nails pressing into his shoulders as she whimpered then screamed as Rowdy settled to the hilt inside her. She could feel every thick inch parting the tender tissue of her pussy, straining it to its limits as fingers of electricity sizzled through and the tension began to increase once again within her.

"God, you're tight." His expression was strained as she stared up at him, fighting to make sense of the sensations ripping through her. "And soft as silk." His forehead pressed against hers.

He grimaced, lifting his head a few inches as he stared down at her, his thumb dragging roughly over her lips as she fought to breathe.

"Lift your legs." His voice was like gravel. "Brace your knees against my hips." He lowered one hand, lifting her thigh as she did as he bid.

"Oh God, Rowdy." He slid in deeper than ever, filling her in ways she couldn't explain. "Oh God, I don't know what to do . . ." She wanted to cry, wanted to ease the furious throb of hunger pulsing in her womb, in her cunt.

"Shush, baby," His voice was strained, his body tight with the effort it was taking as he helped her, positioning her knees against his hips as a ragged moan tore from his chest. "Son of a bitch, you're so fucking tight. I could come just feeling you grip me like that."

The muscles inside her pussy were indeed milking him, rippling around him, driving her crazy with the furious heat building inside them. She stared up at him, feeling the tears on her cheeks, the emotions clogging her throat. She couldn't imagine ever needing anything more than she needed Rowdy.

"Easy now, sweetheart," he warned as she felt his thighs bunching. "If I don't move I'm going to come before you ever get yours. And you have to have yours." A wicked smile crossed his swollen lips as he began to move.

His cock slid slowly from the clutching grip of her cunt as she heard her own desperate groan of pleasure; the thrust back had her crying out in sharp agonizing need, and then there was no stopping him.

He arched back, gripping her legs and pressing them closer to her body as he stared down to where they came together, her gaze following automatically, watching as the slick, glistening shaft of his cock powered in and out of the flattened curves of her cunt. It was mesmerizing, consuming. She could feel raking fingers of pleasure, pain, sharp sensation, and fiery explosions of hunger ripping through her body as she watched him fuck her. Watched his cock thrust in and out, shafting her with furious strokes as the world receded around her.

She came again, screaming through her orgasm, and still he didn't stop.

"Again," he snarled, turning her to her side, her legs bent, pressed to her breasts as he leaned over her, one hand parting the cheeks of her ass as his fingers found the tingling entrance there.

Her back arched, her head falling back as his finger slid inside, pumping in tandem with the thick erection driving inside her cunt, stretching her, burning through her mind as pleasure and pain mixed with the addition of another finger to stretch her tender anus. And still his cock drove into her, stroking furiously over sensitized nerve endings until she was shuddering, convulsing around him, her juices spewing from her pussy as she heard him give a ragged shout and felt his body tighten.

She was still dissolving around him as she felt his release, the hot, furious blasts of semen filling her, burning her, sending her into another quaking paradox of sensation that had her convulsing beneath him as he held his cock deep inside her, shuddering with the pleasure ripping them both apart.

Kelly had lost sanity long before Rowdy's release. She quivered in the aftermath of orgasm, weak, wasted by the emotion, the pleasure that had erupted through her. She felt him collapse beside her, still buried inside her pussy, his breathing harsh, his arms tight as he pulled her to his damp chest.

"Breathe, baby," he crooned in her ear as one hand massaged her chest, reminding her she was holding her breath as it released in a rush, sending stars exploding before her eyes. "There you go, sweet thing," he murmured, his lips at her shoulder as his cock jerked inside her. "Rest for a bit. Just a little bit. Then we'll try it again and see if we can't get it right."

Get it right? Dear God, if that wasn't right then he would kill her if he ever managed perfection.

SIXTEEN

It was still dark when Kelly awoke, her body pleasantly sore as Rowdy slept deeply beside her, sprawled naked on his stomach.

Heat curled low in her stomach as she stared at his shadowed form, a shiver of remembered pleasure echoing through her womb.

Moving quietly, she slid from the bed, searching until she found Rowdy's T-shirt, discarded on the nearby chair earlier that night, and pulled it over her naked body. She couldn't hear anything below, but she doubted Dawg and Natches were both sleeping.

Making her way down the narrow, curved staircase, the faint glow of the television provided a dim light as Kelly headed for the small refrigerator.

She pulled a bottle of water free, uncapping it as she straightened and lifted it to her lips before she caught sight of Dawg.

He was sitting in the shadowed corner between the table and

counter, his eyes gleaming in the darkness as she paused, watching him.

"Rowdy's gonna bitch over you stealing another of his shirts," he drawled quietly as she felt her face flush.

The heat had nothing do with the fact that she was caught stealing more of Rowdy's clothes, it was the sudden question of whether or not his wicked mouth had been the one caressing her earlier.

"He should be used to it by now." She cleared her throat uncomfortably, feeling a tingle of heat curl around her clitoris.

"He's a stubborn boy, though." He shrugged negligently. "You already know that."

Kelly leaned against the counter and watched him curiously. There was a lot she still didn't know about Rowdy and his relationship with his cousins. All anyone seemed to care about was the fact that sexually, they enjoyed sharing their toys.

She ducked her head, knowing she shouldn't have put off learning more about the three men together rather than just focusing on Rowdy. But it was Rowdy who held her heart, not the other two. Though she knew, eventually, they would become a part of the relationship she and Rowdy shared.

"You look like a frightened little doe standing there." His voice was like dark silk. "We've known each other too long for that wariness in your eyes, little girl."

Yes, they had. Dawg and Natches were as much a part of her life as Rowdy was.

"I'm not frightened of you, Dawg," she sighed. "I'm not frightened of any of you."

Maybe she was frightened of herself.

"People make too much out of our little pleasures," he grunted. "As though some insidious evil causes it rather than choice." He chuckled at his own words. "There's nothing evil in it, Kelly. And

Rowdy would never press you for what you don't want. So you don't have to watch us as though we're going to jump you at any minute."

"And the three of you think I didn't know what the hell I was getting myself into when I waited on Rowdy." She pressed her lips together as her own frustration ate inside her. "It's not a matter of not wanting it, Dawg, or even if I do want it."

"You want to be seduced into it. You want the choice taken out of your hands?" He leaned back in his chair, watching her intently.

"I don't want to analyze it to death, that's for damned sure," she snapped. "It's a wonder the three of you found a woman to share if you talked her to death first."

"The other women didn't matter, Kelly." He shocked her with his answer. "They were fun and games—you're Rowdy's future. There can be no misunderstandings, no seduction, no hesitations or hiding from the truth if you accept it. If you accept it, then you accept all of it.

Even the fact that eventually, the man she loved would touch another woman, pleasure her, fuck her. She couldn't accept his cousins' touch without that knowledge.

"I love him," she whispered.

"This won't be easy on any of us." He lifted his shoulders heavily. "Natches and I both love you too, Kelly, not like Rowdy does, but we love you. We've been burning along with him to touch you. But the day will come when one or both of us will find the woman we want for our own. The sharing isn't an every time thing, but it would sure as hell be missed if we stopped."

"Has anyone ever asked you to stop, Dawg?" she asked. "Have you ever considered it?"

Something dangerous flashed in his expression before it was gone just as quickly. "I'd stop if someone I loved asked it of me. If

I knew the woman I loved couldn't handle it." He shrugged his broad shoulders.

"I don't know if I could bear to see him touch another woman, Dawg." A self-mocking smile twisted her lips. "How's that for hypocrisy?"

"Not hypocrisy, sweetheart, honesty," he told her quietly. "That's what makes a relationship like this work, being honest about it. Being true to yourself and to Rowdy. We couldn't ask for anything more than that."

"I won't do this just for Rowdy," she breathed out roughly. "I won't let him touch another woman just because I know it's what he wants. It has to make sense to me. I have to be able to live with it."

"That's true enough." He nodded in understanding. "Any relationship is give and take. You give a little, Rowdy gives a little, and vice versa." He rose from his chair, moving the short distance to where she stood, towering over her.

Kelly swallowed deeply as she felt him surrounding her, his heat, the sensual hunger building inside him.

"Dawg . . ." There was no way to retreat.

She shivered as he reached out, his callused fingers running down her arm and filling her with conflicting emotions. Could she do it? Fantasizing about it was one thing, and Lord knew she had fantasized about it often. But actually taking that step was another matter.

"I want you," he whispered.

"Stop," she protested, shaking her head as denial began to rage within her. A panicked sense of discomfort began to build. It might be what Rowdy wanted, but this wasn't Rowdy. It wasn't his body heating her, his need surrounding her.

"It's dark and shadowed. A lot of truths can be hid in the shadows." Dawg's voice was darker than the night. "As can lies."

Her breath caught in her throat as his head lowered, his lips too close to her own.

"I could seduce you," he whispered. "I can give you that, Kelly. I don't have to wake up with you in the morning. I don't have to face you knowing I used your body against you. Is that what you want?"

"Moron." She pushed against his chest, her hands smacking into his hard-packed muscles as a shadowy chuckle whispered around her. "Get away from me. You're about as amusing as the flu, Dawg."

"Did I make my point?" His teeth flashed in a smile.

She sniffed disdainfully. "The point wasn't needed. Don't make the mistake of thinking I don't understand his reasons. But I'm also still a woman, Dawg, not a plaything. He can get serious about this, or he can forget it."

"Can he get anymore serious, Kelly? He let one of his cousins lick your ass. That's pretty damned serious to me."

Her face flamed as she narrowed her eyes.

"Was it you?"

He crossed his arms over his chest, watching her with a hint of a smile. "One licked, the other watched in anticipation. I ain't tellin' who did what."

A feeling of denial raged through her at the memory. This wasn't fantasy, it was reality, and she wasn't comfortable with it, no matter how much she wished she was.

"You know, Dawg, one of these days you boys are going to bite off more than you can chew in a woman. What are you going to do then?"

"Looks to me like Rowdy has already managed that one," he chuckled as his gaze shot past her. "And here he is to see how much further he can sink into monogamous bliss."

Kelly turned quickly, barely restraining a moan at the sight of Rowdy, naked, hard, his eyes gleaming with interest as he stood at the bottom of the steps. One thing she could say about him, naked or dressed, confidence oozed from every pore of his body. Confidence and pure, driving lust.

He tilted his head as he watched her, his gaze moving to his cousin, then back to her slowly. There was a challenge there, a knowing glint in his eye that assured her that he was well aware that she was wet and aroused herself.

"There you go stealing my clothes again." He shook his head in mock chastisement. "I was hoping you would learn better, baby."

"I think she needs to be spanked," Dawg murmured behind her, sending her pulse rocketing at the suggestion.

She arched her brow as she held Rowdy's gaze. He was grinning back at her, a crooked, self-assured grin filled with carnal intent.

As she watched him, she was aware of Natches moving from the rear of the cabin, watching the scene curiously. The testosterone swept through the room, heavy with wicked hunger and sinful intent. Three predatory males, no matter how they tried to hide the primal instincts that ran just beneath the surface of their lazy humor.

They converged on her, tall, broad, aroused. Rowdy was the only one completely naked, but the other two were following suit quickly. Natches stripped off his shirt, while behind her she heard Dawg's movements, the rustle of his clothes.

Nerves ripped through her, sending shudders of instinctive response to curl through her lower stomach before burning a path of erotic destruction along her erogenous zones. Her nipples peaked. Her lips ached and her sex wept.

"Take the shirt off, baby," Rowdy whispered as his hands gripped the hem, slowly drawing it upward.

Behind her, Dawg stepped closer. The shock of his bare hands running up her thighs had her tensing at the pleasure. She was so wet she could feel her juices dampening her thighs now, running freely from her weeping pussy as they prepared her for the coming possessions.

"Look how pretty you are . . ." Rowdy whispered reverently as she lifted her arms, allowing him to strip his shirt from her body. "You nipples are so hard, flushed. I love tasting them, Kelly. Feeling them in my mouth, the tight little points throbbing on my tongue."

They were throbbing now at the thought of it.

The shirt was tossed aside, but it wasn't Rowdy's hands that cupped the firm globes, it was Dawg's. They slid around her side until both hands were filled with her flesh, the index finger and thumb of each hand gripping a hard point, playing with them, rolling them deliciously.

Her head fell back against his chest as the fingers moved aside. Rowdy shifted, making room for Natches as both men lowered their heads to the upthrust peaks.

Kelly went to her tiptoes as sensation exploded through her. A ragged cry slipped past her lips as a flood of weakening lust ripped through her.

Kelly lost the ability to speak, to see, to do anything but feel as two sets of hard male lips covered the sensitive peaks. Fire engulfed her as damp, lava-hot tongues begin to whip over the tight flesh, and hard male mouths began to suckle erotically.

"Easy, sweetheart," Dawg whispered at her ear as she began to writhe within the hold the three men had created. The feel of their mouths sucking at her sent arrows of near painful pleasure ripping to her womb, her clit. The aching throb was destroying her. "It's okay, Kelly." His hands moved from her breasts, only to be replaced by Rowdy's and Natches's.

207

One arm clasped her to him as he slid his hand down her stomach, moving slowly for the tortured flesh of her pussy.

"Rowdy . . ." His name was a whimpering plea as she felt Dawg's palm cup the sensitized folds of her cunt, one finger tucking subtly against the syrup-laden entrance to her vagina.

Rowdy groaned as he continued to suckle her, his teeth raking her nipple, his tongue flickering over it as Natches caught the tip he held captured between his teeth and pinched at it.

Her cry echoed around her as she twisted against Dawg, silently pleading to feel his finger slipping inside her.

The sensations tearing through her body were violent, destructive. Alternative caresses, suckling mouths, hands over her, hot male groans washing over her. And she was in the center of it, weak, helpless against the eroticism of each touch.

She pressed against Dawg's palm, shattering cries passing her lips at the pressure against her clit. It would be so easy to climax, if she could just press against him a bit more, just the barest friction would allow her to ease the hunger beating at her.

"Not yet, baby," he whispered at her ear, nipping her lobe. "Let your body burn for us, get so hungry that nothing matters except the touch, the need."

She was already burning. Her fingers clenched in Rowdy's and Natches's hair as she felt Dawg's fingers moving, felt him spreading her juices, allowing them to coat the tight entrance beyond as his finger massaged the closed portal.

She felt her anal entrance clench at the caresses, felt it open, milk at the tip of his finger as another hand, she didn't know whose, began to play with the swollen bud of her clitoris.

She was trapped between them, in the middle of the kitchen area, suspended within a pleasure, a heat so intense she could barely make sense of it. Pleading, incoherent cries fell from her lips as she arched back, arched forward, so desperate that she no longer knew which touch would send her streaking toward orgasm; she just knew she needed it.

Yet, it was different than it had been with Rowdy alone. She struggled to push aside the vague unease she felt. The lack of emotional warmth, of sharing that had come from being in bed upstairs, just her and Rowdy.

"There you go, sweetheart," Dawg whispered again as she felt the tip of his finger slide inside her anus. "Damn, you're tight, and hot. Your ass is sucking at my finger like a little mouth, needing more. Do you need more, sweetheart?"

At the same time, hard fingers captured her clit and pumped it wickedly. Oh God, she could come so easy, if she could just get closer.

She relaxed her buttocks as flames licked at the little bud. Simultaneously, the little entrance sucked the hard finger deeper as the pressure eased at her clit, causing her to scream in pleasure and frustration.

Her ass felt filled, and yet she needed more. Her clit was pounding with need, her pussy clenching with it until suddenly, sirens began to rip through her head. . . .

"Fuck . . ." Reality slammed through as she was jerked to the floor, three cursing, furious men covering her as blasts shattered the erotic frenzy with cold fury.

"Get her to the side." She was being pulled, jerked to the side, between the heavy cabinets as the sound of pounding feet and raging curses were heralded by return fire.

Shadows flashed around her in the dark as she scrambled to the corner of the cabinets, her hands brushing over fabric as she felt the shirt she had worn earlier beneath her hands.

Pulling it from the floor, she crouched in the V made by the cabinets and pulled it over her head as Rowdy pressed her tight against his side.

She didn't ask questions, she wasn't hysterical. She followed his lead as he, Natches, and Dawg began to work her closer to the back of the houseboat.

"Bastard shot the hull, Rowdy," Dawg hissed as the gunfire eased.

The computerized alarm was still going nuts, the siren shattering her nerves as the sound of the security personnel on the other end demanded an answer.

She noticed no one was answering. Within seconds they were informed that Lake Patrol had been alerted and was now moving for the area.

"The pumps are working." Natches slid in place with them. "We'll be okay until the patrol gets here."

They were dressed. She felt the scratch of Rowdy's jeans on her thigh, Natches at her rear. Dawg had dragged his shorts back on, but where Rowdy had come up with clothes she wasn't certain.

"I think he's on the cliff overlooking us," Natches snapped. "The trajectory of the shots would be about right for that."

"He'll have to cross the point to get back to the road," Dawg growled. "I'll be back. I'm going after him."

"No . . ." The word was a hollow, raspy sound, jerking from Kelly's throat as she caught at his pants.

Dawg brushed her hand aside, moving through the darkness as the pulsing siren continued to echo through the boat.

"Stay here." Rowdy pressed her against the counters before moving for the alarm box and quickly cutting the sound off.

Kelly listened silently as he spoke to the security personnel, his voice hard, dark, furious.

"Don't move from here until Rowdy comes back," Natches whispered in her ear. "I need to check upstairs."

She nodded in reply, her throat tight, fear and fury clogging her voice until she wasn't certain she could speak. This was because of her. Someone had shot into the boat, tried to sink it, to kill them, because of her. She had placed Rowdy and his cousins in danger, had caused a madman to focus on them.

She wrapped her arms around her waist, staying in place, huddled against the counter as Rowdy flipped on a light in the living area.

She looked up as he came around the counter, his expression hard, his eyes gleaming with rage.

"Come on, baby." His voice was gentle as he reached down for her. "Lake Patrol will be here to escort us to the dock in a minute. We need to get you dressed."

She pulled herself wearily to her feet, gazing around at the destruction. The windows were shattered, glass and debris littering the floor, the paneling splintered from the bullets.

"Come on." He lifted her into his arms as she stared around numbly at the destruction.

Despair tightened in her chest as she buried her face against Rowdy's neck. She could feel her stomach cramping with guilt, with fear. One of them could have died. She could have lost Rowdy, or Dawg or Natches could have been hurt, killed.

"Here." He sat her in the middle of the bedroom floor before moving to the small closet and pulling free a pair of her jeans. "Put these on."

She accepted them silently, bending to pull them over her feet and then to her hips before she took the sneakers from his hand. She sat on the bed, slipped them on, then struggled to tie the laces.

"Easy, baby." As Rowdy knelt before her, she realized the small whimpers she could hear were her own.

He brushed her fingers out of the way before tying the laces quickly, then staring up at her. Something twisted inside Kelly at the gentle emotion she saw in his eyes. Beyond the anger, the determination to kill that she could see raging inside him, she saw his gentleness.

"This wasn't your fault, Kelly." He reached up, cupping her cheek in his hand.

Kelly fought the tears that clogged her throat. Rather than answering, she pulled from his touch slowly, shuddering at the thought that his need for her could end in his death.

"Don't even try it." The snarl that twisted his face had her staring back at him in shock. "Don't think I'm going to let you run from me now, Kelly," he snapped roughly. "The time for running was over the minute you let me fuck that hot little body of yours."

She shook her head desperately, pushing against his chest as she fought to jerk to her feet. She couldn't speak. If she dared to attempt to, she knew the screams of rage and fear wouldn't be far behind.

"Stop it, Kelly . . ." He grabbed her wrists, forcing her in place as she heard the first hoarse cry leave her lips. "It's okay to be scared, baby. I swear to you, we're all okay, we anticipated this, we know how to fight him—"

"No," she protested fiercely, feeling the tears seeping past her eyes despite her desperation to hold them in check. "He's crazy. You can't do this. You can't . . ." She wasn't going to let him do it.

She tried to tear herself away from him, to get away from his touch, his warmth. She couldn't live like this. She couldn't live if anything happened to him, or the others, because of her.

"I will do it." He gripped her upper arms, giving her a brief, hard shake as she stared back at him miserably. "Hear me well, Kelly. I will stop him. And when I get my hands on him I'll kill him. Do you understand me? He will never ever touch you or another woman again. Ever."

Death shadowed his eyes as she stared back at him, incredulous. He would kill, and he would do so with no guilt, no second thoughts, she could see it in his eyes.

"He's trying to kill you all. He won't stop." Her voice was shaky, her insides trembling with enough force to make her stomach pitch. "Because of me. What if you're hurt? What if he manages to . . ." *To kill one of you.* She couldn't say the words, was terrified to let the thought pass her lips, as though giving it voice would make it more real than it already was.

"I won't stop either, Kelly," he bit out. "Listen to me, dammit. I will not stop until he's dead. I will not let that bastard terrorize you."

She opened her lips to argue, to beg, only to be cut off as Dawg moved quickly into the room.

"He got away." He was breathing rough, heavy. "Lake Patrol is moving in and Ray and Maria are right behind them. Natches is on the deck waiting for them."

Rowdy turned back to her. "You aren't leaving with them, Kelly. Don't even consider it."

Her breath caught, feeling the shudders in her belly beginning to work through her body. She had no other choice. She had to leave. And soon, she would have to leave Ray's home as well. She couldn't continue to endanger the people she loved.

"Don't make me gag you." She stared back at him in shock as his voice rumbled dangerously.

"What?"

"You're going to try to run from this. I can see it in your eyes. Leaving town isn't the answer Kelly. And if you try, I'll throw you over my shoulder and cart you out of here like a sack of fucking potatoes. Don't push me."

His lips curled back from his teeth in a powerful snarl as his eyes blazed with green fire back at her. Shock whipped through her at the deadly warning she saw in his gaze, as well as the confidence that he would carry out his warning.

"Don't . . ." She tried to protest, to fight against the sheer force she could feel wrapping around her.

"I mean it, Kelly," he growled, rising slowly to his feet as he pulled her after him. "Don't fight me on this. Not right now."

She felt dazed, overtaken, her mind overwhelmed by the danger and the certainty that if she attempted to run from him, then he would chase her down. He wouldn't let her go. Not now, not yet. Not before he shed blood.

SEVENTEEN

Sheriff Ezekiel Mayes had surveyed the destruction of the *Nauti Buoy* after she limped into dock. His deputies were going through the interior as Kelly, Rowdy, Dawg, and Natches sat inside the small employees' room of the marina.

Ray and Maria stood at the side of the room as Sheriff Mayes took their statements. Kelly could see the knowledge in the sheriff's eyes as he questioned her, his gaze flickering to the Mackay cousins, a hint of disapproval lighting the golden brown depths of his eyes.

"You didn't see anything at all?" His gaze went over the four of them once again. "Hard to believe three tough ex-Marines would let a stalker get the jump on them, especially considering those same Marines were well aware of the danger of the situation."

Kelly pressed her lips together as she clenched her hands in her lap. She had to grit her teeth to keep from defending the men. To keep from revealing the fact that she knew Rowdy had planned this. She knew he had, and it infuriated her.

"Come on, Zeke, you know better than that," Rowdy bit out. "Kelly needed some time out. I thought the cove would be safe—"

"I'm not a fool, Rowdy," the sheriff snapped. "I'm not buying that shit and neither is your daddy." He nodded to where Ray was staring back at his son with a heavy scowl.

"I'm old enough that my daddy's opinion either way doesn't sway me, Zeke," Rowdy snapped back. "Now why don't you let me take Kelly home to rest—"

"Kelly, letting these three mix you up in some crazy scheme to catch this stalker is a bad idea." The sheriff hunched down in front of her chair. "Let me handle this. We'll catch him."

"You haven't yet," she whispered, shaking her head as anger and fear collided inside her.

Damn them all. She felt like a bone in the middle of a pack of wild dogs.

Compassion filled the sheriff's eyes. "I'm not a vigilante, sweetheart. When he's caught, I need the law on my side, not his. Kelly, if these boys suspect someone, I need to know."

"If I suspected anyone, you'd know it, Zeke." Rowdy's voice was hard, cold. "Now leave her the hell alone."

"God, stop snapping around me." Kelly jerked to her feet, causing the sheriff to straighten and stare down at her with a heavy scowl. "All of you. I've had enough for tonight. I didn't see anyone. I didn't hear anything. We were on the lake to get the hell away from that bastard. That was all."

She pushed her fingers through her hair, aware of the strained silence filling the room. She glanced over at her mother, and saw knowledge there. They knew why she was at the lake with the three cousins. She and Ray knew, and though Kelly felt no embarrassment, no shame at the knowledge, what she did feel was a sudden certainty that this wasn't a relationship she could endure.

Not because of the knowledge. Not because of morality. Because she didn't love them. She loved Rowdy, and the discontent, the subtle anger building inside her for days now over his expectations were clawing at her heart. The attack had only reinforced it. She was tired of being controlled. Period. First by a damned stalker and then by her need to please Rowdy.

"I'm ready to go home." She shook her head before lifting her chin and staring around the room. "Now. I need to sleep and I need to think."

"You can go home." Sheriff Mayes nodded. "But I may need to ask you some more questions tomorrow."

"Fine. Whatever."

"Just a minute and I'll drive you—" Rowdy began.

"I'll ride with Mom and Ray," she told him, ignoring the surprise that swept across his face. "I need to think, Rowdy. We can talk later."

"Kelly." He caught her arm as she moved to step past him. "We'll be right behind you."

We?

She moved her gaze over his cousins. She had been in their arms, felt their hunger and their lust, and despite the pleasure, she could feel her anger building. They were like little boys desperate to keep their newest toy close to them.

She inhaled deeply. "Whatever you want to do, Rowdy."

She pulled her arm from his grip before moving to Ray and her mother.

"Sure?" Ray asked her quietly.

"I just want to go home," she muttered. "Now."

Rowdy, Natches, and Dawg moved from the store with them. She was aware of how they placed themselves around her, protectively, shielding her. She felt smothered instead as she moved into the backseat of her stepfather's Laredo.

Within minutes they were heading to the house, a fucking convoy of vehicles. Dawg and Natches were in front of the Laredo with Rowdy bringing up the rear.

"Kelly—" Her mother began softly.

"Not now, Mom." She huddled into the backseat, wishing she could make sense of the emotions clouding her heart, her mind. Trying to make sense of her anger.

Rowdy was taking her over. Forceful. Dominant. He was so certain he knew what she needed, but Kelly had seen what she needed, and it wasn't what he was offering.

It was the reason she couldn't make the choice. Why she fought Rowdy every time he pushed for her to make a conscious decision about her needs. It was why she had wanted to be seduced, because she knew that unless the decision was taken out of her hands, she couldn't make it.

And that drove home the sharp edge of knowledge that this wasn't something she could do. She couldn't let this happen, because if she did, it would shadow her relationship with Rowdy forever. It would be better to lose him now than to have to share him later. If any more of her soul became invested in this, then she didn't know how she would bear letting go of every dream she had ever had. Hell, she didn't know how she was going to do it now.

Maybe she just wasn't naughty enough for the man she loved, or his cousins.

He was a fool. Rowdy followed the Laredo, his thoughts as confused as the emotions he had glimpsed raging in Kelly's eyes.

218

He ached, and it wasn't because of the attack. That just pissed him off. No, he ached because the attack had been a diversion he had begun praying for just before it happened. A way to pull Kelly from Dawg's arms, make certain the fingers filling her tight ass were gone, the touch to her clit no one's but his own.

Jealousy had begun to mar the pleasure even before the sounds of gunshots and the whiz of bullets tearing through the cabin had sent them all crashing to the floor.

What the hell was he supposed to do now? Dawg and Natches had protected her for the past four years from the bastards desperate to get into her pants. His two cousins hadn't touched her because of the understanding of the relationship that would evolve later. Even though Rowdy knew they had hungered for her almost as desperately as he had.

Had he not been so intent on running those last four years, of being certain what he wanted, the attack wouldn't have happened. He would have been there to protect her, to keep that bastard from touching her. But what would have happened to the relationship he had always envisioned?

He realized now that the shift in his desires had begun before he returned home. Hell, before he took that last tour in the Marines. He hadn't wanted to face it, and now it was slamming into his face with the force of a sledgehammer.

He was risking everything he had come home for and he hadn't even realized it. His own arrogance, his own certainty that he hadn't, that he couldn't change. That the sexual pleasures that had always been such a part of his life would remain the same.

Kelly was changing the rules. She was changing him.

Rowdy rubbed at his neck wearily, blowing out a frustrated breath as he turned into the driveway of his father's home, his eyes scanning the well-lit exterior. Dawg and Natches had pulled to the sides of the driveway, keeping Ray's Laredo between their vehicles with Rowdy bringing up the rear.

Turning off the ignition, Rowdy opened the door and stepped from his pickup as Ray, Maria, and Kelly slowly stepped from the Laredo.

With a flick of his fingers he sent Natches ahead of them to check out the house before Kelly entered. His eyes continued to scan the exterior, the hairs on the back of his neck tingling as he moved closer to Kelly. He could feel the bastard out there, watching them.

She leaned into him as his arm went around her. Damn, she was exhausted, terrified. What the hell was he going to do about her? As the warmth of her swept through his body, the possessiveness growing inside him seemed to expand, strengthen.

Leading her toward the house, he kept his senses on alert as Natches slipped in ahead of them, with Dawg following close behind.

"Rowdy, we need to talk," Kelly whispered as they stepped up to the porch.

"We will, baby." He bent his head, kissing the top of her head before leading her into the hallway, his eyes finding Dawg as he made his way along the top of the stairs. Natches had moved into the kitchen, each man checking the rooms thoroughly as Rowdy led Kelly, and their parents, into the darkened living room.

"Leave the lights off for now, Dad," he advised his father as he moved Kelly to the wide chair at the side of the room. "There were signs of a watcher on the hill overlooking the house on this side the other night. The lights will pick up shadows with the thin curtains in here."

"Shit," his father muttered, but the lights stayed out. "I need a drink."

As Ray took care of drinks for himself, Maria, and Kelly, Rowdy went through the house again, checking windows, assuring himself it was safe for the few hours of night left. Dawg was currently set up in Kelly's room, armed with a night vision telescope as he watched the hill across the clearing, while Natches had slipped outside to take watch.

Returning downstairs, he escorted Kelly to his own bedroom. She was quiet, withdrawn, and he'd be damned if he knew what to say to her.

"Grab one of my shirts and go on to bed, darling." He couldn't touch her, if he did, he was guaranteed to completely humiliate himself. How could one man be as big a fool as he was? he wondered. And now, how did he fix it?

She was moving for his closet even as he spoke, and pulling free one of his more comfortable T-shirts. He had to give her credit for knowing what she wanted.

As he stood silently watching her, she stripped down to bare skin, then drew the shirt over her head and smoothed it down past her thighs. His clothes hung on her, but they carried her scent for weeks after she wore them. The soft, subtle hint of woman that only he could smell.

"You go ahead and do whatever you have to do," she told him, her voice cool as she flipped the blankets back on his bed and crawled in. "I'm too tired to deal with it tonight."

"Go to sleep, baby." He came close enough to bend, to let his lips caress the still kiss-swollen curves of hers as she stared up at him. "I'll take care of you, Kelly."

"Yes, you will," she sighed heavily, her gray eyes shadowed. "And tomorrow, I'll take care of you."

He didn't think she meant sexually.

"Kelly—"

"Not tonight, Rowdy." She shook her head firmly. "Tomorrow. I'm just too tired to talk tonight."

221

He could see the adrenaline crashing through her, wiping her out. She was still in shock, fighting the reality of the attack. She would dream later, he knew. And the nightmares could be ugly. He promised himself he'd be back by then, that he would hold her through them, ease her.

"Tomorrow." He smoothed her hair back from her face as she settled into the bed. "I'm going downstairs for a while, baby. I'll leave the door open and I won't be long—"

"I'll be okay, Rowdy," she assured him, a thread of mockery filling her voice. "Go. Just let me sleep."

Rowdy paced the house. Nervous tension was a bitch, and suffering from it wasn't something he normally did. But damn if he wasn't just about to cut his own throat just to ease the thoughts tormenting him.

What the hell had he done?

When he first came downstairs on the *Nauti Buoy*, the sight of Kelly standing next to Dawg had sent his cock to full erection and the blood racing through his veins. Just as it had earlier when his cousin had moved behind her, his lips moving over her buttocks, spreading them, caressing her.

It had been hot as hell, feeling her pleasure as her hot little mouth surrounded the sensitive crest of his cock. Holding back had been iffy. His balls had drawn up in tortuous need, desperate to explode as the pleasure of it had seared his nerve endings.

He had ignored that unfamiliar tension that began to hover at the back of his mind. Fought with it. Then later, as his lips suckled at her tight nipple his eyes had watched as Natches pleasured the other, and he heard the words Dawg whispered to her. How snug she was, how hot, and the lust that filled his cousin's voice had slapped at Rowdy.

Jealousy. Possessiveness. He wasn't used to those emotions, but now they raged inside him until his fists were clenched and violence simmered just beneath the surface. He prayed for the chance to get his hands on the little son of a bitch stalking Kelly. To take out the fury and aggression rising inside him on someone who deserved it. Neither Dawg nor Natches deserved it, but it was building, growing inside him until Rowdy wasn't certain he could contain it.

Stalking back to the living room, he moved to the small bar Ray kept at the side of the room and poured a measure of whiskey into one of the tumblers sitting ready. The liquid burned going down, but did nothing to calm the beast raging inside him.

"Liquor doesn't help, boy."

He turned, his hand tightening on the butt of the pistol he carried before recognizing his father.

Ray stood just inside the doorway, dressed in a pair of dark cotton pajama bottoms and a faded T-shirt. His expression was sober, lined with worry, and his eyes gleamed with knowledge.

"We'll catch him." Rowdy shrugged. "He's losing focus—"

"I wasn't talking about her stalker." He moved farther into the room. "I was talking about what happened on that boat before he attacked."

Rowdy brought the glass to his lips and threw back the rest of the whisky before grimacing tightly. Damn, he didn't need this conversation with his father.

"Let it go, Dad."

"Doesn't set well, does it, Son?" Ray moved closer to the bar, lifting one of the clean tumblers and pouring his own drink. "It starts eating at your gut first thing, tearing at you, making you wonder where your mind was."

Rowdy narrowed his eyes on his father, hearing the knowledge in his voice, the assurance that only came from experience.

"They didn't take her," he muttered, wondering why the hell he was bothering to explain this to his father of all people.

"Might not have, but something happened. Something strong enough to make you panic, to keep you awake. To tear your guts up with guilt."

Son of a bitch.

"She was shot at, Dad, that's enough to shake any man's insides."

Ray sipped at his drink, staring at him over the rim of the glass. Rowdy couldn't hide from the knowledge, no matter how much he suddenly wanted to.

"I know what's going on, Son," he finally sighed heavily. "You think you and those two hardheaded cousins of yours are the only men in this family to think they know what they want in a woman? And in her pleasure?" Ray frowned heavily, his eyes darkening. "You're not. I've tried to warn you since I first caught wind of what was going on, and you've never wanted to listen."

Rowdy watched his father curiously then. Through the years, there had been whispers that Ray Mackay and his best friend had been up to some sexual little games, but nothing concrete and nothing his dad had ever confirmed.

Ray grunted mockingly. "Your generation thinks they know everything. You don't. Mine knew what a reputation was, and we knew what should be kept private and what should be flaunted. Women like Calista James were steered clear of except for a certain few. We knew our actions would always backfire on us, if not at the time, then later, on our wives, our children. I thought I taught you that, but maybe I failed there too."

Ray shook his head as he nodded to the chairs Maria and Kelly had sat in earlier. "Come over here, Rowdy. Let's talk."

"What's there to talk about?"

"Saving face," his father sighed. "Those two cousins of yours

224

have waited nearly as long as you have for Kelly. They don't love her like you do, but when you yank something like that out of a man's hands, he's bound to get pissed. And you don't want that kind of pissed from men you've been as close to as brothers."

Ray leaned forward in his chair, staring back at Rowdy intently. Damn, that look had the ability to send him right back to his teenage years and the memory of his father's chastisements.

He wasn't a teenager anymore, but at the moment he felt as uncertain as one.

Rowdy turned his gaze to his drink, wondering what the hell he was supposed to say. He'd already figured out the fact that he was making a hell of a mistake—he didn't need his father to point that out to him.

"It's tough, being as close to men as you are to Dawg and Natches," Ray sighed. "You three are closer than brothers, you always have been." He shook his head, staring down at the glass in his hand as he grimaced painfully. "I had a friend like that once, Rowdy." He lifted his eyes then. "A damned good friend."

Rowdy stared back at him, knowing what was coming. Knowing he didn't want to hear it.

"It was before your mother." Ray cleared his throat. "And there was this woman. One that made the blood boil in my veins, made me want forever. But I was dumb. Brick dumb. I thought I'd always be the man I was then. That what I wanted sexually would always be a part of my life. And I shared that woman. Because I thought that pleasure was the greatest gift I could give her . . ."

He tossed back the rest of his drink before meeting Rowdy's eyes once again.

"Kelly should have been your sister, Rowdy. If I hadn't been so stupid, I wouldn't have lost Maria all those years ago. She chose the lover willing to love just her, rather than his own selfishness.

Willing to give her all of himself, without the childish need to have it all his own way."

Rowdy's jaw bunched tightly.

"Dad, let it go." Rowdy shook his head sharply.

"You're figuring it out, I can see that in your eyes. The same way I thought I was figuring it out. But I let that bond I thought I had with my buddy get in the way. I was torn between the loss of friendship, and my own wants. And I thought the woman would be there either way. It wasn't the friend I lost, Rowdy. It was the woman. And trust me, when it comes right down to it, Kelly is no different than her mother."

Rowdy breathed in deeply. Damn, he hadn't wanted to hear this. He lifted the whisky before tipping more of the liquor into his glass.

His father was silent then, finishing his drink as Rowdy sipped from his.

"I love her," Rowdy finally breathed out roughly. "I didn't expect this though."

"Love changes us, Son." Ray rose to his feet, crossing the room slowly to set his empty glass on the bar. "Don't make the same mistake I did, Rowdy. Once it's over that first time, once you've let another man claim what's yours and yours alone, you lose a part of your soul. Getting it back is hell. A hell I hope you never know."

Rowdy stared back at his father silently, finally hearing what the other man had always tried to teach him. What was fair, what he wanted alone, wasn't all that mattered. He had begun learning it in the Marines, but it was slapping him upside the head now.

"James Salyers was still a friend when he died, Rowdy. And I grew up and learned some damned hard lessons. Maria gave me a second chance, but that chance came at a cost. A very high cost. The daughter that should have been mine came from another man, and the son I love more than life is about to fuck up not just his own life, but that girl's as well. Watching it and knowing I can't stop it is hell. Remember that while you struggle between what you love and what you want."

As Rowdy watched his father leave the room, a heavy sigh slipped past his lips. Maria's objections to his relationship made more sense now. He shook his head, realizing how well his father, James Salyers, and Maria had kept that secret. Reputations. Theirs was intact, but his wasn't. And now, he was risking Kelly's as well.

Kelly was awake when he returned to the bedroom a little after midnight. Sleep wasn't coming, no matter how hard she sought it. Each time she closed her eyes she saw . . . herself . . . surrounded by the Mackay cousins, their hands touching her as pleasure whipped around her. But it wasn't pleasure she felt in the memory. She felt the dark swirl of shame.

The same emotions she had felt each time she swore she wasn't waiting one day longer on Rowdy and she was going to find someone to love her. To stick around and be with her. Each time she had tried, each time she had attempted to allow another man to touch her, shame had eaten her alive for days later.

The door closed behind him, the click of the lock causing her to open her eyes, to stare through the darkness as his shadow moved toward the bed.

God, she loved him. If she could give him his every desire then she would do it in a second, but some things she knew she couldn't do. Dawg and Natches she couldn't do. And she had no idea how to tell him. No idea how to broach what she knew could destroy the relationship she had dreamed of.

"Everything's quiet," he said softly as he pulled his shirt from his body.

The room was dark, too dark to make out his expression, but she could hear his voice, see the gleam of his eyes.

"I couldn't sleep." She could feel the tension between them.

Rowdy sat at the edge of the bed, pausing before he sighed tiredly and bent to take off his sneakers.

"Rowdy?" She whispered his name, uncertain what to say, what to do as he rose to his feet and shucked off his jeans.

He was naked. As he turned to her she glimpsed the heavy, engorged length of his erection a second before she was suddenly jerked to him.

"Rowdy?" She gasped his name as his lips covered hers, stealing her breath, her startled cry.

And from there, her strength. His hands were hard, dominant as he tore the shirt from her body, tossing it carelessly to the floor before his lips took hers again. Her muted cries built in her head as he bore her to the bed, spreading her thighs, sinking into her.

There were no preliminaries. No foreplay. One moment she was empty, the next she was full, her pussy stretched to its limits as he groaned into her mouth.

She fought to breathe, and she could feel his struggle as well. The harsh sounds that tore from his throat were almost animalistic in their hunger, their intensity. His lips held back both their cries as he began to move, hard, furious strokes inside, sending her nerve endings into shock, the pleasure ripping through her with the same desperation with which his erection thrust into the slick, heated depths of her body.

Her arms wrapped about his neck, fingers pushing into his hair as one hard hand gripped her hip, holding her in place as he moved.

The other arm curled beneath her as he supported himself on his elbow.

He surrounded her. He possessed her. Pleasure became a burning, consuming need as he fucked her with a hunger that swept through her soul. She could almost touch his soul. Then her eyes opened, widened, shock and ecstasy exploding through her as the orgasm overtaking her stole a part of her very spirit. Stole it and merged it with his. Melded them together as he stiffened above her, his cock swelling then pulsing as his release jetted inside her. Deep, almost violent spurts of his seed heated her, triggering another, deeper orgasm, sending stars to explode around her as she screamed soundlessly into his kiss.

"Mine!" The hard, throaty growl that left his throat had to have been her imagination. "Mine."

Possessive. Consuming. *His*.

EIGHTEEN

"Rowdy, we're not going to be able to keep her here." Dawg moved through the living room, checking the windows and their latches the next afternoon. "Your dad's security system is good, but it won't stop a bullet."

"Don't know many that will," Rowdy muttered, tamping down his impatience as he pushed his fingers through his hair and surveyed the living room.

He had been through the rest of the house, just as Dawg and Natches had been over the hill above it. The bastard was hiding there at night, watching the house, and he had a clear shot into every room from one point or another, if one of them messed up and didn't close the curtains well enough.

And that didn't change the fact that his dad and Maria were refusing to leave now. As was Kelly.

"He'll come back at us quick enough to keep us from making headway into security here," Natches drawled from the entryway.

"He was in that clearing across from her room last night. I never caught sight of him, but I could feel him. He was out there. And he's damn good."

Shit.

"We have to get her out of here, Rowdy," Dawg reiterated. "Now. My gut is going crazy with this. Whoever the bastard is, he's lost his damned mind. He won't care who he kills to get to Kelly."

"Your place?" Rowdy's eyes narrowed on Dawg's expression. He could see the expectation there, the excitement.

Dawg's house was an underground masterpiece built by his parents. The outside was cement and stone overlaid with roughened wood siding. The windows were extra thick and after Dawg's return from the Marines, bulletproof. As far as anyone knew, there was only one way in or out. No one knew about the hidden entrance except for the three of them.

Dawg nodded. "It's the most secure."

Rowdy braced himself. He could feel the sexual tension beginning to heat up in the room. His cousins had waited years for this. Hell, they all had.

"I'm not sharing her." The words were out of Rowdy's mouth before he could stop them.

His head snapped up, his jaw tightening as Dawg and Natches stared back at him in surprise.

"Is that your decision or Kelly's?" Natches tipped his head to the side and watched him curiously.

Rowdy found the look testing his temper. Natches liked to push and he liked to challenge things just for the hell of it. Rowdy hated the thought of fighting his cousin over something that should have been settled years before, but he would.

"It doesn't matter whose decision it is." Rowdy pushed the words past his lips, attempting to contain the anger rising from his cousin's question. "It's not happening. We'll move her to the house, but hands off. Period."

Dawg sighed heavily, a grimace contorting his expression.

"Now, son of a bitch, how did I know you were going to go and get all dog-eared fucking jealous?" he griped, his green eyes narrowed in irritation. "Hell, Rowdy, talk about blue balls going on here."

"Talk about too damned bad," Rowdy muttered as his muscles bunched and flexed beneath his flesh in rising tension. Damn, this shit sucked. As though the possessiveness, the emotions he felt for her were a separate being living within his flesh and bone.

"Hell, we can argue over this later," Natches finally grumped. "After I take out my mad on that son of a bitch stalking her. Then we can fight over sharing rights."

"No sharing rights. Period," Rowdy snapped. The only thing that restrained him from taking his cousins apart limb by limb was the fact that he knew them. They weren't pissed, at least not yet. But Rowdy admitted he was getting there fast.

And it was his own damned fault. He was mad at himself for letting this situation get out of control, for letting his cousins believe there would be more here than he was able to accept now.

"Chill out, cuz," Dawg breathed out roughly. "Hell, it would have been nice, but no one's pushing. Wouldn't be worth a shit if both of you didn't want it anyway."

Rowdy narrowed his eyes on his older cousin. There was a vague restlessness in his voice, and he realized it had been there for a while.

"What the hell do you two think you're doing? Growing the fuck up?" Natches snapped then, disgust lining his voice and filling his green eyes. "If I wanted to grow up I would have stayed in the fucking Marines."

Rowdy rolled his eyes. Trust Natches to get to the heart of the matter.

"I guess it was bound to happen eventually," Dawg sighed. "Come on, let's get the little troublemaker hid out in the house and see what we can do to make her life a little safer before she takes on the resident grouch here." He flicked his hand toward Rowdy.

"This falling in love crap obviously sucks," Natches commented as he turned and headed out of the room. "Remind me to steer clear of it why doncha, guys? God only knows what kind of fool I might end up making of myself if I made that mistake." His mock shudder had a grin pulling at Rowdy's lips.

"Careful, Natches, you know what happens when we tempt fate." How many times had they assured themselves the fun and games would never end. And now look where they were.

"Fate can kiss my ass," he grumbled. "Better yet, she can suck my dick. I'm footloose and fancy-free, my man. And that's how I'll stay."

Rowdy eyed his cousin warily. There was lightning striking somewhere, he was certain, and at that moment he decided he didn't want to be anywhere around when Natches finally did manage to fall in love.

"Think about it guys," he muttered. "Do you think I'd ever be able to touch another woman after Kelly? That she could ever bear the thought of it, even if I could? She's my life—"

"All this sugar is just going to give me a toothache," Natches growled as he threw him a dark look. "Get over it already. She would have gone along with it if she had spent awhile between the three of us. She's a fair-minded person—"

"Well maybe I'm not," Rowdy bit out, his tone guttural. "Keep pushing me, Natches, and you're going to get the fight you're aiming for."

Rowdy was aware of Dawg watching them both warily, sensing the tension suddenly whipping between Natches and Rowdy.

"None of you are going to fight."

Rowdy's head whipped around as Kelly stepped into the room, her gray eyes glittering with temper, her face flushed with it.

She was dressed in a pair of those low-rise jeans he liked so damn well. It was paired with a little cami shirt with tiny straps that flashed abdomen and the belly ring that made his dick jerk in his pants. That curvy little body of hers was going to be the death of him.

Surprisingly, Natches backed down from the look in her eye, not that Rowdy blamed the other man—she looked ready to claw all their eyes out.

"Hell, Kelly, you know us. We fight for the hell of it." Natches flashed a smile at her, one that gave a hell of a pretense of friendly amusement, if you discounted the darkening of those pale eyes.

"Save it for someone you can convince." She frowned back at the other man.

Natches grimaced.

"Kelly, you know"—Rowdy leaned against the bar as he watched her—"I can take care of some things myself here."

She was cute as hell as she watched them with a temper tantrum seething just beneath the surface.

"Where these two are concerned?" She flicked her fingers between Dawg and Natches. "Rowdy, I doubt a whole team of Marines could whip those two in line."

"Several might have tried though," Dawg pointed out, his lips twitching in a grin.

She stared between the three of them before her gaze moved back to Rowdy. He could see it in her eyes, she must have caught part of the conversation, but that didn't mean she liked any of it.

He was realizing just how intensely private his little love was, and it shocked him to realize how much that pleased him.

He should have known Kelly would change the rules on him; what surprised him was the fact that she made him like it. It sent a strange little pulse of pride through him, that considering his past, he shouldn't have felt.

"If you're making plans concerning my life or my safety," she said then, crossing her arms beneath the tempting mounds of her breasts, "I think I should be a part of the planning process. Don't you?"

What had made him think she would accept anything less?

"Now, Kelly," Natches drawled then. "We can take care of the detail stuff here. You shouldn't worry your little head about this stuff."

Rowdy and Dawg both blinked back at the other man, wondering if he'd lost his ever-lovin' mind. Everyone who knew Kelly knew you simply did not patronize her, period. She was sharp as a whip and had definite ideas on a lot of things. Pig-headed men being one of those things.

Kelly's eyes narrowed on him. "Just not worry my little head about it?" she asked him gently.

"Kelly . . ." Rowdy cleared his throat, looking for an excuse for his dim-witted cousin.

"More or less." Natches's smile was condescending as Rowdy stared at him in disbelief. When had his cousin decided that women were stupid?

"Kelly, sweetheart, Dad and Maria were supposed to—"

"Don't try to distract me, Rowdy, it doesn't work," she snapped, her dark eyes furious as her stubborn chin lifted, her soft lips tightening in anger as her gaze swung back to Natches.

"Come on, Kelly, we all know Natches can be a knothead,"

Dawg sighed. "Let's not hurt him too bad here. We might need him down the road later to dig ditches or something."

Natches's lips lifted in a grin as his light green eyes stayed locked on Kelly. And suddenly, Rowdy knew his game. He almost laughed when his gaze went back to Kelly and rather than seeing furious arousal glittering in her eyes, he only saw the anger.

His little spitfire wasn't in the least turned on by Natches's confrontational attitude.

"You know, Natches"—she lifted a hand and surveyed her nails for a second before lifting her gaze back to the other man—"just because I'm not exactly a part of the upper crust of this fine little town doesn't mean I don't know its little secrets. Don't make the mistake of thinking I'm one of those slow-witted little blondes you and Dawg have been snacking on lately. Because I'm not. And neither am I at all interested in taming that bad boy thing you have going on. And as for you." She turned to Rowdy.

Rowdy lifted his brow curiously. There was the arousal. It glittered just beneath the anger as she raked over his lazy slouch against the bar. "Before making any plans that concern *my* future, maybe you'll be good enough to discuss them with me first. If you don't mind, that is."

Ouch. The lash of displeasure in her voice actually stung.

"And I think that's our cue to go," Dawg stated with a smile as he straightened from where he was leaning against the wall. "Let's go, Natches."

"Like hell," Natches drawled. "Watching her neuter him is way too much fun."

Rowdy straightened as hurt flashed in Kelly's eyes as she stared back at the other man. Natches's tone was bordering snide, and Rowdy was fed up with it.

"Natches, shut the hell up," he warned softly.

"Why?" Natches asked with apparent joviality. "Hell, Rowdy, I'm taking notes here. Watching you get your dick twisted in a knot like this over her is teaching me what not to do."

He was going to kill Natches.

"Kelly, ignore that fool," Dawg drawled then. "He's just pissed as hell that you're not twisting his dick, that's all."

"And he's getting ready to get his ass kicked." Rowdy moved then.

He stalked across the room, ignoring Kelly's flinch as he pulled her against him, his lips pressing to her forehead as he held her to him, his gaze slicing to Natches in warning.

"We're just discussing the best place to protect you, baby." He rubbed his hand down her arm, feeling her tremble against him despite her anger. "No plans are being made without you. I promise."

"I don't need to be babied." She pulled away from him, but the hurt in her voice was easy to hear and Rowdy promised he was going to make Natches pay for that one. "I just thought somehow, plans that included me were my business. Just forget it."

She turned and stalked from the room as Rowdy turned back to Natches. The minute he heard her moving up the hallway, he jumped for the older man.

"Whoa! Hold on there, boy." Dawg jumped in front of him, blocking him with his wider body as Rowdy growled in fury. "You know how he gets. Dammit, Rowdy, you start a fight in here and Maria's gonna kick all our asses."

"Get the fuck out of my face." He jabbed his finger over Dawg's shoulder, glaring back at Natches as his expression darkened with anger. "And so help me God, you treat her like that again and I'll tear your dick off and feed it to you. You want to be a bastard because you're not getting what you want, then you take it up with me."

238

He knew Natches's problem, and he knew he should have anticipated it. Dawg and Natches both had waited, just as he had, for Kelly. They had hungered, lusted, expected certain things where her relationship with Rowdy was concerned.

This was his fault. As he jerked away from Dawg, he admitted it was his fault, but he'd be damned if Kelly was going to pay for it with Natches's surly attitude.

He paced to the bar, pouring a quick drink and kicking it back as he grimaced at the sting. Natches was damned good at pushing buttons, and, Rowdy admitted, Kelly was a sore spot with him. Hell, he should have known years ago that this wasn't going to work, rather than running from the situation as he had. And he had run. The emotions that damned woman caused to rise inside him threatened his sanity at times.

"I didn't mean to hurt her." Natches cleared his throat uncomfortably. "Hell. I didn't mean anything by it, Rowdy."

Rowdy lifted his gaze. He was so damned close to fighting Natches that he had to clench his fist to hold onto his control.

"She's mine, Natches," he snapped. "I can understand why you're pissed but if you take it out on her again, you'll deal with me. You got that?"

"Yeah, I got that." Natches snorted, though he didn't sound overly concerned at the prospect. "I'm going to go see if I can find a sign of that bastard while you cool off. Hell, son of a bitch needs to die for fucking shit up like this."

He stomped from the living room. Seconds later, the door slammed behind him. Rowdy stared back at Dawg then.

"He'll chill out." Dawg slapped him on the shoulder as he headed from the room. "You take care of Kelly, and we'll watch your back. And when Natches's time comes, we might even watch his."

NINETEEN

Kelly was furious. The anger that sizzled through her carried her through the afternoon and into that evening.

It was the fear making her angry and she knew it. It was making her crazy. And Rowdy, Dawg, and Natches weren't helping matters. They were making a target of themselves rather than her, daring a madman to strike out at them. Endangering all their lives, and it scared her to death. And that's where the anger stemmed. Toward the bastard who thought she should belong to him rather than the man she loved. A monster who wanted to terrorize her because she wasn't the good girl he had decided she should be.

She snorted at that thought. The fantasies she'd had over the years where those three men were concerned were anything but good. But they were fantasies for her. She liked the fantasies, she liked pretending she was daring enough, cool enough, to control Rowdy and his cousins.

But the truth of the matter was that she was anything but cool, calm, or collected when it came to Rowdy. And as hot as the thought of having all three men focused on her was, as hot as it had been in the boat, something still held her back. Made her wary.

"I didn't mean to hurt your feelings."

She whirled around with a gasp, wishing now that she had turned the lights on. Natches was shadowed from the hall light, a dark form leaning against the wide entrance into the room.

"You didn't hurt my feelings," she snapped. "You pissed me off."

He sighed. "I didn't mean to piss you off either."

Natches flipped on the light. He grinned at her as she watched him warily.

"Do you remember how Dawg and I rushed to the hospital after you were attacked?" he asked, his voice soft, a bit sad.

And they had. Ray swore the doctors had almost had to call security to get them to leave the hall outside her room.

"I remember."

He brushed back the long hair from his devilishly handsome face. Natches was a charmer, with the face of a fallen angel and eyes that invited a woman to be bad.

"We knew you were ours even when you were a little girl," he said reflectively. "Not in the sense we knew it after you grew up, but we claimed you. Watched out for you—"

"I love Rowdy, Natches," she whispered, halting what she feared was coming. "And don't try to tell me you love me in the same way, because we both know better."

His lips tightened. "We're a set. You're destroying it, Kelly."

He stared back at her, his light green eyes wary and somber but she could feel the anger in him. She was changing the rules and he didn't like it.

"I don't mean to, Natches," she whispered. "I can't be what you want, I can't do what you need."

"You knew that was part of it," he growled. "Everyone knows that's part of it."

Kelly tipped her head to the side, watching him. Of the three cousins, Natches had always been the most alone. Dawg had his sister after his parent's death, as well as Rowdy's parents. Natches's parents were cold, almost inhumanly so. Scions of the county, with more money than they needed and less heart than anyone Kelly had ever met. How a brother of Ray's could have turned out like that, she couldn't figure.

And Natches had always suffered for it, until he was old enough to leave. Dawg and Rowdy were his family. They were all he really claimed. And though she couldn't see him as needy, she could see the regret that egged at him, the fierce determination not to lose that connection he had with the other two men.

"I'm sorry," she whispered. "What Rowdy does when he leaves me—"

"You think he's going to leave you?" Mocking laughter filled his voice then. "Hell, Kelly, what do you think we were fighting over when you walked in? Rowdy gave us the 'hands off.' He's gone all white-knight possessive on us for some damned reason, and it has to be because you refused to do it."

She stared back at him in surprise.

"He did what?"

"You heard me," he grumbled. "Son of a bitch dared us to touch you. You have his dick tied in so many knots he doesn't know what he wants."

Now, that just didn't sound like Rowdy. Rowdy wasn't a man who didn't know what he wanted. And he always meant what he said.

"I didn't know that was what you were arguing over—"

"Because you're not the one who would have problems understanding the concept." Rowdy's deep, angry voice broke in on the conversation as he stepped into the smaller entrance next to the stairs.

He stared back at Natches, his eyes narrowed, his body corded and tense.

"Hell, back down, Rowdy," Natches sighed. "I just wanted to apologize for hurting her feelings, not take you on."

Natches pushed his fingers wearily through his hair. She could feel the sense of resignation moving around him and the sadness of it pricked at her.

Kelly shivered as Rowdy moved next to her, his arm going around her waist, pulling her against the warmth of his body. As he did she caught the look that flashed across Natches's face. It was so quick that she wondered if she imagined it. Envy, regret.

"I accept your apology, Natches," she told him softly. "And I'm sorry, this isn't what I intended."

Rowdy tensed at her side.

Natches's grin was crooked, charming, but the sight of it made her chest ache. It was a ruse. Natches wasn't taking this well, and of the three men, she wondered if perhaps he was the one who needed the sharing the most.

"Time for me to slip out and see if we can catch our evil neighborhood stalker now." He straightened from the doorway, flexing his shoulders as he turned toward the hallway. "Catch ya'll later."

As he disappeared she felt Rowdy's hands slide through her hair.

"Are you okay?" He tilted her head back, staring down at her with a slight frown.

"I'm not an emotional wreck, Rowdy." She grimaced at the concern in his eyes. "You're suddenly treating me with kid gloves and it's getting on my nerves."

"What do you mean by that?" His frown darkened as she moved away from him then turned to face him.

"You told Dawg and Natches to keep their hands off me?" She leaned against the center island and crossed her arms beneath her breasts as she stared back at him. "Why?"

His eyes narrowed. "We'll discuss this later."

He turned away to the fridge, opening it to grab a beer as she stared back at him in surprise.

"Says who?"

"Me." He unscrewed the bottle top with a hard jerk of his fingers.

"And you think that perhaps this doesn't concern me in some way? That maybe I don't have a say in it?"

"Drop this, Kelly," he warned her, his voice grating as his eyes flamed back at her. "This isn't a conversation I'm ready to get involved in where you're concerned, not right now."

"Fine. I'll drop it." She uncrossed her arms, straightened her shoulders, and lifted her chin defiantly. *Drop it?* Oh she could drop it all right. "I'll drop it completely, Rowdy. And you can go to hell at the same time you find yourself someplace else to sleep. If I'm not able to decide for myself whether or not I'll screw another man, then I'll be damned if I have the brains to decide if I want to screw you."

She stalked from the kitchen, fists clenched, her teeth grinding. God, when he had gotten so damned arrogant? So impossible to deal with? She didn't know when it had happened, but where she was concerned, it could stop now.

When had she become so damned stubborn?

Rowdy watched Kelly as she stalked from the kitchen, then listened to her stomp up the stairs muttering to herself before he moved.

Self-control, he had tried to warn himself. Things weren't exactly stable right now. Between the stalker, his argument with Natches, and his own revelations about himself, he knew his temper wasn't exactly calm. But this was just too much.

Moving quickly up the stairs behind her, he caught the bedroom door as she was attempting to close it, pushing his way in before he slammed it forcibly.

"Did I ask you to follow me?" she hissed, her gray eyes dark and gleaming with irritation as she faced him.

"You didn't have to ask."

Before she could blast him with whatever her lips were opening to say, he jerked her to him, lowered his head, and stole the sound with his kiss.

It was like sinking into ecstasy, fire, all the pleasure he could have ever imagined. He caught her little gasp with his lips, felt her hands grip his shoulders, her nails biting into the fabric of his shirt as he turned and lifted her, pressing her against the wall as he devoured the sweetness of her lips.

Her kiss. He loved her kiss. The feel of her lips softening beneath his, her body straining against him as his hands moved over it, pushing beneath the thin material of her shirt to cup her swollen breasts.

She was ready for him. He could feel it in the way her tongue met his, the hot little moans smothered by his lips. God, he had dreamed of this. Dreamed of touching her. Loving her.

Pulling his head back, he jerked her shirt over her head, staring down at her, fighting to breathe as he watched the heavy lift and fall of the firm mounds.

He loved her breasts. His hands cupped them again, fitting over the fragile lace of her bra, his thumbs raking over the tender tips as he stared back at her.

"You're mine." He could hear the guttural tone of his voice, but he also saw the effect of it in her eyes.

They darkened in hunger as she drew in a hard breath, her tongue licking over her swollen lips.

"I need you," he whispered then, desperately, hungrily. "All of you, baby. Sweet and hot, and crying for me."

He took her lips again before he made a fool of himself. Before he went to his knees and begged her to see, to understand the self-ishness rising inside him. It sliced through him like the sharpest blade. The thought of another man touching what was his, taking the innocence, the sweetness of Kelly was more than he could bear.

"Rowdy . . ." She shuddered in his grip as he released her bra, drawing it from her shoulders before his hands went to the clasp of her jeans.

"This is mine." He worked his hand between them to push her jeans roughly over her hips before cupping the hot, wet mound of her pussy.

His fingers delved beneath the silk of her panties, so desperate for the feel of her that taking time to completely undress her was more than he could consider.

His fingers moved through silken heat, parting the bare folds to sink into the sweet, tight depths of her slick core.

She arched into the touch, pressing against him, driving his finger further inside her as she cried into the kiss. The hot little sounds she made as he touched her had his cock throbbing in demand. He needed her. Needed to taste her, to touch her.

Now. He had to claim her.

The sharp knock at the door had his muscles clenching further in denial.

"Rowdy, we have movement out here." Dawg's quiet voice was dark with imminent violence. "You in on this, man?"

"No." Kelly clutched at his shoulders as he moved back.

Son of a bitch, if he caught the bastard stalking her he was going to rip him apart with his bare hands.

"I'll be back." He pulled her jeans quickly back in place.

"Don't go out there," she cried out, her face paling as her fingers gripped his arm. "It's too dark Rowdy, and you don't know where he could be hiding. Wait—"

There wasn't a chance in hell he wasn't going out there.

"You're mine," he snarled, sealing the claim with a hard kiss to her lips. "All mine, Kelly. And that bastard is going to figure that out at the end of my fist or my gun. I don't care which."

He pulled away from her, jerking the door open and closing it before Dawg could see her, her sweet breasts rising over the lace of her bra, her pale face staring back at him with equal amounts of fear and anger.

The fear was going to be gone.

"Let's go hunting." He took the rifle Dawg handed to him and headed downstairs.

TWENTY

Kelly waited until nearly dawn for Rowdy, Dawg, and Natches to return to the house. Whatever or whoever had been out there had been determined not to be found. They had disappeared, leaving the three men with a growing, restless anger. And a determination to get her where they felt she would be protected.

Despite her objections, Rowdy packed her clothes and loaded her into Dawg's truck as the sun began to rise beyond the mountains.

She was terrified, she admitted. Whoever was stalking her knew how to hide, which only made him more dangerous. The thought of Rowdy, or one of his cousins, paying for the danger stalking her was eating a bleeding wound into her soul.

Finally, despite her objections and her demands that she simply leave town, the pickup pulled into the graveled road leading to Dawg's house.

Kelly knew the moment she saw the house why they had chosen Dawg's as a secure location. She had forgotten about the house, built by Dawg's parents, and set into the base of the mountain that ran through their property outside Somerset. He spent most of his time on his boat, so she hadn't considered the house.

The huge dwelling was set into the side of the mountain, with only the front left in view. Dawg's father had designed and overseen its building, Ray had once said, claiming that he was determined to have the most unique home in the county. And it was that.

It had been meant to be a vacation home, private, out of the way, and as unique as his parents had been. Though Rowdy had often wondered if Dawg's father hadn't been more than the architect he claimed to be. There were too many secrets in the Mackay family, he admitted, and one of these days, he was going to get to the bottom of them.

The face of the house was warm wood, covering steel and cement, with large windows looking out from the kitchen on the left, and the large living room on the right.

It wasn't opulent, or expensively furnished, but it was a huge dwelling with four bedrooms, accompanied by private baths. There was an exercise room and a basement pantry–wine room larger than some apartments she had been in.

The house was built in three levels—kitchen, living room, and exercise room on the ground level, bedrooms above on the top level, and the basement on a third level. She now understood why Dawg's father, Chandler Mackay, had been considered one of the finest architects in the nation.

It had been surprising when Dawg entered the Army then took over the lumberyard his father had owned. Everyone had expected him to step into his late father's shoes and become an architect instead.

Rowdy led her through the large open living room to the wide hallway that opened at the back of it. There, two sets of curved wooden steps led to the other levels. He moved aside as they reached the stairs that led to the upper level, allowing her to move ahead of him.

The steps were narrow, but comfortable, and led into another short hallway and two open doors.

"The left." He nudged her toward the open door, his voice brooking no argument as they moved into the room.

A huge king-sized bed took up the center of the room, draped with sheer curtains that hung from a steel ring in the center of the ceiling and tied at each corner of the bed.

A dark wood dresser and chest, writing desk, and vanity table sat along the walls. Scenic pictures set in frames that resembled windows on the far side of the bed. Behind it, another door opened into what was obviously a large bathroom.

"Nice," she murmured as Rowdy moved in behind her and closed the door before setting her bags on the floor. He must have packed everything she had before they left his father's house.

"It suits Dawg." He shrugged negligently. "Go ahead and get settled in, take a nap if you need to. We'll go out to dinner later."

"I'd prefer to stay here." She turned to him slowly, keeping her expression carefully bland.

"Too bad." He crossed his arms over his chest as he watched her, the dark gray T-shirt he wore stretching over his rippling muscles. "Dawg, Natches, and I decided we're going to eat out."

"I want to be alone." She pressed her lips firmly together. "I told you that."

The argument had raged for hours. She couldn't believe his complete arrogance and stubbornness. He refused to leave her alone for even a second, and he wouldn't hear of her leaving town without him. At this point, he wouldn't even hear of her leaving town with him. She would have settled for that.

"And I said, you can forget it," he repeated, not for the first time as he dropped his arms and moved closer. Kelly stepped back, ignoring his dark frown. "Kelly, baby, you don't have to worry like this, everything will be okay."

"Sure it will." She smiled tightly. "That's why we're staying in a house that could likely defend against an attack from a foreign government and your cousins are packing in enough weapons to defend against an army."

"They're for looks only," he assured her. "We have a plan, I promise."

"Like you did the other night on the lake?"

"Naw, that was just to see how rock-dumb that bastard could get. He's dumb enough to need help breathing at this point. He won't be that hard to catch."

Confidence gleamed in his eyes, even as dread burned in her belly.

"He would have been caught by now if it were that easy." She pushed her fingers through her hair as she shook her head. "You're underestimating him, Rowdy."

"Maybe you're underestimating me," he grunted as his hands whipped out, pulling her into his embrace before she could avoid him.

Heat instantly sizzled across her body, nearly taking her breath as he pressed the hard length of his erection against her belly.

"Want me to help you shower?" He nuzzled his face against her neck, his tongue licking over her pulse erotically as his fingers clenched at her hips.

Kelly gripped his shoulders, certain the weakness in her knees was going to become a permanent thing if he didn't stop touching her so damned much. She needed to think; she didn't need her mind clogged by his kiss, his passion.

"I can manage alone." Her voice was hoarse, despite the strength she attempted to inject into it.

"Hmm." He lifted his head, staring down at her knowingly before whispering, "I bet you can, but can you manage this alone?"

His lips caught hers before she could do more than gasp, covering them, taking them as his tongue licked at the curves, tempting her to play with him.

How she had always longed to play in just such a way with Rowdy. His lips tugged at hers as he stared down at her, his eyes heavy-lidded and darkening with sexual hunger. His tongue stroked over hers, retreated, then came back for more until she was moaning and reaching for him, desperate for the kiss he was teasing her with.

"Hungry for me, baby?" His voice was dark velvet, rasping against her senses as she arched against him.

"I've always been hungry for you," she whispered, nipping back at his lips as his eyes narrowed, his expression becoming primitive, deepening with sexual energy as her hands smoothed from his shoulders to his chest and lower.

She needed him. She had never pretended otherwise. She needed everything he was, everything he wanted and needed to give her.

She gripped the material of his T-shirt, pulling it quickly from the band of his jeans as she allowed her nails to rake his flesh. The trembling response that raced over his body sent flashes of erotic heat tingling between her thighs.

"Take the shirt off, Rowdy." She pushed the hem to his chest before lowering her head, her lips pressing to the hair-spattered skin beneath the flat, hard male nipple that drew her attention. "I want you naked. I want you against me, inside me."

The shirt was jerked from his body and tossed aside. His expression darkened, his face flushing with hunger as he stared back at her.

Kelly murmured her approval as she bent her head, licking around the tight, hard nipple that fascinated her. How she loved Rowdy's lips on her breasts, his teeth scraping her own hard peaks.

She raked over the tight point with a tentative little nip.

"Son of a bitch." He flinched, his hands gripping her hair, tightening in the strands before pressing her to him again. "Again, Kelly. God, baby, do it again."

She did that and more. She licked, sucked, rasped the point until she could feel a fine sheen of perspiration coating his chest and felt his breath heaving.

She moved her fingers lower, struggling with the metal buttons of his jeans, dragging them free and spreading the material apart. He wore no underwear. Rowdy wasn't an underwear-type man, and she knew it. Which suited her fine. It made it easier for the hard length of his cock to push free, rising nearly to his navel, thick and heavy, the head bloated and damp from the silky pre-come coating it.

"Suck it." His voice was a hard rasp as she licked a path down his chest to the hardened flesh below.

"Patience is a virtue." She could barely speak for the lust rising inside her.

"Fuck patience," he groaned, his hands tugging sensually at her hair. "God, baby, do you know how often I dream of watching you wrap your pretty mouth around my dick?"

A punch of excitement convulsed her womb and sent a spasm of response trembling through her pussy.

"You should have savored it last time," she panted. "Maybe I don't want to now."

But she did. She grasped the heavy weight of his erection as she used her other hand to push at the band of his jeans. A growl of impatience tore from his throat as he moved, toeing off his shoes before quickly disposing of his jeans.

Each second it took him to undress, her palm stroked his cock, up and down, tightening at the base before loosening and running up the silky shaft once more. Until his hands were in her hair again, clenching in the strands, sending darts of heat to rake across her scalp as lust slammed through her bloodstream. Prickles of sensation, of need, raced across her flesh as emotion erupted through her chest.

Rowdy. She had dreamed of him, lusted for him, waited for him. Now, everything she had ever prayed for was being threatened because of one careless act on her part. Because she had waited. Because she had wanted Rowdy to seduce her rather than take her. Had she belonged to Rowdy before he left last year, then the attacker would have never targeted her. And she could have belonged to him. He would have tried to fight it, but he had wanted her as badly as he did now. He had hungered as much as she had.

She lowered her head the last inches as she bent to him, taking the mushroomed head between her lips as her tongue stroked over the throbbing crest.

"Oh fuck," he growled, his hands tugging at her hair, pulling it just enough to light a sudden blinding flame of need inside her.

She liked the pain. Not true pain, the spark of intensity, the erotic burn that emphasized the pleasure. She liked it, and she wanted more.

Kelly wrapped her fingers around the shaft of his cock, pumping it with slow, measured strokes as she began to suckle the head with a growing hunger she could no longer control. She wanted to take all of him. Wanted to feel his cock pulse in her mouth, feel his semen spilling onto her tongue.

"Here, sweetheart, let me help you take those clothes off." His fingers were pulling at her shirt, tugging at her hands and her head until she released his flesh to have the shirt stripped from her body.

"Come here, darlin', turn right around for me." Rowdy turned her as his hands stripped her jeans over her thighs before tugging them free of her legs as he slipped her shoes from her feet.

His lips touched her thigh as he undressed her, her knee, his tongue licked, his teeth rasped.

It was taking too long and it was taking forever and she was certain she was going to scream from sheer excitement as she felt him push her over the bed, his hard, callused hands parting her buttocks just before hungry lips began to caress the hidden flesh.

She couldn't breathe. Feeling him move, she knew he was reaching for the tube of lubricating gel on the bedside table. Knew what was coming.

Cool lubricated fingers eased into the narrow crevice seconds later, massaged the rippling entrance to her ass as she cried out her pleasure. "There, baby," Rowdy's voice whispered across her senses. "It's just for me. Just feel good, sweetheart. Just for me."

One hand held her in place as the other slowly, methodically prepared her rear.

"I want you there, Kelly," Rowdy groaned as she felt his finger slide fully inside her before retreating. "I need you there. I want to part those pretty cheeks and watch your sweet ass suck my cock in."

She couldn't stop the ragged cry that left her throat, or the overwhelming hunger for him. Rowdy was making her crazy. His fingers were pumping inside her anus now, two stretching her, making her burn in ways she had never imagined.

She could feel the juices weeping from her pussy, thick, silky, soaking the bare curves as he teased her clit with a finger, making her hips jerk and sending talons of need ripping at her womb.

She needed . . . oh God, she needed his fingers pumping inside her pussy, filling her there as the rocketing sensations overwhelmed her body.

She could feel her rear entrance being stretched further, slickened, heavily lubricated as Rowdy kept up the pressure on her clit, kept her begging for more.

Her hips were churning, driving his fingers deeper inside her. He was breathing hard, almost as hard as she was.

"More, baby." Another finger joined the first two, working inside her, stretching her until she was burning alive for more, ready, willing to plead for more if only she could find the strength to speak.

"Oh God!" She shuddered, her back arching at the fullness stretching her.

"Three fingers, Kelly," Rowdy growled as his arm latched around her waist, holding her upright. "Three fingers buried in that tight little ass. When I pull them out, you'll be ready for me." He pressed on her shoulders until she was lying over the bed. Rowdy moved her, arranged her as he pleased, propping her knees on the mattress as he pressed her shoulders down.

All the while he worked his fingers inside her, pulling nearly free, spreading more of the cool gel over them before working them inside her once again.

"Fuck. So fucking pretty"—she felt his hand smooth over her buttock as he pulled his fingers free of her grip—"so pretty, and so damned sweet—"

"Rowdy . . ." Her fingers clenched in the blanket as she felt the bloated crest of his cock tuck against the entrance.

"Let it hurt, baby," he whispered. "Just a little bit. Let yourself feel how the pleasure and the pain mix, how it can make you fly like nothing else does."

He pressed closer.

Kelly held her breath, feeling the nerve-laden tissue begin to part, to suck him in, rippling around him as it began to burn.

She was fighting to breathe through the pleasure. Through the burn. Through sensations that tore through her mind and left her dazed with the explosions of heat burning through her body.

"Damn. You're tight, sweetheart." He pulled back, pressed forward again, working the thick crest into her further with each stroke.

Below, his fingers circled her throbbing clit, stroked down the parted slit, and massaged the entrance to her vagina. She pressed back, desperate to feel them inside her.

"Rowdy!" She screamed his name as she felt the head of his cock pop inside her. A hard, blinding stretch of tissue that had her arching, had her nerve endings flaming as a finger speared inside the depths of her pussy.

Rowdy slid inside her to the hilt then. His hands were tight on her hips, holding her steady as the hard rasp of his breath echoed in her ears. Part growl, part groan, his pleasure was vocal, physical, wrapping around her as it blended with her own. This was what she wanted. Needed. Just this. Just with Rowdy. He moved then, slowly, dragging his cock nearly free before pressing forward again. The movement sent violent waves of pleasure tearing through her as she begged Rowdy for ease.

"God, yes, baby. You're so sweet. So tight. So hot," he rasped, his voice dark and rough as he began to thrust inside her slow and easy.

"Yes." She reached back for him. "Please . . ." She needed him deep inside her. Needed his erection tunneling into her harder as his fingers teased her pussy. "Now . . ."

He gave her what she was begging for. Slowly. Teasingly.

His fingers caressed the swollen folds of her pussy a second be-

fore his hand retreated, only to return. Her eyes flew open, a startled cry leaving her lips as she felt the buzzing vibration of the vibrator he pressed against her vaginal opening. The thick tip entered
her pussy, burning her further. "Damn, you're so fucking tight."
She could feel the perspiration that covered her skin, that dripped
from his.

Kelly shook her head. "Take me. Please . . ."

She heard him, felt Rowdy press the vibrator upward, working
inside her slowly. Her anal muscles flexed around the invading
cock as her pussy convulsed around the vibrator filling her. The ta-
pered head of the toy pressed forward, making room for the following shaft.

It was unlike anything she could have imagined. As Rowdy
filled her ass with his cock, he filled her pussy, filled her until she
was certain she could take no more, only to learn she could take
more. Much more.

By the time the toy had seated fully inside her, her screams of
pleasure had turned to raspy, incoherent pleas. Sweat coated her
body as her juices coated her thighs. She was slick all over, wet and
pierced and dying for more.

"How's that, baby?" Rowdy leaned over her, his chest pressing
against her lightly as he fucked into her slow and easy. "Can you
take it?"

"Please . . ." She was crying, so desperate to come she was
shaking from the need. "Fuck me. Please. Please . . ."

He moved. His cock and the vibrator began to power inside her
in tandem. The friction, the overwhelming intensity of pleasure
consumed her. At first slow, tentative, then faster, harder, he began
to thrust inside her with strong, powerful strokes.

Kelly writhed between Rowdy and the toy, the sensations of the dual penetration, of the pleasure flowing between them, just them, no one else, sent ecstasy screaming through her system.

She couldn't survive this pleasure. It was burning, intensifying, stealing her mind, her body. She felt each stroke tightening her womb, pushing her closer, deeper into the maelstrom overtaking her.

She was going to explode. She could feel it, flew closer to it, feeling the rapture build, the pleasure, so deep, so intense, so overwhelming . . .

Rowdy's name was on her lips. A scream of fear, of ecstasy as she felt the orgasm rip through her. It tightened her body, her vagina, tore through her and flung her into a pleasure she couldn't fight, couldn't resist.

She felt Rowdy stiffen, felt the heat of his release, the hard shudders that suffused his body, and a blinding fiery blaze of emotion that had her screaming his name.

As the hard, wracking shudders eased from her body she collapsed against him, wasted, exhausted, certain she couldn't open her eyes if her very life depended on it.

TWENTY-ONE

Rowdy walked from the bathroom half an hour later, dressed in fresh jeans and a shirt before moving to the bed and the shoes he had left forgotten beside it. Kelly still slept. A hard, hopefully dreamless sleep. Sprawled on her stomach, one arm tucked beneath the pillow, her cheek rested on, breathing deep. She looked innocent, sweet, and untouched.

It was hard to believe she had been a wildcat less than an hour before. The sweet little kitten sleeping so calmly bore no resemblance to her, he thought with a smile. Rowdy shook his head, the smile creasing his face further at the memory. He had always known she would be a firecracker in bed, ready and willing for any adventure he could give her. She was earthy, lusty, and she liked that sharp little edge of pain he enjoyed giving.

He reached out, smoothing back a thick swathe of hair from her cheek as emotion overwhelmed him, tightened his chest, and reminded him of what he could have lost. If he had given in to the demand that he take her the year before, the attack might have never happened. Hell no, it wouldn't have happened, because he would have demanded reassignment. He couldn't have left her. He had known that then. Once he had her, there was no way he could have walked away.

He was crazy about her. So crazy in love with her that it terrified him clear to the soles of his feet. She was young as hell, and still so innocent it broke his heart.

Leaning forward, he pressed a butterfly kiss against her forehead before tucking the sheet closer over her shoulders. Minutes later he was striding into the living room where Natches and Dawg waited on him. Natches had his head back on the couch, eyes closed. Dawg just looked grouchy as he stared back from the chair he sat in.

"Bastard!" Dawg grunted as Rowdy dropped into a chair across from him. "Guard duty sucks."

There was a gleam of envy in Dawg's eyes, despite the amusement in his tone.

"Did guard duty pay off though?" Rowdy lifted a brow, staring back at his cousin questioningly.

Dawg grinned in satisfaction. "Guard duty paid. I slipped out the doggie hole and found a nice little perch topside. We had some definite movement."

Natches's eyes opened as he straightened in his seat, his expression going as darkly dangerous as Rowdy felt. Evidently this wasn't information Natches had been given, which surprised Rowdy.

"What kind of movement?" Rowdy asked, paying attention to the dangerous, predatory light that gleamed in Natches's expression as Dawg continued.

"Little fellow, barely taller than Kelly. Dressed in hunting gear with a hooded mask. He was being real careful. Watching the house from heavy cover. I couldn't get a shot."

"Did you recognize anything?" They were getting close. The stalker was losing his grip on reality if he had followed them so quickly.

Kelly's stalker was obviously beginning to crack, and that was what they needed. Just a small fracture in his self-control and they would have him.

Dawg shook his head. "I watched him as best I could. Maybe something will trigger if I see him around anywhere." A grimace twisted his expression. "Catching him might not be easy, but I have a feeling he'll make another move soon."

Of course he would, he considered Kelly his. The fact that the Nauti Boys had her, were possibly sharing her, would be too much for his tenuous hold on reality to survive.

"I'll take guard duty from here on out," Natches spoke up then, his voice bland, unassuming. Dangerous. A good ole boy attitude covering a steel core of determination.

Rowdy stared back at him curiously. Natches had changed in ways that were hard to put a finger on. He had returned from the Marines only months before Rowdy had, quieter and a hell of a lot harder than he had been when he went in. That hardness was more than maturity and confidence, more than a soldier who had seen battle in the sands of another nation. Despite his vow that he had never grown up, somehow, Rowdy knew better.

"Fine." Rowdy nodded slowly. "You take watch. We'll head into town in the morning, take Kelly shopping, do some stocking up. We'll let the bastard see what he's missing. If he's the nutcase I suspect, he'll hit by tomorrow night."

"Are we going to give him an opening?" Natches's voice softened.

"We can't make it look too easy. He has to work for it." Rowdy sat back in the chair, considering their options. "Dawg, weaken the security monitor on the kitchen window, and in the shrubbery beneath it. Make it look natural, something he can get through. He's broken the women's security systems so he's not a stranger to it. Let's see what the bastard's made of."

Dawg nodded sharply as Natches continued to watch them with a hard, merciless stare that assured Rowdy that he wasn't the only one waiting to shed blood.

Rowdy turned his gaze back to Natches, realizing in that second that he had seen the look in his friend's eyes before. He had seen it in another man's eyes, a Marine assassin. He had worked alone, disappearing for weeks at a time and returning with that same dead, cold chill in his eyes.

Hell. He blew out a silent breath as Natches met his eyes, his expression never changing. What the hell had Natches gotten into while he was in the service?

"Go ahead and set up," Rowdy told him quietly. "Let me know before morning how you want to play it."

Dawg's head had lowered, proof that he was aware of a truth that Rowdy hadn't been privy to. A truth he still wasn't certain of the details to.

"I'll go public with you when you need me to," Natches said softly. "I'll use the bolt-hole otherwise."

The bolt-hole, or dog door as Dawg had amusingly named it, was the single, secret entrance into the house from a shrub-hidden door several hundred feet around the base of the hill. Dawg wasn't the trusting sort, and his time in the Marines hadn't helped his trust issues any.

"Boys, we need to talk when this is all over and done," Rowdy sighed, watching the weary resignation in his cousins' eyes. "Keeping secrets among ourselves isn't a good thing, ya know?"

Dawg grunted, a sound of wry amusement that was typical Dawg. Natches's lips quirked into a smile.

"A good drunk maybe," Dawg growled as he rose from his chair and paced across the room toward the kitchen. "Until then, boys, I need food. You want me to take mess duty?"

Rowdy's eyes met Natches's in shock, as his cousin's widened in horror.

"Hell no!" They both came out of their seats, rushing for the kitchen as they heard pans rattling beneath the stove cabinet and remembered Dawg's past attempts at manning a stove. The memory wasn't a pleasant one.

He had checked on his girls. His special good girls. Kelly was weak—she was allowing herself to be degraded, to be taken. Oh, how he had hoped she had been the only one. He had prayed, prayed so long and hard that his good girls were waiting on him.

He curled into the corner of the small dark apartment, rocking himself gently as he stared at the first of his lovers. He had thought she was so pure, so sweet. With her long, silken blond hair, and her innocent blue eyes. She had a soft voice, one that stroked the senses and made him think of his mother before she became a whore. Before she had turned his father away, before his father had stolen him away for his mother's sins. They had to punish her. She hadn't been a good girl.

He sniffed, realizing he was crying. He hated crying. Crying never helped, tears made a man weak, he remembered that from his father's lessons. A man had to do what he had to do. His father had been weak. The old man had cried, he had raged but he had left the depraved creature he had married rather than punishing her.

He should have punished her. If his father had punished his mother, then she wouldn't have been so bad. She would have been the good wife and mother she should have been. If she had been a good woman, then she wouldn't have lost her son.

He flinched at that memory, shaking his head to force it back from his mind as he reached out to touch thick strands of hair that flowed out from his good girl's head.

He touched the silken strands, rubbing them between his fingers, remembering how soft and sweet she had been. Before she had let herself grow weak. Before she had let another man convince her to be bad.

He stared at the man, a tight smile crossing his lips at the sight of the nude man, laying half on the bed, half on the floor. He wasn't dead, but he would soon wish he was.

The girl. He sighed wearily as he let himself stare at the blood staining the carpet. She stared back at him sightlessly, her china blue eyes reflecting the horror of her punishment.

Kelly must have somehow convinced this one that she could be bad, too. How, he wasn't certain. He could have sworn his girls didn't know about each other. He had taken pains to be very careful. But Kelly was so bad, so depraved, that she would have found a way to convince the others that they too could escape him.

They belonged to him. They were his good girls. He wouldn't allow another to touch them, not like his mother had.

He pulled himself to his feet, careful to pick up the knife and clean it of the blood that stained it. Her blood.

"You'll always be my good girl now," he whispered as he stepped around the blood and moved for the spare bedroom.

He had hidden there for hours, waiting for her to come home. Waiting to assure himself that she was a good girl. Only to listen in pain and fury as another man touched her.

He fought back his tears again as he entered the dark room and headed for the window he had used to slip inside the apartment. He had bypassed her security. How easy it had been. She had thought she was safe from him. That she could disobey him as his mother had disobeyed his father. She had found out wrong. Just as Kelly would have to learn as well.

TWENTY-TWO

The next morning, Kelly would have preferred to enjoy the awakening caresses Rowdy was bestowing as she swam toward reality rather than the warm, sensual dreams twining around her. Unfortunately, the moment was interrupted by Dawg's growling message that her mother and Ray were on their way, and they had better get their asses ready before the arrival. His words, not hers.

She had enough time to shower and dress, never realizing the kind of devastating news her parents would bring.

"Her name was Dana Carrington." Ray's voice was low, angry. "She was murdered, and her boyfriend was molested."

Kelly sat in shock, listening as Ray recounted the murder that had taken place the night before. She sat at the kitchen table, her hands wrapped around her coffee cup as Rowdy stood behind her, his hands resting on her shoulders as she felt fear tremble through her.

"Kelly." Her mother leaned forward in her chair, staring back at her worriedly. "I called your aunt Beth in Montana, she wants you to come stay—"

"No." Rowdy's voice was hard.

Kelly's gaze flickered to Ray. He glanced at Rowdy in concern, but said nothing more.

"She's not safe here, Rowdy—" her mother protested.

"She won't be any safer there," he argued as Kelly tightened her fingers on the coffee cup. "At least here, Dawg and Natches and I have a chance of catching this bastard."

"By letting him think she's screwing all three of you?" Maria came out of her chair then, her cry filled with fear as she faced Rowdy. "For God's sake, Douglas, what if using her doesn't work? What if he gets to her—"

"Enough," Rowdy growled warningly.

"Kelly, listen to me, whoever this is has killed now. He won't stop . . ." Her mother stared back at her, her eyes damp with tears, her lips trembling.

"That's enough, Maria," Rowdy protested.

"Let her have her say, Rowdy." Ray shook his head regretfully. "She's her mother."

"All of you stop it!" Kelly's palm cracked on the kitchen table, sending an enveloping silence to fill the kitchen as all eyes turned to her. Ray and her mother, Dawg and Natches, Rowdy, she could feel their gazes boring into her as she lifted her head and stared back at her mother.

Kelly drew in a deep, hard breath. Fear was like a snake coiling in her belly, striking at her chest in an effort to be free.

"Rowdy's right," she whispered. "He won't stop killing now. If I stay here, there's a chance he can be caught—"

"Oh God, Kelly, listen to yourself," Maria protested desperately. "That girl last night is dead. He raped her boyfriend while he was unconscious. He's not sane."

"And I can't run." She shuddered at the thought of being terrified of the dark for the rest of her life, of being terrified of what could happen. But even more, she knew there were a lot of things Rowdy would allow, but he would never let her go. "We have to face it. Now. Here."

God, for a minute she wished Rowdy were less intense, less determined. She wished she didn't know him as well as she did.

"Come on, Aunt Maria," Dawg grunted as she continued to glare at Rowdy. "You know lookin' at him like that don't work. He's just going to get in a bad mood and pout on us all night long if you do."

Maria flashed her nephew by marriage a dark look. Dawg grinned back, flashing strong white teeth through his gaze remained hard.

"You boys are going to get her killed," she snapped. "This isn't a game you're playing here. It's Kelly's life."

"Which makes it my life," Rowdy assured her. "I'll be damned if I'll let this bastard hurt her more. Now stand the hell down and we can talk about this reasonably, or by God we won't talk about it at all."

Ray breathed out wearily.

"He's right, Maria. You know he's right. She can't run all her life," he said, the regret heavy in his voice as Maria gasped in surprise.

"Ray, you don't mean that. She would be safe—"

"She'll never be safe as long as that bastard is on the loose, Maria." He grimaced, shaking his head. "We both know it. She has to make her stand here."

"I won't have it—"

"I said I've heard enough!" Kelly scraped her chair across the floor, coming to her feet and pushing her fingers through her hair with an edge of frustration.

"Kelly . . . I'm scared for you," Maria whispered. "If Rowdy is so determined to stay with you, then the two of you can go away for a while."

"This isn't something I can run away from." Kelly swallowed tightly as she stared back at her mother.

"You mean he won't let you run away," Maria accused. "Don't let him risk your life like this, Kelly."

"I'm letting him save it," she whispered. "Because without him, I'm dead. It won't matter where I go, or how long I stay, he'll find me. Just as he found the other girl. He won't let it go."

"He would have," Maria bit out. "He left that girl alone until she found someone, and he would have left you alone if Rowdy hadn't drawn you into . . . this . . ." Her arm swung out to encompass Rowdy, Dawg, and Natches.

Heat flamed in her cheeks as she breathed in roughly, staring back at her mother, hating what her mother suspected, hating that the danger she was in now was tearing at them all. No explanation would make a difference; her mother would no more believe that she wasn't sleeping with all three men than the stalker would.

"This is my business," she said softly. "Remember that, Mom. And don't forget it. My relationship with Rowdy is my business, and it will stay that way. Period. I love you, but I can't deal with fighting with you right now. I want you to go home."

"No—"

"Mom, go home." She strengthened her voice, fought back her tears, and stared back at her mother firmly. "I'll call. I promise. But this isn't going to help anything, and it's sure as hell not going to make this easier. For my sake, just go."

"Kelly . . ." Rowdy's protest as she moved quickly from the room was ignored, as was Ray's curse and her mother's cry.

She couldn't handle the combined pressure, or her mother's fears. Her own were choking her, strangling her with tightening bands of remembered horror as she escaped the tension building in the kitchen.

She had tried to tell herself that the man who attacked her would go away. That it would stop. That it couldn't be worse than what she had already endured. But now the nightmare was growing worse. Her stalker had become a murderer.

She rushed into the bedroom, carefully closing the door behind her as she capped her hand over her mouth in an effort to hold back her screams of horror. She wasn't the only one at risk now. She had known when the shots were fired into the boat that the stalker was going to try to hurt Rowdy. It hadn't sunk in though, not all the way to the bone, until Ray and her mother dropped their bombshell.

"Kelly, open the door." Rowdy wiggled the doorknob as he spoke on the other side of the panel. His voice was soft, gentle, nearly breaking her resolve to hold back her tears.

Pressing her lips together she turned the lock before moving away, unaware she had locked it in the first place. She moved to the center of the room, wiping her fingers over her cheeks in an attempt to dry the tears from her face.

The door opened then closed as silence engulfed the room for long seconds.

"I don't want him to hurt you," she finally whispered, keeping her back to him as she wrapped her arms over her breasts. "What will I do if he hurts you, Rowdy?"

She heard the male snort behind her, mocking, filled with stubborn pride. She turned to him slowly, wishing, praying, that none of this had happened. That she could have had her dream of holding Rowdy without the danger that surrounded them.

He was staring back at her tenderly, but there was no missing the spark of rage behind the tenderness, or the pure confidence that poured from him.

"What happens if you run, Kelly?" he asked her, moving toward her, a slow, predatory movement that had her heart racing in anticipation even as fear overwhelmed her. "Can you stay one step ahead of him? Can you live your life knowing he can strike at any minute? Knowing that eventually he'll get tired of just watching you, and find a reason to kill you instead? Just as he found a reason to kill that girl last night?"

"I'm not stupid." Her breath caught as his hands cupped her shoulders, his thumbs smoothing over the flesh the straps of her shirt left bare. "I'm scared, Rowdy," her voice lowered. "I'm so scared."

"That's natural," he whispered. "Do you know I'm scared too, Kelly?"

She stared back at him in surprise.

"Scared you won't trust us to protect you. Scared you'll leave, that he'll hurt you in ways you won't be able to come back from. That I'll lose you forever. That's what scares me, Kelly. Hell, it terrifies me."

"Don't . . ." She shook her head, shaking at the throb of emotion in his voice, the pain that threaded through it.

"I'd rather die than see that, Kelly," he whispered painfully, his eyes tormented, dark with emotion. "Don't you understand, sweetheart? I love you until I can't breathe without feeling it move through me, feeling your presence around me. You're my heart. My soul. I won't let that bastard take that from me. If it means I have to lock you up for your own protection and listen to you rage for a lifetime, I'd do it. Anything, Kelly, to keep you safe."

The tears were streaming down her face now, shudders whipping through her body at the sound of his voice. Her big, tough Rowdy, his tone soft, thick with emotion, his eyes brilliant with it.

"I love you so much, Rowdy." Her hands moved from his chest, no longer pressing to hold him back, but moving to his shoulders as he drew her to his chest, holding her close, secure against him.

"It's going to be okay, Kelly." She felt his head lower, felt his lips move over her forehead. "Everything's going to be fine, babe. I'm not stupid, or careless. And Dawg and Natches sure as hell aren't. We're going get through this. All of us, baby."

She lifted her head for his kiss, needing it, desperate to fill the dark places moving through her soul with the fire of his hunger, his need. She could feel his cock straining beneath his jeans, pressing against her stomach as she drew his head down to her.

"Kiss me, Rowdy," she whispered. "Kiss me like I dream—"

His lips stole her words as a hungry groan filled the air. His groan, her whimpering cry of need as she felt the heat and lust moving from him, into her.

Her lips opened as her arms curled around his neck, pulling him closer to her as he tilted her head back, sipping from her lips, licking at them, nipping until they opened as she was crying out for more. Needing more. His tongue was a stroke of fire, his hands were everywhere. Hunger heated the air, filled her body and whipped around her like forked fingers of lightning tingling over her body.

In those moments there was no stalker, no danger, no death or pain. There was only passion. There was only Rowdy.

Amazement flared through Rowdy, not for the first time, at the pleasure he received from just kissing Kelly. Holding her head between his hands, feeling her silky hair fall over his hands, feeling her lips like hot satin beneath his.

And her taste. She intoxicated him. Nothing but Dawg's white lightning had ever had the power to affect him so quickly, until Kelly's kiss. Her touch. Her passion.

He groaned against her lips as he let his tongue dip past them, feeling hers waiting, tangling against him like damp silk and sending his senses spinning.

A man shouldn't be so weak in the face of a kiss, he thought with a sliver of amusement. But damn if she didn't sap his will to resist her, to keep from taking her again and again.

And he was going to have her again. Now. He was going to lay her back on that big bed and sink inside her until she screamed his name.

He backed her toward the bed, keeping his lips on hers as his hands moved from her head to wrap around her back before gripping the hem of her shirt and pushing beneath it. She had the softest skin he had ever touched. Everything about Kelly was different, better, hotter, and sweeter, and with each touch he only wanted more.

"Let's get you out of these damned clothes," he muttered as he tore his lips from hers, his eyes lifting to stare down at her.

Her lips were swollen, cheeks flushed with arousal, and her pretty gray eyes were dark, stormy with hunger. Damn, he liked her hungry. She was like a little tigress, scratching and mewling and uncaring of anything but the pleasure she was attaining. The pleasure he was giving her.

Getting undressed was a matter of a few ripped seams, some buttons popping, and strangled curses as they both struggled with stubborn jeans. But within seconds he was tumbling her back to the bed, his lips zeroing in on her hard, peaked nipples as the taste of her filled his mouth.

God, she was sweet. Arching to him, hoarse cries leaving her lips as he suckled at the tight little points. Her head was thrown back, her hands gripping his head, holding him to her as he went from one swollen mound to the other.

All the while her hot little body twisted and writhed beneath him as her thigh caressed the tight length of his cock. He could feel his balls tightening with the need to fuck and to do it now. It was always like this with Kelly. He couldn't wait to get inside her, to feel her silken heat clasping him, rippling around him as he thrust into the liquid fire of her tight little pussy.

And that heat was so close. He could feel it whispering over the head of his erection, drawing him to her. He wasn't going to be able to wait long, he knew. Long enough maybe, maybe, to ease down her straining body. He did just that, laying quick little kisses down her abdomen, licking at her skin, tasting her with every cell of his body. Just long enough to spread her thighs and settle between them before dipping his head for one quick little taste of her sweet, juicy cunt.

His taste buds exploded as he slid his tongue through the syrupy slit before circling the tight, swollen bud of her clit. Sweet, tart, silken ambrosia that entangled his senses and kept him coming back for more.

Her cries echoed around him as he enjoyed the taste and feel of the slick folds of her flesh. Silken and bare, her pussy flowered open for him. Peaches and cream and soft syrup, and he was a man with a taste for this particular fruit. Especially when those gorgeous legs lifted and her feet propped on his shoulders to allow him maximum access.

He could happily drown in her. He licked at the sweet cream, tasted the hunger and passion that rained from her. His fingers caressed the tender opening to her vagina, teased and tempted her before working inside her. His senses exploded with the heat that surrounded them, with the moist, rich juices that flowed from her.

He ached for her. His cock throbbed like a demon's kiss, but the thought of leaving the succulent flesh beneath his lips was more than he could consider. Not while she burned like this for him. Not while her cries filled the room and her lithe legs spread wide for him.

He licked around her straining clit, grimacing as her pussy tightened further around his fingers. His dick was screaming in pain, begging to push inside her. He pulled his fingers back, pushed inside again and flicked the little nubbin with his tongue as she screamed for more, begged to come.

Not yet. God, the taste of her, the feel of her. He wanted to feel her coming around his cock, not his fingers. He wanted to feel the tight muscles rippling around his erection, sucking the semen from the depths of his balls, and sending his head racing with ecstasy.

He pulled his fingers from her, groaning at the effort it cost to pull back from her, to lift his head from her tender pussy and force himself to rise over her.

He pushed her legs back as he moved, opening her further for him as he pressed the head of his cock against the moist, flexing entrance to her pussy.

She stared up at him, her expression dazed, her eyes the color of storm clouds as her hands lifted to his chest. Her palms pressed against the hair-roughened muscles, her nails biting into his flesh.

"Now," she whispered. "Please, Rowdy, now."

He pressed in the barest fraction, his breath catching at the heat that surrounded the tip of his cock. Looking down, he watched as the smooth, naked lips of her sex parted, glistening with her juices and hugging his cock as he began to work inside her.

Flames traveled from the sensitive crest to his tortured balls as he fought to breathe. Release was an agonizing need that sent fingers of electrified pleasure racing up his spine. He couldn't come yet. Not yet. He thought of baseball, fishing, auto mechanics, and cleaning his gun, but each subject fizzled within his mind as he sank further and further into her heat.

Shaking his head, he plunged in the last inches, growling at the tightness, the suckling heat. He was a man on the verge of madness, control gone, only the wild need to fuck and mate spurring him now.

He didn't stop with one thrust. Pulling back, he began fucking inside her deep and hard, snarling at the pleasure that built with each stroke, at the extreme sensations overtaking his body. His thighs bunched, his balls nearly drawing into his body before he finally felt Kelly explode.

"Fuck. There, baby. So sweet and hot. Come for me, Kelly. Come for me so hard . . ."

Her pussy tightened around his cock nearly to the point of pain as it began convulsing around him. Liquid heat engulfed him, burned him, then sent him careening into a mad, furious drive toward his own pleasure.

"God yes! Sweet baby"—the words ripped from his chest, from his soul—"God help me, I love you."

The release exploded through his body, drawing him tight as an animalistic snarl left his lips. He buried his cock to the furthest depths of her before he felt the harsh, blinding explosions tearing through his scrotum. Pleasure was ecstasy, destructive and consuming as he felt his semen spewing inside the hot depths of the sweet cunt wrapped around him. It held him on edge, milking spurt after spurt of rich seed from his body before the last shudder tore through him and left him wasted.

Rowdy collapsed at Kelly's side, barely retaining enough sanity to keep from falling atop her. He was gasping for air, rippling echoes of pleasure still racing up his spine as he used the last of his strength to drag her into his arms and cushion her against his chest.

"Okay . . . that was wild enough," she panted weakly against him. "You could have warned me first."

"Would have had to suspect first," he mumbled. "Go to sleep or something. Let me rest."

"I'm not sleepy." But her voice was weak, drowsy. "We were going to shop. I heard Mom and Ray leave after we came up here. We could go shopping before they come back for the next round of arguments."

"Nap." He groaned. "Just nap. God, you just killed me. I gotta sleep."

A soft laugh against his chest was the last thing he heard as he sighed deeply and let himself drift off. Dawg and Natches could watch her for half an hour; she had wiped him out.

Kelly rose from the bed, a frown furrowing her brow as she found a loose T-shirt and shorts before heading to the bathroom. She was hungry—breakfast had been set aside because of Ray and her mother's visit, and she was feeling it now.

She forced herself not to think about the reason for that visit. If she thought about it then the fear would take over. The helplessness and overwhelming dread threatening to attack her lingered at the back of her mind, though, shadowing her thoughts.

She cleaned up quickly before dressing and leaving the bathroom. She glanced at Rowdy where he lay facedown on the bed, breathing deeply in sleep, before leaving the room. The beginnings of a smile tipped her lips as the need to curl up against him unfurled inside her.

At the same time her stomach growled warningly. Sex with Rowdy became a secondary need in the face of her hunger. But, she reminded herself, she *had* worked up a bit of an appetite with the sex part.

She moved slowly down the narrow staircase, listening for

Dawg and Natches. She couldn't hear either of them, but the television was playing in the living room. She knew Natches had intended to sneak out somewhere, and she wouldn't put it past Dawg to be hiding as well.

She was surprised to see him lying on the couch instead. He was stretched out in what had to be an uncomfortable angle. His head was hanging over the side as he lay on his back and one leg bent at an odd angle, his arm falling to the floor.

Kelly tipped her head, staring at his dozing posture before shaking her head in confusion at it. She had seen some odd sleeping angles, but that one took the cake.

Restraining a soft laugh, she tiptoed through the living room and made her way into the kitchen. Despite the television, there was a heavy silence in the house that bothered her, made her wary. The moment she entered the kitchen she knew why.

She stopped in shock at the sight of Natches, facedown on the floor, a trail of blood oozing from his temple to stain the floor beneath him.

Her heart slammed into her throat, stealing her breath and the screams that tightened her chest. She gasped for air, certain she was going to smother, knowing the terror filling her would kill her before anything else could.

Rowdy. Oh God, she had to get to Rowdy. She turned, the blood rushing through her veins as her mind screamed at her to run, only to slide to a stop as she moved back into the living room.

Eyes wide, her lips parted in shock, she stared at the form standing in the middle of the living room, a gun pointing toward her chest.

TWENTY-THREE

It took Kelly a moment to realize that she knew him. She blinked in surprise as she recognized the young deputy who had come to the apartment with the police the night of her attack and again to Ray's house the night her bedroom had been destroyed. He had been so quiet she had barely remembered him being there.

"They thought they could catch me." He smiled back at her, his hazel eyes gleaming with triumph as he waved the barrel of his weapon toward where Dawg lay on the couch. "They thought they were better than me because they were big, tough Marines."

His voice was soft, almost girlishly so. His expression was benign, calm, terrifying.

Deputy Carlyle. He hadn't been on the force long, a few years maybe. He was easy to overlook with his nondescript, plain features and quiet voice.

"Deputy Carlyle?"

"Barnes-Carlyle. John," he answered her then. "My mother's maiden name was Barnes, did you know that?"

She shook her head.

"Why are you doing this?" Oh God, had he killed Dawg and Natches? From the corner of her eye she tried to make certain Dawg was still breathing, but she just couldn't be sure. Natches had seemed to be breathing, but was that wishful thinking or had he been?

He sighed as though in regret.

"I didn't mean to make them pay, but I guess the past is catching up on all of us." He glanced at Dawg before his gaze came back to her. "I lost count of the beatings I took from my father because of what your lovers did with my mother."

"What are you talking about?" She shook her head, confused.

"Loren Barnes was their lover," he snickered. "She was my mother. Dad stole me away from her a few years before she seduced them into her bed. She was such a whore. One man was never enough for her."

Kelly remembered Loren Barnes. She had died several years before, an older woman, perhaps her mother's age. There had been a rumor that the Mackay cousins had been her lovers years before, but Kelly knew none of them had ever confirmed it.

"That doesn't tell me why you've done this." She couldn't breathe, fear was strangling her, weakening her, and she knew right now she couldn't afford to be weak.

He looked at her in surprise, his thin lips curving into a smile.

"You don't know who I am, do you, Kelly?" he asked her.

She shook her head slowly, suspicion and horror beating at her.

"My poor little girl," he whispered, confirming her worst fears. "And you were such a good girl at one time. You know I'm going to have to punish you now. You were supposed to be mine."

"I didn't ask for your mark," she yelled back, fury rising inside her. "I didn't want you, John. Love is given freely. You can't force it."

He shook his head as his eyes glistened with tears, his lips wobbling with some demonic emotion.

"You didn't give me time," he pouted. "You would have told me you loved me."

"I knew I didn't love you." She edged back as his head turned from her. If she could get to the kitchen and he chased her, then she could use the hall exit to get back to the stairs. All she needed was a head start. "I've always loved Rowdy, John. Always."

"No! Mine!" he screamed back at her. "I'll show you, you're mine then I'll kill you."

He lunged for her. Fury lit his expression as rage transformed his face and he rushed her. Kelly turned, sliding on the slick floor as she heard an enraged howl of fury echo through the house a second before the sound of two bodies impacting pulled her up short.

Gripped the door frame, she turned back, shock filling her as she watched Rowdy struggling with the smaller man. Rowdy was bigger, but the blood at his temple showed the earlier blow that was now slowing his reflexes.

The gun John had carried slid across the room as he fought to get to it. Kelly rushed for it, crying out in rage as a hand snagged her ankle, bringing her to her knees.

Her head turned as she saw the knife in John's hand, and Rowdy's reach to grab at his wrist as the other man aimed at her leg. She kicked out, breaking loose before scrambling for the weapon.

Her fingers latched onto the handgrip as she flipped over, bringing it up with both hands as she fought to get a clear shot.

The two men were snarling now, wrestling for the knife as she heard the sounds of sirens in the distance. The gun shook in her hand as she blinked back her tears, terrified that the deputy would manage to actually find a way to wound Rowdy with that knife. There was no way to shoot yet. No way to be certain if she did, that she would miss Rowdy.

There had to be something she could do. But if she did the wrong thing, it could mean Rowdy's life. She prayed, sobbing in terror as she watched the two men grapple until the knife was between them a second before Rowdy jerked the other man closer to him.

They both froze.

A whimper left Kelly's throat as the front door crashed inward, and as though in slow motion, she watched Deputy John Barnes-Carlyle slide slowly from Rowdy's grip to collapse on the floor.

His head turned toward her, his hazel eyes filled with shock and surprise.

"My good girl . . ." he whispered before his gaze dimmed and his body went limp.

Kelly stared back at him, the sounds of police filling the room receding to the background as adrenaline began to crash inside her. She lifted her head as the gun dropped in her lap, watching as Rowdy began to move toward her, only to have the sheriff block him as the room continued to fill up. She could hear her mother, or was it merely wishful thinking? Rowdy was yelling and Sheriff Mayes was barking orders.

She knew she should get up, knew she should do something. But all she could do was turn her gaze back to the dead deputy as she heard his final words ringing in her ears. "My good girl . . ."

She wasn't his good girl. A sob tore from her throat as she pushed to her feet, fighting past the shock winding its way through her. He was dead. He was dead, and Rowdy was surrounded by the police.

"Let him go!" she screamed out hoarsely, fighting past Sheriff

Mayes as she struggled to get to Rowdy. She kicked at someone, her fist landed against another, but they parted, staring back at her in shock as she flung herself into Rowdy's arms.

"Thank God! Baby." Rowdy's arms closed around her as his voice whispered in her ear. "Sweet Lord, Kelly. Don't ever terrify me like that again."

She was crying and couldn't stop. She could feel the sobs shaking her body as her arms tightened around his neck.

She could hear Rowdy explaining the deputy's insanity as he held her close. Somehow, he had managed to regain consciousness and call the police, informing them of who was there and what was going on as he slipped down the stairs.

They were prepared, but questions had to be answered. Dawg and Natches were brought around by the medics and the house continued to fill with people. But Kelly refused to leave Rowdy's side.

She held on to him through the evening, answering questions when she had to, but otherwise remaining silent as the knowledge slowly filled her mind that it was over. The stalker had been John Barnes-Carlyle, and he was gone. He was dead. It was finally over.

TWENTY-FOUR

Kelly stared around the living room the next morning, amazed that there was nothing left, not so much as a speck of blood, to prove that the night before had been no dream.

The only proof left was the egg-sized knots that had been left on Dawg's, Natches's, and Rowdy's heads. John Barnes hadn't come to the front door, he had known about Dawg's back entrance through his father, who had spent years spying on the Mackay cousins, and used it to slip into the house.

He had gotten Dawg first, while Natches was outside getting the last supplies from his truck. When he came in, he had seen the same thing Kelly had, what appeared to be Dawg napping on the couch.

He had moved into the kitchen with the supplies, where the deputy had moved in behind him and knocked him unconscious as well. He had waited until Kelly had left the bedroom upstairs, hiding in the other room until she started down the stairs, before he had disabled Rowdy. Or thought he had.

Rowdy had been coming out of his nap as he was struck; the blow had dazed him, taking precious minutes for him to get his bearings enough to struggle from the bed.

The sheriff had called that morning after running a night-long investigation on his dead deputy. He had indeed been Loren Barnes's son, kidnapped by his father several years before the Mackay cousins had become her lovers.

There was a long history of abuse as a child, foster homes, and disappearances that hadn't been followed up on at the time. As the full story emerged, everyone who had known him on the force had been shocked. His father had molested him for years, punishing him for the supposed crimes his mother had committed. Richard Barnes, the father, had been insane, and his insanity had been forced upon his son until it had warped his view of women.

Four women had paid for that crime.

"Feeling better?" She turned her head as Dawg moved from the kitchen, followed by Rowdy and Natches.

She stared at the three men, feeling the tension that suddenly filled the room, the intensity in their eyes. She had known this was coming, had known Rowdy's cousins would soon put his decision to the test. She could see it in the ready tension of their bodies. There was none of the expected anger in Rowdy's expression though. His body was relaxed, easy, his gaze simmering with amusement.

"Do we have a problem?" She crossed her arms over her breasts and stared back at the three curiously.

"Rowdy's being greedy," Dawg grunted. "How do you feel about that?"

"I'm rather greedy myself, Dawg," she informed him fondly. "I can't do it."

"We wouldn't hurt you." She could see the frustration in his face. "Hell, Kelly, our cousins in Texas have survived just fine."

The Augusts. They didn't even live in Somerset and they had a reputation here.

She breathed in deeply.

"I'm not Marly or their other wives," she informed them as Rowdy straightened, slowly tensing.

Dawg glared back at Rowdy then. "You didn't even give us a chance—"

"You don't love her, Dawg," Rowdy snapped, striding across the room to Kelly's side.

When he turned to face Dawg and Natches, his arm curled around Kelly's back, pulling her closer to his hard body.

"We love her enough," Natches protested, his jaw pulsing tightly.

"Oh give it up!" Kelly stepped away from her lover, staring between the three men incredulously, laughter bubbling from her throat at their fierce expressions. "Geez, do I look like a bone between the three of you?"

They stared back at her in surprise.

"Dawg, how many times did I flirt with you, just for the hell of it, while Rowdy was gone?"

"You did what?" Rowdy turned to her in surprised irritation.

"Save it." She rolled her eyes back at him. "You were gone, so the jealousy is a little late." She turned back to Dawg. "And I'm waiting on an answer, Dawg?"

Dawg shifted nervously, rather like a little boy caught in a fib.

He cleared his throat, glancing at Rowdy with a grimace.

"You belonged to him first."

"I'm his always, Dawg," she informed him gently. "Now, forever, and always. And that's my decision. Not Rowdy's. And it's one you won't change."

"I told you she was trouble," Natches griped. "Dammit, Kelly, we didn't ask you to mess things up like this." He cast her a brooding glare.

"You're welcome." She smiled back placidly.

They weren't angry, she could see it in their eyes, feel it in the affection in their gazes.

Natches turned to Dawg and lifted his fist.

"We're the last."

Dawg lifted his fist in return, touching it to his cousin's. "The last."

He appeared firm, decisive. Kelly tilted her head and watched both men curiously. Natches might never let go of the more extreme needs, but there was something there in Dawg's expression. Something hesitant. Something uncertain.

"Let's go." Rowdy's arm hooked around her waist, dragging her toward the stairs.

"Where?"

"To bed," he growled.

"But, Rowdy, I'm not sleepy."

"I promise, you will be. Later . . ."

She was laughing as he swept her into the bedroom.

Look for
Lora Leigh's sexy new book

Nauti Nights

Coming fall 2007 from Berkley Heat